DURARARA!!

DRRR!!

13

D0925847

OCT 0 1 2019

RYOHGO NARITA

ILLUSTRATION BY
SUZUHITO YASUDA

Design: Yoshihiko Kamabe (ZEN)

Ikebukuro is much the same.

The city is always changing as its people and buildings rise and fall with the times.

But I think it should be fine if one thing, at least, stays constant through it all.

...In fact, I think the city stays the city precisely because of that.

Well, it's about time for us to part ways.

The next time we meet, let's hope that something between you and me remains the same.

I'll be praying as much, at least.

Daioh TV's *Wandering Around the Town Squad*

—An excerpt from the raw footage of the episode in which

Yuuhei Hanejima walks around Ikebukuro

"...When I walk around Ikebukuro, I feel like I'm back home.

"I've been living here since I was a child, and I still live here now...

"So maybe saying 'I'm back home' is a strange way to put it.

"But it's like each time I walk down the same street or intersection, I feel something different.

"...It's not always good memories, I suppose, with vending machines flying...

"...street signs torn out of the ground, thugs getting tossed onto the roofs of tall buildings...

"...but there's something kind of nostalgic about all of it.

"When you live in the same city for a while, you make memories there...

"So maybe when I say 'I'm back home,' I'm referring to the memories themselves.

"Just us walking and talking here is a new memory, for example...

"...one that'll get added to the top of the pile that is this street.

"No matter how the town or the people change, the memories will always be there, just as they were.

"All these people walking around—the salarymen and the students,

Those three were often beholden to the whims of such forces, just as their whims affected others as they raced through the city like a breath of fresh air. Perhaps it wasn't always pleasant seeing what they did.

They changed as they went; they grew and evolved, and sometimes they sank deeper into the depths, entangling one another without realizing, until at last they came back to the same place.

The trio reunited as different people than they were when they started, but whatever it was they saw in one another, only they would know.

If you're concerned for them, the only thing any of us can do is have faith.

Faith that there's something within them remaining constant since they left the starting line.

Shinichi Tsukumoya's Closed Blog

You want to hear about the end of the Dollars?

...At best, I can only tell you the story from memory.

Mikado Ryuugamine, Anri Sonohara, Masaomi Kida.

These three raced their way through the Ikebukuro area, making waves all the while—and yet barely anyone noticed.

They did quite a number on this place in just a year and a half at Raira Academy.

They've changed considerably, and not just because of the process of adolescence.

For better or worse, the city changes people.

New environment, new people, new life.

"the housewives and the children, the street gangs,

"even the Headless Rider—

"they all have memories of this town that they can return to, that they can call 'home.'"

(The previous footage was entirely cut in the editing process.)

"I love this city.

"So I hope everyone else loves it, too...

"I hope you create memories that make you want to come back here.

"I'm sure Ikebukuro is hoping you'll come back, too."

VOLUME 13

Ryohgo Narita
ILLUSTRATION BY Suzuhito Yasuda

NEW YORK

DURARARA!!, Volume 13
RYOHGO NARITA
ILLUSTRATION BY SUZUHITO YASUDA

Translation by Stephen Paul
Cover art by Suzuhito Yasuda

This book is a work of fiction. Names, characters, places, and incidents are the product of the author's imagination or are used fictitiously. Any resemblance to actual events, locales, or persons, living or dead, is coincidental.

DURARARA!! Vol.13
© RYOHGO NARITA 2014
First published in Japan in 2013 by KADOKAWA CORPORATION, Tokyo.
English translation rights arranged with KADOKAWA CORPORATION, Tokyo,
through Tuttle-Mori Agency, Inc., Tokyo.

English translation © 2019 by Yen Press, LLC

Yen On
150 West 30th Street, 19th Floor
New York, NY 10001

Visit us at yenpress.com
facebook.com/yenpress
twitter.com/yenpress
yenpress.tumblr.com
instagram.com/yenpress

First Yen On Edition: September 2019

Yen On is an imprint of Yen Press, LLC.
The Yen On name and logo are trademarks of Yen Press, LLC.

The publisher is not responsible for websites (or their content) that are not owned by the publisher.

Library of Congress Cataloging-in-Publication Data
Names: Narita, Ryōgo, 1980– author. | Yasuda, Suzuhito, illustrator. | Paul,
    Stephen (Translator), translator.
Title: Durarara!! / Ryohgo Narita, Suzuhito Yasuda, translation by Stephen Paul.
Description: New York, NY : Yen ON, 2015–
Identifiers: LCCN 2015041320 | ISBN 9780316304740 (v. 1 : pbk.) |
    ISBN 9780316304764 (v. 2 : pbk.) | ISBN 9780316304771 (v. 3 : pbk.) |
    ISBN 9780316304788 (v. 4 : pbk.) | ISBN 9780316304795 (v. 5 : pbk.) |
    ISBN 9780316304818 (v. 6 : pbk.) | ISBN 9780316439688 (v. 7 : pbk.) |
    ISBN 9780316474290 (v. 8 : pbk.) | ISBN 9780316474313 (v. 9 : pbk.) |
    ISBN 9780316474344 (v. 10 : pbk.) | ISBN 9780316474368 (v. 11 : pbk.) |
    ISBN 9780316474382 (v. 12 : pbk.) | ISBN 9781975358198 (v. 13 : pbk.)
Subjects: | CYAC: Tokyo (Japan)—Fiction. | BISAC: FICTION / Science
    Fiction / Adventure.
Classification: LCC PZ7.1.N37 Du 2015 | DDC [Fic]—dc23
LC record available at http://lccn.loc.gov/2015041320

ISBNs: 978-1-9753-5819-8 (paperback)
        978-1-9753-8469-2 (ebook)

1 3 5 7 9 10 8 6 4 2

LSC-C

Printed in the United States of America

A tale of twisted love comes to a close.

The grotesque creature silently watched the city from above.

It extended paths of shadow and rode through the sky on the back of a horse that was equally monstrous.

Despite it being the middle of the night, the city below still flickered with thousands of tiny lights.

The creature surveyed this view, as if the land and the starry sky had switched places, in total silence.

It wore pitch-black knight's armor. The head, which rested under the pit of the armor in the grip of the creature, far from the neck, featured wide-open eyes.

But its mouth stayed shut.

The creature was called as such because despite its features, it was certainly not human.

No human being could be alive with its head separated from its shoulders.

So in that sense, her form was indeed abnormal.

But there was no way to know what lay within her heart.

For whether human or inhuman, the heart has no set form to begin with.

CHAPTER 10
A Tiger Dies and Leaves His Skin

Raijin High School—in the past

"Hey, Orihara. You had quite a fight yesterday," chirped Shinra Kishitani as he approached the young man, who was reading a magazine. They'd been friends since middle school, and currently Izaya Orihara was sitting on the landing of the stairwell that led to the roof.

For his part, Izaya narrowed his eyes. His lips pulled into a subtle smile, and he offered with some annoyance, "Fight? Whatever are you talking about? That monstrous amoeba nearly murdered me—that's what that was."

The "fight" Shinra was referring to was a brutal battle to the death, itself practically a bad joke, that started after he had brought Shizuo Heiwajima and Izaya Orihara together.

"What is up with him?" Izaya complained. "I lured him right into that accident, absolutely perfectly, but I didn't expect that he'd take a hit from a truck and just walk away without a scratch."

"Fascinating, isn't it?" Shinra pressed. "You said that you loved humanity, so I thought you might take an interest in him."

"That's not a human being. That's a wild animal or a monster."

"Oh, I don't know." Shinra shrugged. "I'm hoping that you two will learn to get along, though."

Izaya shot him a venomous look. "Why?"

"Because unless you learn to get along, you and Shizuo have the worst chemistry imaginable," Shinra said simply. "Based on what I saw yesterday, someone is going to die. At the very least, one of the two of you might."

"You're exaggerating."

"But if either you or Shizuo calms down a bit, that might be a different story."

"You were the one who introduced us to each other, Shinra," snapped Izaya.

"You go to the same school. I just thought it would be easier for you to be friends if I was in the middle. But if it doesn't work out, then it's not meant to be. If you guys try to kill each other, then I'm only out one or two friends."

He said it like a joke, but Izaya knew that when Shinra gave off that sad, troubled smile, it was a sign that he felt serious about something.

"Well, look who's above it all."

"If one…or both of you die, I'm sure I'll be sad about it, but I can live with that result."

"What a swell guy to have as a friend."

"I can't help it. Every last human being in the world could die, and as long as my beloved girlfriend survives, I'll still be happy," Shinra said with a distant look in his eyes. Whatever he was imagining, his mouth curled into a dopey grin.

"Ugh, you're so creepy. I feel sorry for whatever woman you fall in love with."

Izaya had a pretty good idea of who his "beloved girlfriend" was, but he chose not to mention that. Instead, he returned to his magazine.

Unfortunately, that was when Shinra decided to get philosophical. "Ah yes…have you ever heard the quote, 'A tiger dies and leaves his skin, but a man dies and leaves his name'?"

"?"

"Shizuo would be the tiger. If Shizuo dies, the pelt that surrounds him…the stories of his superhuman power would be passed on and treasured, taking on a life of their own and becoming urban legends," Shinra said, as excited as a grade schooler who had spotted a fascinating insect—while speaking about his friend as if he were a fascinating insect.

"And he wouldn't just be a tall tale," Shinra continued. "He'd be an urban legend that actually existed! In fact, it might be only after his death that Shizuo Heiwajima is truly complete—as a being that transcended humanity."

Izaya felt himself getting irritated.

Him? Living on as an urban legend? A being who transcends humanity? Nonsense. He's nothing more than a dumb beast.

Izaya realized that even considering their extravagant fight yesterday, he was extraordinarily annoyed at Shizuo Heiwajima. "And you're going to autopsy that monster and get famous that way?"

"Sure, I'd like to give him an autopsy, out of scholastic curiosity. But I don't have any special interest in dissecting men, nor do I wish to become famous for it. And I have no hobby of dissecting girls, either. Although I will admit that my affection for my beloved started with dissection," Shinra said rather ominously.

"...?" Izaya was confused at first but decided that this was just Shinra being Shinra. "So assuming that tiger will leave his skin, how do *you* plan to leave your name, as a person? I'm kind of holding out hope that you'll go down in history as a horrific serial killer."

"As a person...?"

Shinra thought it over. His smile vanished. He looked toward the light coming down from the roof above.

"I want..."

♂♀

Ikebukuro, atop a building under construction—present day

Which of them was first to move?

No one witnessed the moment happen.

Perhaps even they themselves were not aware of it.

Neither Shizuo Heiwajima, who had turned into a pure system designed to destroy the man before him, nor Izaya Orihara, who still retained his rational human mind.

They were atop a building under construction, shortly before dawn.

The battle to the death started without even a provocation to initiate it.

*   *   *

To the two longtime foes, this fight was an undeniable turning point. But for such a momentous occasion, it certainly started in unmemorable fashion.

Then again, given that their mutual hatred essentially stemmed from the feeling of *I just don't like the guy*, perhaps it was also fitting that it happened unceremoniously.

Their astonishing, overwhelming battles, going back to school days, made you doubt the accuracy of that old saying "The more you fight, the closer you really are."

There was no high-minded chivalry in this duel, no respect for the other side whatsoever.

And in the case of this stunning battle in the wee hours of the morning, there was once again not a shred of respect for the other combatant. Not once did either of them ever view the other with the positive aspects inherent in the word *rival*.

So when they met again on the upper portion of the construction site, there was not a single word of dialogue between them.

The only exchange of words was the phone call that Shizuo Heiwajima received from Izaya Orihara as he climbed up the stairs of the building.

Less than a minute earlier, when Shizuo slowly opened the door to the top of the building, where construction was still ongoing, the first thing that stung his nose was the odor of evaporated gasoline.

Then he realized that it was coming from the liquid flowing along the ground at his feet.

But Shizuo didn't show any signs of panic. Even when flames shot up around him the next moment, he barely blinked.

Not because he'd expected it, nor because he'd instantly thought of some means to counteract it. It was just that the fury compressed into his body dulled the ordinary human senses, leaving him incapable of typical reaction.

"..."

Ordinarily, that kind of lapse in focus would be fatal—but Shizuo grabbed the door in silence, wrenched it off its hinges, and stepped over it.

That was all he did.

But the abnormal physical strength with which he performed the feat flattened the flames spreading at his feet and caused a gust of air that pushed back the wind blowing in from outside. The flames practically danced in the resulting eddies of air.

Shizuo used the trampled door as a stepping-stone to leap forward, using the swirling force of the flames as momentum. Parts of his clothes were singed, but he was able to get clear before they actually caught fire.

Before the secondary effects of the heat and the lack of oxygen could inflict any damage on him, however, a steel beam hoisted on the crane swung at him like a pendulum.

The beam was moving with enough force that it would easily go straight through a typical automobile—but once again, Shizuo barely batted an eye.

His right arm was still dangling at his side, ever since he'd deflected the forklift minutes earlier, but the anger in him dulled both his pain and his common sense.

He swung his good arm upward, delivering a solid uppercut to the oncoming beam. In the moment of impact, the steel crumpled, and the floor under construction made an unpleasant sound around Shizuo's feet.

But despite being in the midst of the two expressions of force, Shizuo was unhurt.

The deflected beam slid loose of its supporting wires and plummeted back down onto the construction site.

He glanced toward where it fell, and he caught sight of a man. It was Izaya, who showed no sign of alarm or reaction of any kind when the giant piece of metal crashed right next to him.

The two men were united in their lack of surprise at dramatic changes in the situation, but unlike Shizuo's, Izaya's face was fixed into a cruel smile, and he at least displayed enough intelligence to calculate how to kill another person.

From Izaya's perspective, however, he wasn't killing a "person" at all.

This was the beginning of Izaya's quest to vanquish a monster.

In this case, the monster wasn't evil, and Izaya wasn't the hero.

The battle to the death wasn't undertaken on any basis of good and evil at all. The two of them were both, in their own way, in a place far from any concept of righteousness and wickedness.

All the unconscious restraints were gone. All there was to do was face the other.

Nothing until now had risen to the level of a battle to the death. Those were like introductions.

The two men faced off, glaring each other down—until the urge to kill condensed into the space between them and exploded outward all at once.

Which of them was first to move?

There was a moment in time containing the answer to that question, one that no one would ever be able to answer later.

The slaughter began without a clear point of initiation.

Just thick, boiling air seething with heat.

♂♀

Ikebukuro—Russia Sushi

In the middle of Shizuo and Izaya's battle to the death, there was activity happening elsewhere.

It was the time of sleep in the city, when several hours still remained until dawn.

The time that even the twenty-four-hour karaoke booths, the bars that stayed open until morning, and the seedy girlie clubs saw reduced foot traffic. And yet…

"Well, dammit."

Tom peered out through the barricade erected behind the window out of tables and other furniture. He was watching the steady gathering of people outside the building who sported bloodshot-red eyes.

They weren't rioting, nor were they zombies in search of a meal.

They just stood out there, facing the restaurant, smiling silently.

But that was even *worse* than the alternative.

"Am I having a nightmare or what?" Tom lamented, squinting through the glass.

Next to him, a man with a shaved head doing the exact same thing muttered, "Saika possessed them."

"Huh? You know something about this…uh, buddy?"

"It's Kine."

"…Oh, right. I'm Tanaka. So…you know what that means, Mr. Kine?"

Kine? As in…the former Awakusu-kai Kine?

Tom had cleaned up his tone of voice a bit, sensing that his conversation partner was a "professional" gentleman. The hairless man, Kine, furrowed his brow and said calmly, "Well, it's probably a waste of time trying to convince you to believe me, so I'll put it simply and say that it's kind of like a hypnosis that makes people into slaves."

"…Hypnosis?" Tom repeated. But based on the view of the outside, it did seem to make more sense than, say, a zombie invasion. "Well, whatever. If it's hypnosis, that means someone did it to them, right?"

"You get right to the point."

"I can't do the job I've got now unless I can process new information quickly… So you got any thoughts about who the hypnotist is…?"

"I've got a few ideas, but I can't imagine any of them would want to surround this place," Kine replied.

Tom sighed and hissed back at the nearby employees of Russia Sushi, "Hey, what about you guys? Is there any kind of dangerous bullshit this place is getting sucked into?"

Denis shot Tom a nasty glare and said, "I don't know. Why don't you speak for yourself?"

"I don't think I've done nothin' to get a hypnotist pissed at me… Well, I guess there was that one person I saw outside. Who was that again…?"

"It doesn't have to be you specifically. Could be folks who have a problem with Shizuo," Denis pointed out.

Tom envisioned the boss of the company he worked for—and then his subordinates, Shizuo and Vorona.

"…Well…yeah, I guess you have a point there. But why *me*, then?"

"Probably means you've got more personal sway than you realize," Denis offered as he continued calmly cleaning up the interior of the restaurant.

"I think you've overestimated me," Tom said with a shrug.

Then Simon returned from the back, smiling. "Hey, we have sleepover here tonight. I have many fireworks ready, too."

There was something that looked like a dirty sack in his hands. Apparently, he'd been digging it up from under the floor of the kitchen.

"Don't bring all that dirt over into the restaurant," Denis snapped, but Simon just grinned and pulled something out of the sack. When Tom saw what it was, his cheeks twitched, and even Kine's expression darkened.

It was clear from the look of the object, which resembled a black spray can of hair mousse with a handle and pin attached to it, that it did not belong in a sushi restaurant or in any Japanese city to begin with.

Simon gestured with the black tube—a military flash grenade—and spoke in his typical tone of voice, as if nothing about the scene was any different than usual.

"Edo is famous for fires and fighting. But fighting no fun, makes your face flush. Replace fires with fireworks, and everyone friends, no fighting."

♂♀

Ikebukuro

"Are you all right, Sonohara?"

"...Yes, sorry to worry you."

"You shouldn't push yourself if you can't do it. Want to rest somewhere?" asked Saki Mikajima, who had noticed that Anri Sonohara was looking pale and uncomfortable.

"I'm fine..."

Anri's voice was clearly unsteady, but Saki seemed to conclude that she wasn't going to get the answer she was looking for and didn't press the issue any further.

The girls were making their way to a specific destination.

They considered taking a taxi, but since the place was close, they leaned toward walking the distance instead—and right around the point that they passed by Ikebukuro Station, Anri suddenly found herself racked with a powerful anxiety.

On the inside, something much more reliable than simple animal intuition was giving her unmistakable signals: The Saika slumbering within her was stirring.

What…is this…?

Even during the Night of the Ripper, when Haruna Niekawa brought forth a great new influx of Saikas, she had never felt a stirring of this scale.

Part of that was the fact that she hadn't fully accepted Saika yet at the time, but she could tell that the trembling from the cursed blade within her was abnormal beyond whatever difference that would make.

It felt like the Saikas were resonating. Like she was on the inside of a gigantic bell, and the roar from the outside was reverberating directly into her body.

This mental resonance blasted Anri's mind. It made her see spots.

But she couldn't stop now.

After talking with Saki, Anri decided that whatever trouble was happening at the moment in Ikebukuro, she ought to involve herself in it.

Izaya Orihara had hinted to her that Mikado Ryuugamine and Masaomi Kida were in the path of some terrible oncoming disaster. He was not the kind of man whom she trusted at all, but there was something in his vague, suggestive words that she found highly believable.

And both Anri and Saki shared that view.

I wonder if Saika's surge…has something to do with them…

What if someone aside from her caused Mikado and Masaomi to be made part of Saika? The thought sent a terrible shiver down Anri's back.

Fortunately, her fears were unfounded.

But as it happened, Mikado and Masaomi were indeed caught in the midst of a terrible ordeal.

It just didn't have anything to do with Saika.

♂♀

Abandoned factory—late night

"Now, let's see... Which one of these numbers belongs to Mikado Ryuu-ga-mi-ne...?"

The cheery voice was quite at odds with the oppressive setting of an abandoned factory in the middle of the night.

"Aha, there it is! Wow, when you see it with the kanji and everything, 'Mikado Ryuugamine' sure looks imposing," Chikage Rokujou chattered happily as he fiddled with the cell phone. "Emperor of Dragon Peak—hah!"

The phone's owner, Masaomi Kida, sighed and said, "I told you, he's not going to answer a call from some number he doesn't recognize. The guy's really shy and suspicious like that..."

It wasn't clear whether Chikage was actually listening to him, because he went ahead and read the number off Masaomi's phone, inputting it into his own smartphone. "But that was the old Mikado Ryuugamine, right?"

"..."

"If the guy's cracked as much as you say he has, he'll pick up. Trust me," said Chikage, smiling confidently. He pushed the call button on the screen.

But many rings later, there was no indication that the call was going to be answered.

"..."

"..."

"Wanna pretend that conversation never happened?"

"...Sure, sounds good."

To break the awkward silence between the two, Chikage launched into conversation again, as if nothing had ever happened.

"Doesn't he have a social media account somewhere? Like on Mix-E or Twittia? Something he would definitely look at, rather than ignoring by default."

"You really are exhausting all your options, huh...?" Masaomi said, abandoning any pretense of respect for his elder. Then he sighed again and thought it over. "Someplace he would look... Maybe a Dollars-related web forum..."

"Don't really want a lot of people seeing this."

"Hmm… Social media, huh…? But whatever he might potentially be doing, I'm not linked to him, so… Oh!"

Masaomi snatched the phone out of Chikage's hand, remembering something out of the blue. He connected to the Internet in a hurry.

"Maybe he's still checking that one chat site every day…"

A dozen or so seconds later, when the chat room filled the screen, Masaomi's eyes bulged.

♂♀

TarouTanaka: I don't understand what you mean. Who is Kujiragi? What are you after?

NamieYagiri: You're the one who's after something. What do you think you're doing?

NamieYagiri: Why don't you look around yourself?

NamieYagiri: I just want to bring an end to what's going on. So help me.

NamieYagiri: You have no idea about anything, and yet you're connected to everything.

NamieYagiri: Wake the hell up. You're the key.

♂♀

"What is this?"

Chikage peered over Masaomi's shoulder and said, "Whoa, this chat looks pretty gnarly. What's up with that?"

"It's not usually like this…"

On the screen, a woman named NamieYagiri was taking TarouTanaka—the handle name of Mikado Ryuugamine—to task with blistering force. It was all just on a screen, of course, but her posting was powerful enough that it practically grabbed the collar of the reader.

"Yagiri…? Does that person have something to do with Seiji?" Masaomi wondered, thinking of the boy he'd known from school. Confused, he continued reading.

And after a while, he froze up again.

It wasn't only Mikado.

There was another familiar name in the chat room.

♂♀

NamieYagiri: Same question about your girlfriend, Anri Sonohara.
NamieYagiri: You know that she's a monster, too.
NamieYagiri: You must have seen her with a katana at some point.
NamieYagiri: Want me to tell you what she did during that incident with the street slasher?

♂♀

Abandoned factory

"…"

Masaomi was frozen, unable to continue scrolling down, so Chikage picked up the slack.

"Oh, Anri? Yeah, she had a katana."

"No…wait. Hang on. There's just too much…I can't wrap my head around…"

"See? You think you know your friends, but you know them a lot less than you realize, huh?" Chikage sagely mocked. It was easy for him to say, since none of this had to do with him. He snatched the phone away and checked the web address, typing it into his own smartphone.

Then, eyes sparkling like a child who'd thought up a good prank, Chikage began typing his own text into the chat room.

♂♀

Tokyo—abandoned building

"Mr. Mikado! Mr. Mikado!"

Despite it being late in the middle of the night, Mikado Ryuugamine showed no signs of sleep. He heard the sound of his underclassman from school and the very reason he'd been *dragged down* into this position—Aoba Kuronuma.

Mikado put the object he was holding into a box and turned to face Aoba, who came up the stairs a few moments later.

"What's the matter?" he asked, like it was any old interaction.

Aoba waved his phone and said, "You saw how some weirdo was jacking up the chat just now, right?"

"Yeah, but that's not an issue anymore. I'll have Kanra, the administrator, delete all of it tomorrow."

"No, I'm not talking specifically about the troll... I got curious, so I was watching the chat after that," Aoba said, showing him the screen of his phone, "and some other weirdo showed up going on about Masaomi Kida..."

"..."

Mikado's brow furrowed the tiniest bit. He grabbed his laptop in silence and used it to connect to the wireless hot spot they were using for Internet. When he logged in to the chat room, he found a very one-sided message waiting for him there.

♂♀

Chat room

Rocchi has entered the chat.

Rocchi: Pardon me for interrupting the bloodbath in here.

Rocchi: Uh, can everyone see these posts?

Rocchi: Man, it's been so long since I was in a chat room. Everyone's moved on to social media now, y'know?

NamieYagiri: Who are you?

NamieYagiri: You have nothing to do with this. Butt out.

Rocchi: Based on your name, I'm guessing you're a woman? It's a cute name.

Rocchi: It'd be nice to have a proper chat in person sometime, so I'm sorry, but I'm gonna have to butt in for just a moment. I really am sorry.

Rocchi: For one thing, it's not exactly true that I have "nothing" to do with this.

Rocchi: Mikado Ryuugamine, right?

Rocchi: You got that call earlier.

Rocchi: You really shouldn't ignore a call like that.

Rocchi: What, you can't pick up a call from an unfamiliar number? Well, now we know each other, right?

Rocchi: Though the truth is, we did meet before this.

Rocchi: Anyway, my point is, you should answer your phone.

Rocchi: Once you see this message, go and dial back the number that called you about five minutes before this post.

Rocchi: Otherwise, who knows what might happen to your buddy Masaomi Kida, huh?

Rocchi: You don't want your friend getting hurt any worse, do ya?

NamieYagiri: Shut up, nobody cares about any of this.

NamieYagiri: Save it for later.

NamieYagiri: Ryuugamine, you have a duty to uphold first.

Rocchi: And how's Seiji doing, Sis?

NamieYagiri: What?

Rocchi: Oh, come now, you don't want Seiji seeing you rampaging like this, do you?

NamieYagiri: How dare you threatenlkbe kujehbb ubakjbkm

Kuru: Oh my, what a strange turn of events.

Mai: It's exciting.

$$♂♀$$

Abandoned factory

"Hey, you can't just go typing whatever the hell you want. On the other hand…what the hell is happening in this chat room?"

Masaomi hadn't been in the chat for almost half a year, but it was still an important place to him. He felt disturbed at the way it seemed to be careening toward collapse.

Before he could say anything else, however, the sound of a ringtone echoed off the walls of the abandoned factory building. Chikage saw that the number on his screen was the same one he'd typed in minutes ago, and he grinned.

"Hey, it's from your pal."

"…!"

Masaomi couldn't hide his surprise. That had worked out better than he'd expected. He reached out for the phone without thinking.

"Whoa, whoa, whoa, hang on. I'm the one who has to answer it."

"No, I'm the one who has business with..."

"Once he finds out you're safe, he's gonna hang up. I'll answer."

Chikage stretched his finger toward the answer button, glanced at Masaomi, and added, "Oh, and...before I go through with this, *sorry.*"

"?" Masaomi frowned at that. Chikage put the phone to his ear.

"Yo."

"*...Are you Rocchi, then?*"

"Yeah. I'm glad you checked my messages so promptly. The truth is, we've met before."

"..."

"Do you recognize my voice?" Chikage asked. His tone was light, while the voice on the other side of the phone was flat and unemotional.

"*You're...Chikage Rokujou, aren't you?*"

"Wow, nice one. Round of applause for this guy. Listen, I'm sorry about what happened back there. I should've believed it when you said you were the boss of the Dollars."

"..."

Sensing that Mikado wasn't going to give him a response, Chikage continued, "I'll be straight with you. Your friends, these...Dollars? Have been messing with us again. And I'm here to square up that account."

Masaomi's mouth fell open, but Chikage held up a hand to silence him. He must've been formulating an idea, so Masaomi chose to stay quiet and listen for now.

But then Chikage closed his hand into a fist and used it to rap against Masaomi's cast.

"...?! Urgh?! Ah...*aaah!*"

Waves of pain enveloped his broken bone. Masaomi involuntarily yelped with pain.

Then Chikage pulled the phone back away from Masaomi and snarled quietly into the phone, "You heard him. If you can't meet me man-to-man, your friend here's goin' somewhere very far away."

A few minutes later, the phone call over, Chikage cackled and smacked Masaomi's head.

"There we go. Now we've got a destination. You're my hostage, and I'm gonna hand you over in public. That seems like a fair compromise to me."

"...Since when did I become a hostage? Dammit, that really hurt, you know!" Masaomi protested, but Chikage just shrugged.

"Hey, I did apologize before I did it, didn't I?"

"You don't think I could have played along without having to inflict actual pain?"

"Actually, a good spontaneous scream's a lot harder to pull off than you think." Chikage hummed.

Masaomi exhaled and shook his head in disgust. "Fine, fine, whatever. So where are you handing me over to Mikado?"

"Oh yeah. It's a place that even I'm familiar with. I remember it well."

Chikage swung his arms in big circles, like he was warming up for some kind of athletic performance.

"There's an all-girls school right nearby."

♂♀

Abandoned building

"You're not going to go there alone, are you?"

Aoba looked over at Mikado, who was staring without emotion at the phone he'd just finished talking into.

"Huh? I mean… Oh yeah, I guess he didn't specify any details about the number of people."

"Rokujou is the name of the guy who we messed with first. You don't need to go for yourself. We can go and get Mr. Kida back," Aoba suggested casually.

Mikado thought it over. "That reminds me, how exactly do you guys see Kida anyway?"

"How…? He's your friend, right?"

"But he was your enemy and the leader of the Yellow Scarves, wasn't he?"

"Maybe to my brother, but it wasn't like *we* were fighting directly against him," Aoba replied, shrugging. "To be honest, I don't have any hatred for Mr. Kida, but neither do I have any fondness. If you said that we should go and rescue him, we'd follow your orders."

"Okay, that's good to hear. But Masaomi might not think very highly of you guys. He might look like a frivolous guy, but he's always been very serious at his core."

"…"

As they talked, Aoba sensed a change in Mikado.

Can't help but notice that the way he refers to him keeps changing, between Masaomi and Kida…

Maybe it was nothing, but he couldn't help but feel that it was actually very important.

Perhaps Mikado himself didn't even realize what he was doing. Maybe he wasn't fully conscious of what kind of connection he had to Masaomi Kida personally—or to all the people he knew, including Anri Sonohara—or what he wanted that connection to be.

At least, that was how it seemed to Aoba. He watched, silent.

And then, when Mikado wasn't looking, he let the corners of his mouth tuck into a sneer.

Yeah, he's just so fascinating. He's the best.

Then, watching the back of the broken boy standing before him, Aoba let the smile vanish and asked, "By the way, why did you designate that particular location?"

The place Mikado mentioned during the phone call for the exchange to go down was a location Aoba knew well. While it was the middle of the night, it was also a fairly noticeable locale.

"…"

It was certainly a reasonable question to ask, but Mikado merely went silent. He pondered it heavily, like a computer asked to do something beyond its processing capacity, and when he spoke, it was slow and halting, trying to convince himself of the words as he said them.

"It's…an important…place."

"An important place?"

"As I think you know already…it's the place where it all began, for me and for the Dollars," Mikado said, nostalgia and fondness wreathing the name of the gang. He smiled boyishly. "But Sonohara and Kida weren't there at the time."

He wasn't even talking to Aoba anymore. In fact, it seemed that he was thinking of his reasoning for that choice after the fact, bit by bit. That was how it seemed to the younger boy.

But it was true: The place was very special to Mikado Ryuugamine.

It was where the Mikado of now got his start, when the ordinary and extraordinary completely switched places.

The intersection in front of Tokyu Hands.

It was the start of the major road that passed by the Sunshine building—or, alternately, the end of it.

It was an answer that came to Mikado naturally. And in his case, inevitably.

He made the decision as the Dollars' founder and as a member—in order to welcome Masaomi Kida, who wasn't there on that day.

If possible, he hoped Anri would be there, too.

But despite his desire, Mikado had to keep his hopes under control, knowing he couldn't be that selfish.

That was because he knew that after this, something bloody and ugly was likely to happen there.

A part of him was aware that Anri's secret was far more gruesome than a typical youth rivalry, but he still refused to intentionally get her involved.

Or perhaps it was still a bit of youthful stubbornness that remained within him.

♂♀

Ikebukuro—apartment bar

"..."

In the meantime, a man in a line of work that was completely removed from youthfulness looked hard at his screen, just as Mikado had.

"What's this, then?" grunted Akabayashi, lieutenant of the Awakusu-kai.

The old scar on his right eye was bothering him. He was sitting in a special unlicensed bar built into a private apartment that had been outfitted for business, collecting information for his own purposes.

What Akabayashi was examining was not one of the several Dollars-related message boards or a report message from his errand boys, the gang called Jan-Jaka-Jan. It was a chat room that he'd been introduced to by a girl he helped take care of.

The chat room was oddly well-connected with what was going on in the city, so Akabayashi made it a point to pop in at least once a day, both for information and to check on his patron there, the girl who was like a niece to him.

Something odd was going on in the chat now.

"What's the matter, Mr. Akabayashi?" asked the middle-aged bar-keeper, who must have noticed his expression.

"Oh, just some trouble with work."

"Ah, I see."

The bartender did not ask further. Whether he was aware of what Akabayashi did or not, he clearly came to the determination that it wasn't worth asking about.

But Akabayashi gave him a lilting smile and offered freely, "It's odd. I'd say that we took a shot from a direction that I wasn't expecting."

He looked back at his smartphone. In the chat, a woman named Namie Yagiri was throwing a tantrum and tearing into Mikado Ryuugamine. That alone would strike Akabayashi as nothing more than some internal Dollars trouble, but what alarmed him was when the real name of the girl who invited him to the chat room appeared in the conversation.

♂♀

NamieYagiri: Where is that headless monster?

NamieYagiri: Same question about your girlfriend, Anri Sonohara.

NamieYagiri: You know that she's a monster, too.

NamieYagiri: You must have seen her with a katana at some point.

NamieYagiri: Want me to tell you what she did during that incident with the street slasher?

♂♀

Normally, one might take statements like that as the ramblings of a person undergoing a psychotic break.

But Akabayashi understood them perfectly.

And that was unfortunate, because the words that this Namie woman was saying did indeed relate directly to Anri Sonohara.

Monster.

Katana.

Street slasher.

The old scar on his right eye itched.

A searing pain assaulted his brain, centered around the scar—as though the prosthetic embedded into his socket was radiating the heat itself. But Akabayashi just took off his sunglasses, pressed his eye lightly, and smiled sadly to himself.

Calm down already. You're not some kid in puberty.

He reflected fondly on his past.

His first love had come late for a man of his type, but it was very hot and painful.

The woman seemed barely human. She pierced both his eye and his heart.

The mysterious blade was contained within her body, and her eyes burned red, marking her as the slasher.

Akabayashi could clearly remember the first woman he'd ever fallen in love with.

She had been a blade personified and yet died from a blade wound through the stomach.

But Akabayashi knew more than that. Not from seeing it for himself but out of personal certainty.

She—Sayaka Sonohara—had cut off her husband's head before running the sword through her own stomach.

Where had the katana housed in her body gone?

The police said they never found the murder weapon. So even though the wound looked exactly like a self-inflicted one, they couldn't rule it a suicide without the weapon there, too.

Had the police coroner found anything abnormal with her body? If they had, perhaps they hadn't announced it to the public because it was too abnormal—but what if the sword was still intact and well after Sayaka Sonohara's death and had moved on to inhabit someone else?

In that case, the most likely host by far would be none other than Anri Sonohara.

The thought had occurred to him a number of times, but he'd always laughed it off as a nonsensical daydream.

And yet just a few lines of text from this chat room had given him clear evidence.

The katana that pierced his eye had moved on to Sayaka's daughter, Anri.

Heat bloomed on the right half of his face.

The moment that his conjecture seemed more likely to be truth, he felt his own cold blood suddenly roar to a boil.

But that was where the surge stopped.

Akabayashi stilled the throbbing in his eye with force and pushed his emotions back into the memories of the past.

I said, calm down. Anri inherited a memento of her mother. That's all this is.

If this were back in his more short-tempered days, he might have already been out the door. This meant that a part of the woman he loved was still alive within her daughter.

But Akabayashi was too mentally mature to hold some kind of twisted romantic affection for Anri, a girl young enough to be his own daughter.

The one I fell in love with…was a crazy woman named Sayaka Sonohara. Not that buzzing, annoying sword.

Recalling the flood of obnoxious "words of love" that flooded into him the moment his eye was slashed, Akabayashi drained the last of his drink and called out, "Hey, bartender."

"Yes, sir?" the other man asked.

Akabayashi gave him another lilting smile. "Let's say you were in love with a woman, and she didn't choose you. She ended up marrying another man."

"Uh-huh."

"And say her daughter was in some kind of trouble, real bad stuff about to happen. If you wanted to help the girl get out of it, would that qualify as 'not being over it'?"

"..."

The bartender thought it over, returned the glass he was polishing to the shelf, and said, "Whether you can't get over the girl's mother or not, you don't strike me as the kind of person who would intentionally turn a blind eye to the child of an acquaintance being in danger, Mr. Akabayashi."

"Well, you might think too highly of me. You can close me out now," Akabayashi said, getting up from his seat and pulling out his wallet. He didn't really need to ask the man that question. He just wanted an excuse to go ahead with it.

But it was true gratitude that he felt for the bartender as he took his time leaving the little room.

He was going to poke his nose into this incident but only in the way that a proper man on the underside of society would do.

♂♀

Along Kawagoe Highway

"...This is the apartment building."

"And is this person really going to be that helpful?" Saki asked, not to cast doubt on Anri's offer but just to get some reassurance.

"Yes, she's a very helpful...person..."

The hesitation around the word *person* was not simply an unconscious hitch of the tongue. Anri looked up at the building. It was a place she'd been a number of times. It was the home of a mutual acquaintance—and savior—of both Anri Sonohara and Mikado Ryuugamine: Celty Sturluson.

The troubles that surrounded Mikado and Masaomi seemed like too much for Anri herself to solve. And for one thing, she had no idea where the two of them even were at this moment.

So she didn't want to make things worse for anyone, but she also really wanted someone to speak to. The first person who popped into her head was Celty.

But it was already late into the night. Society did not approve of two young women walking around on the streets at this hour, but Anri, at least, wasn't worried about prowlers or delinquents bothering them. She harbored a weapon inside of her that no half-hearted attacker could ever overcome.

Just because the girls were able to go around in search of a solution at this hour didn't mean that Celty would be available at the drop of a hat, however. Anri felt that a sudden visit at the door in the middle of the night would be in poor taste, so she had at least tried calling on the way. But despite multiple attempts, she got no response from Celty, who was usually very prompt in responding, even in the middle of the night.

"Maybe she's asleep already."

"I suppose so... Oh!" Anri had a sudden epiphany and pulled out her phone again. "Maybe she'll be in the chat room."

"Chat room?"

"Yes...there's one I use online. I actually interact with her more often there than by text messages."

"I see. Then I'll try contacting Masaomi. He didn't answer yesterday, but maybe since it's a new day, he'll be in the mood to talk," Saki suggested, opening her bag so she could get out her cell phone.

Most likely, Masaomi was avoiding talking to her in order to keep her at a safe distance from all the trouble, Anri thought, but there was still a greater-than-zero chance that he might pick up, so she let the other girl go ahead and glanced down at her own phone.

"Huh...?"

Her expression tightened.

"What's the matter?" Saki asked. It was clear that something abnormal had happened. She paused, her thumb hovering over the buttons of her phone.

"Oh no..."

A woman calling herself Namie Yagiri was raging in the chat, throwing around Mikado's and Anri's names. For the moment, Anri's mind went blank; she was unable to process what was happening.

Then Saki peered over her arm at the screen and said, "Hang on. Is the chat room you were talking about...the one that Kanra runs?"

"Huh?" Anri was startled to hear the name of the chat room's moderator from Saki's mouth. "Miss Mikajima, you're familiar with this chat?!"

"Yeah. I go by the username Saki. And on that topic, Bacura is Masaomi."

"…!"

It was all so sudden. Anri froze all over.

And though it was without malice of any kind, Saki made it worse by continuing, "Also, Kanra is Izaya Orihara… Did you know that before you joined?"

"…I…? …?! …Huh?"

Anri's mouth opened and shut without anything to show for it. She couldn't process this.

Not only was she unable to keep up with the string of revelations, the murmuring of Saika inside her was getting stronger and stronger.

Then, right as the dizziness was getting so bad that she might faint, Anri heard a familiar voice.

"Anri…?"

It was a voice she'd heard the other day, but at this moment, it felt old and nostalgic and comforting.

The voice of the girl who had always come to Anri's aid when the bullies were picking on her in middle school. The friend who had accepted her on her side of the picture frame—and acknowledged the metaphor of the frame altogether. The bright and shining host whom she'd lived off when she thought of herself as a parasite.

Anri looked up, suspecting that she was just hearing things, and stared into a familiar face.

"Mika…Harima…?"

Normally, she would never expect to see this person at this hour, at this place.

Mika Harima rushed over to her old friend. "What's the matter? What are you doing out so late…?" she asked, her voice loud and clear.

Anri stammered, "I…I wanted to talk to Celty about something… But what about you…?"

Mika Harima had been to this apartment before, too, to teach the group how to cook *sagohachi*-style pickled sandfish and other tricky dishes. They'd hunched around a hot pot together, so Anri knew that

Mika was familiar with Celty and Shinra, but it was still abnormal to run across her in the middle of the night like this.

"Uh…some stuff happened, y'know? In fact, there's stuff happening right at this moment, too…"

"?"

Anri gave Mika a quizzical look; it wasn't a particularly helpful explanation. Just then, a group of people came into view over Mika's shoulder.

"What the—? Is that Anri?"

"…Hey, it's the Sonohara girl…"

"Don't push it, Kadota!"

It was the van gang but without Karisawa present. That seemed ominous to Anri, but more worrisome than that was the paleness of Kadota's face and the obvious pain with which he was walking.

Behind them, she could also see Seiji Yagiri, his arm over the shoulder of an older woman. He was unsteady on his feet, too, but unlike Kadota, he didn't look pale or weak.

"…Oh, Sonohara. What's up wi…*ung…*"

"Seiji! Don't hurt yourself; the anesthetic hasn't worn off yet! Forget about that girl possessed by the cursed blade!"

"Cursed…? What are you talking about, Sister…?"

Huh?

Yet again, Anri found confusion taking over. And to make things worse, the sickly-looking Kadota did his best to put on a brave face and told her, "You should get out of the area for a while."

"Huh?"

"Remember that slasher who attacked you a while back? The one with the bloodshot eyes…"

"…!"

A nasty chill crawled over Anri's skin. Not one of Saika's murmurs but a feeling of fear from Anri herself.

Was it Haruna Niekawa, or Kasane Kujiragi, or the third party that Kujiragi said she would "sell" Saika to? Whoever it was, Anri was certain now that another slasher had appeared under Saika's influence. She clutched her trembling fists.

And then Kadota added the devastating clincher:

*   *   *

"There's some people around with their eyes all red like that slasher...but there's *tons of 'em.*"

♂♀

Ikebukuro—shopping district

"...What is this?"

Erika Karisawa hid in the darkness from the lights of the city, clutching her phone.

She was peering out at a major road from a narrow alley between two large buildings. And she was looking at a crowd of people.

It wasn't as many as one would expect in the middle of the day, but it was still far too many for this hour of the night.

She'd seen this once before: a year and a half ago, when the Dollars held their first meetup. But the aura surrounding the people occupying the streets was not at all like that gathering.

They were all just loitering around, not going anywhere, standing still like automatons waiting for some order to fulfill.

And most alien of all—their eyes were a deep crimson, to the very last man.

Karisawa recalled the same event that Kadota did. The incident with the street slasher, half a year ago.

It was exactly how the slasher had looked, up until they'd hit him with Togusa's van. It hadn't been the end of it all, given that the Night of the Ripper had happened a few days later, when dozens of people were attacked at once. But even then, she hadn't expected to see a return of that phenomenon out of nowhere.

"If I was gonna get lost in a two-dimensional situation, I'd have preferred a sports manga over a horror movie," Karisawa grumbled, in characteristic fashion. The entire reason that she was here was because she'd gone looking for Kadota after he'd left the hospital without warning. It was by coincidence that she'd spotted this sight.

The group of red-eyed people approached the occasional ordinary pedestrian who passed by them and gave their victims a simple, easy scratch, like a zombie. The pedestrian would spin around at the pain, angry—but within a few seconds, their eyes would be just as blood-shot, and they would promptly join the group.

Karisawa herself had been watching from a distance, until a number of the red-eyed gang noticed her and began to approach, forcing her to run and hide where she stood now.

Yumasaki called her a couple of times while she was hiding, but she declined the calls, wary that answering the phone might draw atten-tion by the noise and cause her to lose concentration.

"And a phone going off? That's such a death omen," she murmured to herself. That kind of monologuing sounded confident, but in fact, she was nearly trapped at the moment.

He did send a text message, however. It said, "Kadota's fine. He's saying either come to the black market doctor's place or go home and hide."

It was a relief to learn that Kadota was okay, but that meant the big-ger question now was if she could actually safely escape this alley or not. Careful not to get too distracted, she typed back, "Kind of stuck right now. If anything happens, you can have my hard disc and dou-jinshi, Yumacchi." Then she went back to watching the crowd for a chance to escape.

It looks like the people are getting scratched by their nails... I wonder if I'll be a slasher, too, if they get me, Karisawa thought, remembering Anri.

The other girl, unlike this mob with their bloodshot eyes, actually glowed from her eye sockets when she swung her katana around. It seemed certain that there was some connection between them, though.

Maybe that was why she was being singled out by the slasher. But Karisawa didn't mistrust or bear a grudge against Anri. She simply smiled sadly to herself.

Rather than being made one of the zombie horde, I'd rather get sliced clean with Anri's katana, so I could be a katana wielder, too. Actually, I'd rather have a giant scythe instead. Just like Death.

Whether she simply felt no impending danger or was acting blithe to drown out her fear, Karisawa was still being utterly herself.

♂♀

"What the...?"

A boy in an area not particularly close to Karisawa's saw the gathering crowd and took out his phone. He was a Blue Squares member and was here scouting out the location of the "transaction" on Aoba's orders.

"Hey, Aoba, is this a festival night?"

"What do you mean?"

"There's a whole lotta people out at this hour."

"Is it Toramaru?"

The boy glanced at the mob again. But none of them seemed to be members of a motorcycle gang. They were all normal types, like salarymen and young adults going home from drinking with friends.

"Nah, they're all ordinary—businessmen, office ladies...a few kids in school uniforms."

"This late at night? Well, watch for a bit longer, just in case."

"Got it. I'll call if I learn anything."

The boy hung up the phone and approached Sixtieth Floor Street.

Then he noticed something. The density of the crowd seemed to increase as he went in one direction.

What's going on?

The people were gathered between the intersection next to Tokyu Hands and the building with the bowling alley inside. Right around where those Russians ran the sushi restaurant.

The boy approached, wondering whether there was a hostage situation in there or something—when he passed by a pedestrian and felt a sharp pain on the back of his hand.

"Aah...," he hissed. There was a little cut on the skin of his hand. He must have scratched it on something when he passed by.

He spun around, wondering whether he should yell at the man.

And then he realized that the scratch was throbbing, pulsing.

...

He stopped. Examined the wound.

......*ve.*

Just a little scratch. Nothing serious.

l ov e

The bleeding had almost stopped already.

ove lo e love l ve

But the itching didn't stop. The pulsing was only getting stronger.

I love you I love you I love you I love you I love you Mr. Nasujima I lovelovelove

And then the boy noticed.

I love you I love your flesh your hair your soul blood voice memory future everything

The throbbing wasn't pain; it was a voice that was echoing throughout his *love you love you love you love you love you love you love you love you love you love love love love love love love lllllloooooooovvvvvvv vvvvvvvveeeeeeeeeeeeee.........................*

"...Hey, Aoba?"

The boy was back on the phone; this time his eyes were abnormally red with blood and shining emptily.

"What did you learn?"

"Turns out there was some kind of unannounced idol concert, so it's just a bunch of people loitering about after it finished. If anything, it's good cover for messing around."

"Okay. Then I'll tell Mr. Mikado about it."

When the call was over, the boy looked to the man standing across from him.

"Well done," the man said. "Very good acting."

"Thank you...*Mother*," the boy replied, then wandered unsteadily away among the throng.

The man, Takashi Nasujima, watched him go, chuckling, and said to a man and woman standing at his side, "This is interesting. Mikado Ryuugamine's actually going to come right out here into the open. And with a motorcycle-gang leader from Saitama and Masaomi Kida, to boot."

"Yes, Mother," said the woman, Haruna Niekawa, with empty eyes.

But the man next to her, Shijima, was more confused. "What? Mikado Ryuugamine?"

Nasujima ignored his question. He smiled happily with the information he'd just gained. He'd been giving all the Saikas under his command a constant order—*"Bring me any useful information you learn"*—and the boy who'd wandered away had done the job admirably.

Nasujima, too, had his eye on Mikado Ryuugamine, the founder of the Dollars. He was considering whether to put him under Saika's control tonight or threaten him into behaving, like he had with Shijima. But if the boy was going to come here all on his own, that was a happy surprise.

And not only that—there was another bird coming home to roost.

"Masaomi Kida. There's a name I didn't expect to hear tonight."

When Nasujima was a teacher, Kida had caught him sexually harassing Anri Sonohara and used that knowledge to threaten him. He wasn't a teacher anymore, but at the very least, he still felt the anger and hatred of being mocked and toyed with by a student.

"Sounds good. I can take him over and make him dance naked. I'll record it, upload it to the Net, then undo his mind control and see how he reacts."

Nasujima chuckled to himself over his trashy idea, then glanced toward Russia Sushi. "I was thinking of just tearing down the place all at once, but I wouldn't want to cause too much trouble and put them on edge."

So he decided to have the crowd lay low for now. More important was how he was going to get Shizuo Heiwajima's supervisor under his control while inside the restaurant.

Nasujima had a few of his Saika-possessed victims standing outside of Russia Sushi with one of those old cell phone signal jammers that used to be popular years ago. In fact, it had been tampered with to augment the effect. If he walked a few yards closer, his own phone would stop working.

The restaurant's landline had already been cut, and there were no signs of a broadband or cable TV wire.

Nasujima had cut off all means of contact with the outside world, putting him at an overwhelming advantage over whoever was inside of Russia Sushi.

But he wasn't completely filled with confidence. Shizuo Heiwajima remained a source of anxiety and a target for his caution.

Not only did he have the trauma of being beaten by Shizuo in the past, but it also seemed that Saika itself viewed Shizuo as a special human being somehow. Therefore, he needed control over Shizuo's boss—his Achilles' heel—without drawing Shizuo's attention. If that monster showed up now, it would all be over.

Nasujima placed a phone call to another number, but it did not get picked up.

"Tsk…damn info dealer. Can't get him when I actually need him," Nasujima swore, conveniently ignoring the fact that he'd stolen money from that same man's office.

Next, he called the secretary of Jinnai Yodogiri, the man he was planning to betray in order to take over his business. As far as Nasujima knew, the secretary's information network was trustworthy. She might even have knowledge on what Shizuo Heiwajima was doing right about now.

But she, too, did not pick up the call.

"Shit, doesn't anybody around here answer their damn phone?" he snapped, ignoring the fact that he was calling in the dead of night.

But of course, he didn't know that at this moment, both Izaya Orihara and Yodogiri's secretary, Kasane Kujiragi, were in the same building.

Or that, more importantly, Shizuo Heiwajima himself was there with them.

♂♀

Building under construction—lower levels

Down in the lower levels of the building where Shizuo and Izaya were fighting to the death, the foundation was very strong and mostly complete. The interiors were entirely finished in parts.

But given that the only lights were the fluorescents in the hallways, it was still quite a barren sight and not much better than a cleared-out empty building.

It was in this environment that three young women faced off.

This was not a glamorous scene or a bright and chatty one. Each of the women had suffered equal physical damage.

"Ha-ha! You two are good," said Mikage Sharaku, a woman built like a street fighter, enjoying herself despite the wounds to her cheeks and arms. "I underestimated you. I shouldn't have."

The other two, Vorona and Kasane Kujiragi, gave her expressionless looks.

"In typical times, this phenomenon would cause my entrails to boil, but at present I deny to do battle with you," said Vorona.

"I agree with her. I have no reason to fight you."

It wasn't a three-sided fight. Vorona and Kujiragi were heading to the top of the building, and Mikage was trying to interfere with their progress. On the other hand, Vorona and Kujiragi did not know each other well and were not capable of teaming up against their foe.

If Slon had been here instead of Kujiragi, Vorona would be three or four times as deadly, but it wasn't until moments ago that she even learned Kujiragi was capable of fighting at all.

All she knew was that the other woman wasn't weak but in fact had superhuman athleticism of her own. Mikage sensed as much through their pugilistic exchange. She gave her a cocky smile.

"I guess it's true that you can't judge a person by their looks. I never expected someone who looks as brainy as you to be a good fighter."

"You have overestimated me. If I were truly brainy, I would not be in this place at all. And if I were as powerful as you make me out to be, I would be leading a different life right now."

"Look, I'm not talking about some vague crap like your 'strength as a person.'" Mikage looked toward the third woman and said, "Vorona, right? I wish I could've fought you at peak condition instead. Though knowing you, I bet you'd just use a gun or something."

Vorona glared and pursed her lips. She'd suffered bruises all over her body from the steel beams dropped off the building's roof. And in fact, she *did* have a gun, which had gotten trapped under the pile of beams.

Still, Vorona knew that even if she were in peak condition, the woman she was fighting was not one to be trifled with. She could be partially armed and still lose that battle.

As evidence of that, Mikage was currently fighting two capable women—even if uncoordinated with each other—and had stopped them short.

In between Vorona's practiced martial arts and combination attacks, Kujiragi would strike with inhuman reflexes and speed. That was the kind of impromptu combination work that would take down any novice fighter, even a man with bulging muscles.

But Mikage blocked all of Vorona's hits with her palms and evaded Kujiragi by just a hair. And in the moments when the two women switched attacks, she even countered with kicks of her own.

While Mikage wasn't getting away scot-free, neither side was able to totally neutralize the other. The fight was turning into a stalemate.

If Shizuo was some djinni or spirit that transcended humanity, then this woman was an amalgamation of advanced technology.

Normally, Vorona would be delighted. If she could destroy this woman, who had pursued the extremes of human strength—or if she herself was utterly destroyed—then at last she could measure the strength of humanity.

But though she was facing an opponent who might fulfill her long-held wish, Vorona was not in the mood to celebrate.

Across from her, guarding the way to the stairs, Mikage smirked. "Want me to let you in on something? Whether you go up there or not, it won't make a difference," she said, grimacing with frustration that she couldn't be there to see it. "This is a fight beyond that kind of interference, I bet."

The building itself seemed to back her up there, as a dull crash from above traveled downward.

"The combatants up there are a guy whose body quit being human and a guy whose brain quit being human," Mikage said.

With absolute certainty, Vorona replied, "There is no inevitability that a fight should be valid. There is no possibility of victory over Sir Shizuo. It is the direction of my duty that should stop the beating of his heart."

"You sure talk some crazy Japanese…," Mikage said with a grin as she shook out her hands. "As to your statement, I'll admit, I didn't think Izaya stood a chance against that monster, either…but the truth is, I've never actually seen what he can do."

"?"

"He'll happily lead a person to their downfall, but he doesn't use his own violence to directly destroy a person. I mean, he's got that whole shtick about loving humanity or whatever."

Mikage glanced up at the ceiling for a moment, looking anguished that she couldn't actually be up there to see their fight.

"So I think this might actually be the first time he's ever used all his power and seriously attempted to kill a human being."

♂♀

Building under construction—upper levels

"Ah… What a view."

Izaya let his eyes travel down from the starless sky overhead.

"I think the view of the night under a sky without stars is the height of beauty. It's a crystallization of human industry," he said entirely to himself, the words melting into the darkness.

Izaya Orihara was not, in fact, holding any kind of conversation with *the man who knelt at the center of the construction site.*

That was Shizuo Heiwajima, grimacing with anguish on the ground.

It was an unthinkable sight: Izaya sat unharmed atop the steel beams of the building frame, looking down at Shizuo, who bore a number of wounds all over his body.

They'd been inflicted by wire and nail-gun traps that Izaya had set up.

All the traps would be instantly fatal to a normal person, but they were little more than scratches to Shizuo. They shouldn't have had the ability to bring a being like Shizuo Heiwajima to his knees—and yet that was exactly where he was, on the floor of the building.

"…"

Shizuo said nothing. He merely glared up at Izaya, sitting off to the side, his expression pained. In fact, he was finding it difficult to even breathe, not that he wanted to say anything if he could.

It was not pain or blood loss that stole the freedom of his monstrously powerful body.

The first things to assault him were dizziness and fatigue.

There was no way he'd be feeling tired given the situation, but by the time he was aware of the abnormal feeling in him, it was already too late.

All the strength had left his muscles. He could no longer stand on his own.

It was lack of oxygen.

Just as simple as oxygen deprivation. It seemed unlikely, happening in a construction site that was little more than vinyl covering over steel building frames, but it was indeed none other than a trap set by Izaya.

The fire, the crane attack, and all the other traps were nothing more than red herrings meant to hide the existence of this one.

Specifically, it was the fire-extinguishing system that had already been built into the building. Izaya tampered with the pipes from the carbon dioxide gas tank meant to snuff out fires, filling the building with the gas very quickly.

It would not have worked without Izaya's brilliant calculations, predicting the wind direction and flow of air and guiding Shizuo to the place where the oxygen concentration was lowest.

It was thanks to the unprecedented level of murderous intent in Izaya's mind—a true aura of lethality shrouding his brain, perhaps—that his concentration hit peak values.

However much gas was being pumped into the area, regardless of it being outside, the spot where Shizuo was standing had dangerously low levels of oxygen. He inhaled, not realizing this, and quickly lost full control of his body.

In fact, if the oxygen levels had been any lower, he might have fallen unconscious. And if the fight had been taking place in an enclosed interior, Shizuo could have died from lack of oxygen.

But sensing that an "enclosed space" was always temporary given Shizuo's strength when in a rage, Izaya chose to employ this strategy instead.

How does one kill a creature to whom guns and blades mean nothing? The answer, to Izaya, was suffocation.

And as a result, the monster who'd taken a hit from a truck without blinking was now helpless on his knees.

But there was no joy or arrogance on Izaya's face.

Shizuo Heiwajima was still alive.

*   *   *

That simple fact meant that he was in the presence of a threat to his very life.

Perhaps if there had been no wind blowing between the buildings or if the night had been perfectly still, the situation would have been different. In any case, it was fortunate for him that his strategy was effective enough to stop Shizuo in his tracks in an outdoor environment at all.

How many minutes would it take before he recovered from the lack of oxygen? How many seconds?

Izaya couldn't put on his usual confident grin, because any estimates based on normal human physiology meant nothing here. Normally he would have been running and darting about, smiling cockily as he fled, but there were two reasons he wore no such smile now.

He was full to the brim with loathing for his opponent.

And he knew, on an instinctual level, that one wrong movement would lead to the end of his life.

I don't care if I die.
But I don't want it to be at the expense of this monster surviving.
The monster can't live among the human beings in a world without me.
Pretending to be human, pinning down humanity with his strength.
Love, hope, malice, plotting, intelligence, technique, experience.
All the things that humanity has built, he ruins.

"...Yeah, that's right."

The words spilled right out of his mouth.

But whether they were meant for anyone aside from himself, as his eyes narrowed with turgid black emotions, no one could say. Not even the man who said them.

"I ought to kill you, whether there's a good rationale or not."

Any display of emotion had disappeared from Izaya's face. He stood atop the steel beam and took out an object.

It was an old-fashioned box of matches, with the name of some business or other on it—the same implement he'd used to burn the chess pieces in his apartment a while ago. He lit a match and dropped the little spark below.

The wind had already blown free the extinguishing gas that was meant to remove the oxygen that might fuel any flames.

Now there was a different kind of gas surrounding Shizuo.

The flammable gas that had been flowing across the outside area from the moment that he'd first emerged there.

As he watched the match falling toward him, Shizuo could also sense the odor of the gas filling the space around him. But no one could say whether he currently had the brainpower needed to process that information accurately.

All that was certain was he hadn't recovered from the damage the lack of oxygen had caused, and he wouldn't be able to generate the same kind of wind he had earlier when kicking down the door.

So he couldn't leap out into the open air. The gas surrounded him on all sides. He was trapped.

And then the flame of the match reached the layer of gas.

Red light flashed against the starless night sky.

♂♀

Ikebukuro

Because it was late at night, only a very limited number of people witnessed a part of the night sky turning red.

But within the confines of a dense metropolis, even a limited number can mean quite a lot—in this case, several hundred people.

Mysteriously, however, the light vanished nearly as quickly as it appeared. From a distance, it was as though the roof of a specific building flashed, then returned to darkness in less than a minute.

But many of those witnesses failed to detect something off about the phenomenon.

The blinking aircraft warning lights atop the building in question had vanished as well.

Only a handful of those witnesses actually noticed what happened.

There were Shingen Kishitani and Egor, looking up at the building under construction from its base.

And also, watching from the window of a distant building, a man whose eyes were bloodshot red.

The man's skin was peeled off here and there, his flesh scraped away, as if he had wrenched his way free from some kind of *physical bondage*. He had done a minimal amount to stop the bleeding, but there was plenty of blood on his clothing.

He watched the distant sight as if he were gazing upon someone beloved, with those bright red eyes. And he *did* know what happened.

On the roof of a building about two-thirds of a mile away, *a shadow had plunged from the sky, scooped up a flame that was about to burst throughout the area, and extinguished it within its darkness.*

At a brief glance, it was as if the light had rapidly dwindled. But the man, who had observed the freakish shadow longer than anyone and knew it better than anyone, understood immediately how it had extinguished the fire, even from a distance.

It was as though the night sky had a will of its own and had chosen to put out the fire.

And in knowing what it did, the man exulted.

Exactly *because* he knew what it had done.

Saika's accursed words of love surged within him.

When Kujiragi possessed him with Saika's power, she commanded him to stay put and behave.

But he used his *own* love to pin down both of these things—and spoke the name of the one to whom he dedicated his unstoppable love.

Moaning, singing, his own word of love escaping his throat.

"Cel......ty......"

It was just a name, but to him, it was a word of love.

He hadn't driven out Saika's curse, the way that Akabayashi once had, by gouging out his own wound. Instead, he had repeated Haruna Niekawa's method, mastering Saika's mad song of love from the inside.

He was able to overwhelm Saika much faster than Haruna had— perhaps because Saika loved "humans," while what he loved was "inhuman."

Did he even know what had happened to himself?

The man cut by Saika, Shinra Kishitani, faced the darkened sky with red eyes and smiled.

Full of love for what seemed to be the dark of the night itself that coated the city.

♂♀

Raijin High School—in the past

"So if that tiger's going to leave his skin behind, as a person, how will *you* leave your name behind? I'm kind of excited about the thought of you being remembered as a serial killer."

"As a person...?"

The smile vanished from Shinra's lips as he looked up at the light coming down from the rooftop door. He imagined a great shadow beyond that light, sucking up everything into its midst.

"I don't need to leave anything behind."

"But I thought people died and left their names behind. If you're not a tiger or a human, then what do you intend to be?"

"Good question. If I'm not a person or a tiger, then I guess I'm going to be some kind of weird folklore monster," Shinra joked—or made what could only be taken as a joke—smiling worriedly.

"But if I could be with her...then I wouldn't mind not being human."

Chat room

Kuru: Well, well. My, my. For claiming that she would flame Ta-rouTanaka until he showed up, Miss Namie does seem to have given up posting all of a sudden.

Mai: Mysterious.

Mai: Maybe she got hungry.

Kuru: We can only hope the reason is as benign as that.

Kuru: But who do you suppose this "Rocchi" is? This message board is supposed to be accessible by invitation only, so I would assume that Rocchi must know one of the members. Or perhaps Masaomi Kida is in fact a member of the chat, and Rocchi threatened him into giving up the address. Who could this Masaomi Kida be...?

Mai: This is shameless.

Mai: Ouch.

Mai: I got pinched.

Kuru: Be that as it may, since neither Rocchi nor Namie has left the room, I would assume they're still watching?

Mai: Exciting.

Rocchi: Yo, I'm here.

Mai: Yo.

Kuru: Oh my. So you're still around. Very clever of you to stay quiet and spy on the chat, pretending that you are away.

NamieYagiri has left the chat.

Kuru: Oh my. Already giving up, Miss Namie? Or did she have some pressing business to attend to?

Mai: I pressed the trapdoor button.

Rocchi: Sorry about that. I was just planning a party with my friend.

Rocchi: Are you two girls, by the way?

Rocchi: Because I've got a bit of time until the party.

Rocchi: Do you mind if I hang out here and chat until then?

Rocchi: Is that okay with you?

Kuru: Oh my. Should you really be talking to ladies in such a forward manner online? You never know, we might be men pretending to be women.

Mai: Gender undisclosed.

Mai: Mysterious!

Rocchi: Nah, I can tell. You're not pretending. You're both girls.

Kuru: That's a very entertaining guess, but do you have evidence? I believe that you might be better suited to writing rom-coms than playing detective. The Internet is the shining darkness of the modern world, where no one can see the other's face. What makes you so certain of the fact that I must be a woman, just because my manner of communication is so blatantly feminine?

Rocchi: A hunch.

Rocchi: I can tell from the writing when someone's a cute girl.

Mai: You're scary.

Mai: You're a philanderer.

Rocchi: Can't deny that one.

Kuru: What a strange gentleman. Oh, pardon me. I did not take into account the possibility that you might be a woman.

Rocchi: Well, that's the question, isn't it? Am I cool for bearing the burden of the shining darkness of the modern world?

Kuru: Anonymity is a thing of the past, after that previous outburst. Miss Namie has most crudely revealed the identities of those who inhabit this place. This entire chat room was predicated upon a delicate balance—made of a group of people who know each other but do not know each other's aliases. Now it is ruined and must be reset. No score, no game, no future.

Mai: That's sad.

Rocchi: I mean, it sure sounds like you know who everyone is.

Kuru: Yes, we had the pleasure of the superiority of knowledge, knowing all and being mere observers. Now this valuable place of play will be lost to us. It is a shame, but I suppose there is little one can do but chalk it up to the work of fate.

Mai: Very sad.

Rocchi: That's not true, is it?

Rocchi: There are many things you can say when you're not looking the other person in the face, but there are also lots of things you can say because you know who you're talking to, right?

Kuru: Oh my. Such as what?

Rocchi: A confession of love.

Mai: Incredible.

Rocchi: Of course, you can also do that when neither party knows the other very well and get into a load of trouble because of it.

Rocchi: I mean, look, I don't know the first thing about this chat room.

Rocchi: But since I happened to be here for its ending, it would be nice to get to know you.

Kuru: You really will say whatever you want, won't you? Who in the world are you?

Mai: Who are you.

Rocchi: Just a passing ne'er-do-well.

Rocchi: And I'm heading to a ne'er-do-well party in Ikebukuro.

Rocchi: I wouldn't go outside until the night is over, if I were you.

Kuru: Oh my. You speak exactly like a certain someone I know. Just when I was preparing to head out into the city, to relieve myself of the loneliness of knowing this special place has been irrevocably broken.

Mai: We're in sync.

Rocchi: Pardon me.

Rocchi: But in fact, this place isn't special.

Rocchi: Out there, in here—it's all the same.

Rocchi: I mean, when you pass people on the street, you both might as well be anonymous, right?

Rocchi: You never know where an acquaintance might be hiding in plain sight.

Rocchi: And that can break down out of nowhere, just like this message board.

Rocchi: Well, so long.

Rocchi has left the chat.

CHAPTER 11
Like a Dragon Given Wings

Hallway, Raijin High School—in the past

"Hey, are you ready to be up and walking around already...? Oh, why do I even ask?"

"...Oh, it's you, Shinra. Where's that cockroach? I'm gonna squash him like the bug he is, until he says he's going to change schools," growled Shizuo bitterly as he passed Shinra in the hallway.

Shinra shrugged and jokingly responded, "You got hit by a truck, and rather than worrying about your own health, your first priority is hitting others? But I guess you've grown as a person, since you're not destroying the school campus itself until Izaya shows up."

He sighed, then glanced at Shizuo's hair. "To be honest, I was stunned when I saw you with blond hair after all that time. I thought you'd finally turned into a bad boy."

"...Oh, shut up. I didn't dye it blond because I wanted to."

"Then why? You can get your way on anything with force alone. Why would you dye it blond if you didn't want to?"

"It was an older guy in middle school who told me to do it... But whatever, that doesn't matter. What class is that mosquito bastard in?" Shizuo demanded, his temple pulsing. He was seething with anger despite the fact that he'd just met the guy the day before.

"Are you intending to get kicked out of school? At least control your-self while in the building." Shinra cackled.

Shizuo clicked his tongue but did as his schoolmate said, this time turning his anger upon Shinra himself. "And what the hell were you thinking, introducing me to that filthy little trash bug?"

"Oh, come on. He's the only friend I made in middle school, so I wanted to introduce him to you, the only friend I made in elementary."

"Let me give you a warning. Choose your friends carefully."

"Really? *You're* going to say that, Shizuo?" Shinra quipped to his old friend with a grin. "Look, at least take it easy at school. You don't want to get expelled right at the start of the school year and cause your fam-ily a bunch of grief, do you?"

"..."

The mention of his family made Shizuo's scowl even deeper. "Fine, fine," he grumbled. "I guess I can wait until after school to kill him."

"Can we at least remove 'killing him' from the options? What is it that has you so furious about him?"

"...I just hate guys like that, who talk around people in circles but don't actually do anything on their own."

"Ah, I see now."

It was quite a bold statement for Shizuo to make about the personal-ity of someone he'd barely met, but Shinra didn't push back on it. He knew that Izaya was exactly the kind of person Shizuo described.

Instead of arguing, he smiled and said, "But if you're going to go down that route, I'm also a person who's all talk."

"That's true. You annoy me all the time, too," Shizuo said with a mean glare.

Shinra backed away in a hurry. "H-hey, don't look at me like that. Whoa, whoa—easy, easy. Let's be cool."

Shizuo's brow stayed furrowed as he stared at his old friend. "The thing is, you might tell a lot of really stupid-ass jokes, but you don't just lie for the hell of it. That, at least, makes you better than that fleabrain."

"I think you're confused. I'm not some pure, innocent soul, and I'll lie if I need to."

"...You're dumb enough to talk about wanting to dissect people in broad daylight. Why would you even need to lie?" Shizuo said, intending it to sound like casual conversation. Shinra thought that one over.

"Hmm… Good question. I'm in love with a girl."

"So?"

"If I needed to, I would lie in order to fulfill my love for her. I would be a villain."

"Okay, fine. Hey, if you wanna be a villain for the sake of the woman you love, knock yourself out," Shizuo shot back, annoyed at the sappy romantic talk.

But Shinra waved his hand in denial. "No, it wouldn't be for her sake exactly. It would be for my sake."

"What?"

"If I was going to lie out of malice, it would be to her."

"What do you mean?" Shizuo's brow furrowed even deeper. The other students were steering so clear of him, they wouldn't even venture into the hallway.

"I mean, I really, really love her. In fact, it's probably closer to a desire to own her than to love her. So if she was drifting away from me for some reason…I would do whatever it takes to keep her at my side, even if it meant being a villain. I might even kill a person."

Even Shizuo had to take this admission in silence. Eventually, he said, "Nah…that's no good. If you killed someone, she wouldn't want anything to do with you anymore."

"Yeah, that's right. Which is why I'd keep it a secret from her. Or maybe I'd lie and say, 'It's your fault I became a murderer!' and make her feel really guilty about it. Then maybe she'll stay with me forever."

"You're kind of a piece of shit, huh?" Shizuo let out a huge sigh and looked at Shinra with pity in his eyes. "I think the reason you don't have many friends is because you say whatever's on your mind like that."

"I didn't think I'd ever hear that from you…but I won't deny it."

"What kind of love is it that makes life worse for the other person? If that's love, it's a pretty twisted strain of it."

"Look, I'm not saying I wouldn't rather have it a different way, right? I'd prefer to lead a normal romantic life and be able to say stuff like 'As long as I can pledge my life to you, I don't need anything else!' That would be best of all," Shinra said, nodding to himself, as proper as you please.

Shizuo gave him a disgusted look. "I feel really sorry for whatever woman you fall in love with. Just don't be surprised if she stabs you when she finds out what you're like."

"I don't know... She's really sweet, so maybe at the end of it all, she'll actually forgive me."

"At least you've got a field of flowers in that skull of yours...," Shizuo said, shaking his head. He was tired of the topic. "But whatever. If it comes to that, I'll smash you up into the sky so your woman won't have to."

He meant it as a way to tell off Shinra, but the other boy just smiled. Whether he was serious or joking, Shinra said, "I'd appreciate it if you did. And I'd appreciate it even more if you do it softly enough that I don't die."

"I'm not as tough as you, after all."

♂♀

Building under construction—present day

The flame of the match acted as a trigger, sending up a huge amount of heat and light from the flammable gas filling the area and causing dull sounds of destruction.

Izaya stood atop the beams, but he'd moved to a safer location away from the searing waves of heat after he dropped the match. But even then, the gusts of wind from the gas explosion sent jets of raging heat right past him.

He had to hold tight to the steel pillar to protect himself and ensure the gust didn't knock him off. That was enough to pull his eyes off Shizuo for the moment.

There was always the possibility that Shizuo could be entirely burned to a crisp, without oxygen in his lungs, and still come after him. At the very least, Izaya expected, he wouldn't be able to escape with his legs paralyzed like that...

But then he noticed something off.

The darkness around them had somehow gotten thicker.

"...?"

This wasn't typical night darkness. The light of the flames was being sucked up directly into the sky—such was the abnormal dark around the building.

It was often said that the stars were invisible in the city because of the illumination around you, but in this case, it was as if the sky had snuffed out all the light on the surface of the planet.

And not just the light. The wind, heated and fueled by the fire—even the flames themselves—vanished into the darkness. A shadow reaching down from the sky was grabbing the fire and devouring it.

Izaya recognized this shadow.

"…"

And realizing that he knew what this mysterious shadow was, he narrowed his eyes and muttered, "I thought it had no memory… What does that monster think it's doing?"

For just a moment, he gazed up at the sky. There were no stars above, nothing at all but unnatural darkness.

But he couldn't afford to pay much attention to it now. He was in the midst of a battle for his life.

Out of the suspicion that the shadow might seek to interrupt or interfere with their battle, Izaya gave it a bare minimum of caution as he searched for Shizuo Heiwajima below.

The flame had not spread far but was collected into a small area, probably due to the effect of the shadow. Yet he did not see a human figure amid the fire.

Where is he?

Izaya squinted, looking for the figure of a man charred to a crisp. Then he felt a dull shaking at his feet and grabbed the steel beam for support.

An earthquake?

It was fierce and yet muffled, like the earth itself was rumbling and rocking.

No, that's not it.

An ordinary person would chalk it up to a quake. But Izaya knew.

There was no coincidental tremor right at this exact moment. There was one possible source that was far more likely, given the circumstances.

Izaya gripped the corner of the pillar and gazed into the center of the shrinking, focusing flames.

And then he saw it. Right in the center of the fire.

There was a large shadow, right around the spot where Shizuo had been kneeling earlier. But it was not in the form of a human figure consumed by the fire.

It was a massive hole in the floor with cracks spreading away from it like the web of a spider. A shiver ran down Izaya's back.

That monster. Did he punch through the floor with his upper-half strength alone?

Moments ago, Shizuo had been paralyzed on the floor due to lack of air. He was able to move his torso but hadn't recovered enough oxygen to use his legs to stand.

So he had used whatever muscles he could to inflict enough damage to break through the floor. Perhaps it had been with his fists or elbows or forehead; Izaya couldn't tell.

All he knew was that the smashing sound he had heard earlier along with the burst of heat and light hadn't been from the explosion but had been the sound of the floor crumbling with the force of Shizuo's blow.

Did he fall through a hole to escape?! Or maybe...

There were two possibilities.

One was that he had punched a hole in the floor and escaped the flames by falling through it.

The other was that, like a grasshopper slamming its legs against the ground for greater recoil, the sheer force of hitting the floor had buffeted the rest of his body clear out of the center of the flames.

In either case, there was just one conclusion to be drawn.

Izaya leaned forward atop the steel beam, looking down the length of the pillar beneath him to its base. And there he saw...

"..."

...the figure of Shizuo Heiwajima—clothes, skin, and hair singed here and there—grabbing the base of the steel beam with a look of absolute fury.

Uh-oh!

Izaya tried to leap away to safety, but a larger shaking threw off his momentum. The beams around him bent and twisted as the very foundation of the wall of the building began to crumble.

Shizuo pried the beam he was holding out of the frame of the building and held it the way he normally held streetlights and electric poles when he removed them and swung them around.

As Izaya fell, off-balance, from his previous foothold, he saw the metal beam swinging straight at him.

"Guh..."

Out of either calculation or pure instinct, Izaya instantly twisted, swinging his shoe out to catch the beam.

The next moment, the sole of his shoe made contact with metal—and Izaya's body was struck toward the starless mound of the sky, a baseball diamond without pitcher or fielders.

Ikebukuro

"...Kinda weird, huh?"

Chikage was on the way toward their transaction point, with Masaomi walking next to him.

"Yeah, sure are a lot of people out and about."

"Exactly... Doesn't feel like the hours before dawn."

They were going to get to the trade-off spot ahead of time and scout it out, to see whether they could learn how many people Mikado intended to bring. Perhaps there was an emergency staircase at a nearby restaurant or other late-night establishment that they could use as a vantage point.

But on the way there, the two noticed that something felt off. Not only did Masaomi, as a resident of Ikebukuro, sense it, but even Chikage, from distant Saitama, could tell that something was wrong.

"I'm getting a bad feeling about it. This crawling on my back? It's like when the yakuza would get involved with my gang."

"Don't scare me like that...," Masaomi said, cheek twitching, but he didn't seem particularly afraid. There was *one* concern on his mind, though: "I just hope that Izumii asshole doesn't interfere..."

Chikage had put the hurt on them at the parking garage, but they weren't the type of folks who gave up easily.

"Can't believe they're bringing in guys like that..."

"Hey, anyone can join the Dollars, right? I heard there are little grade school kids, too."

"But even still…"

Masaomi thought back to how Izumii and his gang had nearly brought down the Yellow Scarves from within. It was a galling memory.

"Anyway, better to steer clear of that guy in the shades," Chikage said cheerily as he glanced around them. "That's the kind of guy who'll hurl Molotov cocktails at anyone he decides is an enemy, even in the middle of broad daylight."

They were still keeping their distance from the shopping district and not approaching the crowds directly. During the day, they might have slipped in among the throng, but they weren't careless enough to wander over into an abnormal situation.

"Got any ideas as to what this is about? I mean, I'd believe it if you told me there was a World Cup match today or somethin'."

"I dunno… Do they look weird to you, too? It's like they're just wandering back and forth…"

A cold sweat began to trickle down Masaomi's back. The eeriness of the sight was starting to surpass curiosity into the realm of horror.

Don't tell me this has the Dollars' fingerprints on it, too…

I guess all those people there…could be Dollars, perhaps…

But then again…

Masaomi had heard the legend of the Dollars' first meetup, but this seemed strange even for that.

"Fine, fine. Let's get inside somewhere, just in case," Chikage suggested and headed for a nearby door. "As long as we can get onto the roof."

"We gotta plan it a *bit* more than that," Masaomi said, chagrined. He glanced at a different nearby building. "Let's go to that one. The rooftop has a good view, and it's easy to get up to."

"You've been on the roof there?"

"I was going all over the place back in the days when we fought with the Blue Squares. My worst adviser, Orihara, seemed to be oddly well-informed about them," Masaomi said, his face twisting at the bitter memories of the wars in the old days.

Chikage cackled and clapped him on the shoulder. "Well, listen to you, juvenile delinquent. I guess I can turn a blind eye to your past exploits in this case, then."

"…Like you aren't about to engage in trespassing yourself."

♂♀

Inside a van

Togusa's van featured an anime decal all across one side of it, thanks to Yumasaki. Normally, it had the space for four to relax in relative comfort, front seat and back, but now it had twice that population density.

Togusa was in the driver's seat, while the injured Kadota sat in the passenger seat.

In the middle row were Namie and Mika, with Seiji seated between them, while the back seat contained Yumasaki, Anri, and Saki. If Karisawa were along as she usually was, they'd be over capacity—but she was not in the vehicle.

She'd been out on the streets searching for Kadota when all communication from her had stopped. The rest of the group decided to head toward the Sunshine area of Ikebukuro to find her, where things tended to be busiest.

"I think you girls should have stayed behind," Kadota said to the two girls in the back seat, conveniently ignoring that he was still injured and had no business being there. "How about if you lie low for a while? I'll ask Shinra's mom if she'll take you in for a bit."

But Anri shook her head. She looked more fervent than usual. "No…I will go, too. I have to go."

Kadota saw her eyes through the rearview mirror and sighed. At first, Anri had been too confused to process the entire situation, but from the moment she learned that Karisawa was in danger, she insisted on coming along.

"Did something happen with you and Karisawa?" he asked.

"She…she helped me in various ways when I was having trouble," Anri replied, her head drooping just a bit, as she recalled all that had happened in the last few days.

If Karisawa hadn't been there, then Izaya Orihara's words alone might have succeeded in destroying Anri's will. The realization gave her a fresh appreciation for what Karisawa had done for her.

It was why she had made up her mind—to face all the *aches* related to herself.

When she looked up again, Kadota wore a pensive expression.

"Huh? What's up, Kadota...?" Togusa asked as he was reaching to turn on the engine. He followed Kadota's lead and looked into the rearview mirror at Anri. "H-hey, kid! What happened to your eyes?"

The rest of them all turned to look at her. One thing was immediately apparent.

Anri Sonohara's eyes were glowing red.

The red light shone through the lenses of her glasses, flickering and floating within the van like will-o'-the-wisps. Kadota and Yumasaki had seen Anri fighting with glowing red eyes in the park before. But they'd never been able to confront her about that and hadn't planned to ask her in the future.

Anri looked at the rest of them with those powerful red eyes and stated, "I think that the slasher in the neighborhood is related to me."

She steadied her breathing and suppressed her normal hesitant tone of voice to produce something far harder and stronger than anything they'd heard from her before.

"And that's why...I need to go."

♂♀

Commercial building—rooftop

On the spacious roof of a building that contained multiple restaurants and bars within it, Chikage and Masaomi secretly surveyed the city around them to get a better picture of what was happening.

For being the middle of the night, there were just too many people around.

And they were especially clustered in the area they were planning to go next—the block in front of Tokyu Hands. But that spot in particular wasn't the densest; that honor seemed to go to the block before that, heading to the bowling alley.

"Can't see that way around the building... Did something happen around Russia Sushi's area?"

"Something's fishy about what they're doing. It's all mechanical or something, like they're on a loop... Like a character in the background of a video game level, ya know?" Chikage suggested. But while he seemed nonchalant, Masaomi was unnerved by the sight.

"Shit... What's going on over there...?"

"Are their eyes red, too?"

"Huh?"

"It's hard to make out from here... In fact, you can't really make out the sidewalk from here, because of the highway."

From their position, the crossing bridge over the Metropolitan Expressway was angled such that it blocked the intersection where Sixtieth Floor Street met Otowa Street.

"If only this building were as tall as the Amlux or Sunshine buildings, we'd have a real clear view of it." Masaomi groaned, tilting his head sideways to look at the Amlux building across the expressway from Tokyu Hands. But it seemed impossible to sneak onto the roof there, and even if the Sunshine observation decks were open twenty-four hours a day, it would take several times as long to get over to that one.

"Still, it's an improvement having a better look at Sixtieth Floor Street, ya know?" said Chikage, watching the streets below. But then he spotted something that looked *off*.

Around the entrance to Tokyu Hands, there was a new group that looked noticeably different from the generic crowds elsewhere. To a person, they wore blue beanies and ski masks, creating a vivid distinction from the rest of the nighttime masses.

When he saw the smaller group of blue, Masaomi clenched the roof's railing.

"There they are... It's the Blue Squares."

♂♀

Outside of Russia Sushi

"...Some new customers?"

Nasujima noticed the van stopping in front of Tokyu Hands to let out a group of boys wearing eerie shark-pattern ski masks and grinned to himself.

"Don't mess with them yet. Just control the ones taken over with Saika, got it? I'll give the command when it's time. Don't want to create an opening that the folks in the sushi place will use to escape."

"...Yes, Mother," said Haruna, her eyes dull. He rubbed her head and smiled.

"Mikado Ryuugamine, huh? All I remember is that his name stuck out and he was otherwise completely forgettable," Nasujima said, trying to remember his old student, but because it had been a different class than his own homeroom and Mikado had been a boy, he couldn't recall the face.

"Anyway. So the boss of the Dollars is a guy without any notable features, eh? Kids these days are crazy." He chuckled to himself. He looked over the blank-faced Haruna and the terrified Shijima.

"Education's not what it used to be, is it?" asked the former teacher. Neither Shijima nor Haruna said anything about the irony.

♂♀

The rooftop of a mixed-use building

"So which one's Mikado Ryuugamine? See, I'd never forget a girl's face, but..."

Chikage scanned the area. Masaomi focused on one specific point in the crowd.

"Shit...there are a couple of guys with the same build as Mikado wearing ski masks, so I can't tell which one might be him..."

Even at a distance, Mikado's innocent, babyish face would stand out among the Blue Squares. And Masaomi had eyesight good enough to just barely pick him out at this range, despite the darkness.

"I see. So they were trying to avoid their leader getting taken out by an ambush right off the top," Chikage said. "Or maybe he's still in the car...but I can't see it because of the damn expressway!"

"They used cars a lot, so I doubt they're walking or on bicycles."

"Dammit, can't see. Stupid expressway... Why does it have to cost so much?" Chikage complained, which was neither here nor there.

But Masaomi had a different concern. "You know, before we came up here…I saw the big road under the expressway, but it seemed like there were way fewer cars than usual…"

There was no way to confirm that from this angle. The only thing visible was the stream of cars whizzing along the raised expressway, unconcerned with the problems below.

"Lots of people but no cars? Even weirder."

"Something's wrong with Ikebukuro today…"

"Well, at least the crowds actin' weird don't seem to have nothin' to do with these guys in blue," suggested Chikage, who turned his back toward Masaomi. "Well, it's almost time. I'm gonna go down there. You stay here."

"H-hey, aren't you gonna need me?"

"You're the wild card. The main event. I'm gonna tear their masks off, so you watch from up above and come on down when you see your friend. If he's not among them, then I'll make them tell me where to find him, and I'll call you with the answer."

The expressway blocked their view of the group, leaving them without even a solid head count of enemies. And yet Chikage spoke as though losing wasn't even a potential outcome; to him, victory was a given.

Abruptly, Masaomi called out, "Mr. Rokujou!"

"What?"

"Um…thank you."

"You can thank me later. When you do it at this point in the movies, that's a sign that I'm gonna die after this," Chikage said, waving him off with a bitter smile and heading down the stairs. "Plus, you don't know if you'll want to thank me for the results yet."

"Huh?" Masaomi frowned.

Chikage shrugged and said, "I might get so carried away that I wallop your buddy along with the rest of 'em."

♂♀

Residential area

Manami Mamiya was an agent of vengeance.

She lived to make life miserable for Izaya Orihara in every way possible, you might say.

Her life should have ended in a real-life suicide meetup. But now, there was an engine that kept her alive—her hatred for Izaya, who had insulted and dismissed both her intentions and her despair.

So in a way, you could say that Izaya was the one keeping her alive. Manami knew this herself but didn't particularly care about it one way or the other.

If she got the chance to see Izaya die a miserable death, his face twisted with horror and gloom, it would all have been worth it. And that conclusion allowed her to do many horrible things without a second thought.

For example, tossing a severed head into the open space in front of Ikebukuro Station in the middle of the day. This announced the existence of Celty Sturluson's head to the world at large and stole one of Izaya's advantages.

She hadn't actually calculated how this would hurt Izaya. She just knew he would hate it, and so she did it.

Now, for the same reasons, she was engaging in a new activity without considering the finer consequences.

"...So this is the next one," she muttered coldly to herself as she stared up at a small building in a residential area of the city.

It was one of the hideouts of Jinnai Yodogiri, a broker and enemy of Izaya Orihara's—at least, according to the information recorded on the computer in Izaya's office. She had stolen a plethora of information from that computer and copied it to a USB stick she kept in her pocket.

Now she was traveling to the various hideouts recorded in that list of information, hoping to hand over Izaya's data to Yodogiri for free, if she could find him. But though she'd visited over ten of the addresses so far, none of them showed any sign of being occupied.

She even sneaked inside a number of them, but she had nothing to show for it. She knew this was an extremely dangerous thing to do, but she didn't even care if Yodogiri spotted her and killed her.

As long as an enemy formidable enough that Izaya would be wary of him ended up with Izaya's data—that was all she wanted. It would be unfortunate not to actually see Izaya suffering for herself, but if she died here, then that was as far as her energy to live got her, nothing more.

It was a very warped way to rationalize her own actions. And that rationale took her to the back door of this building, too. Through the clouded glass, she could see the lights turn on.

"..."

Cautiously, she focused all her senses. She heard the lock open from the inside, and then a young man's face emerged from the opening door.

His pajamas were covered in red stains here and there, and he was dragging one foot in what looked like a cast. Whatever was going on, it was abnormal. He was either the victim of an attempted murder or perhaps the perpetrator, coated in the blood of his prey.

And then there were his eyes, clearly bloodshot behind his glasses.

"...It's the Saika-possessed," Manami muttered, though not out of fear. If Saika was controlling him, then he must be one of Haruna Niekawa's pawns.

Perhaps Izaya had foreseen what she was up to and sent him there to Yodogiri's hideout ahead of her. But as soon as the thought occurred to her, she realized it might not be the case.

She recognized this man.

She'd seen him in a photograph when studying every bit of information about Izaya Orihara she could find, for revenge.

He was...the unlicensed doctor...

Shinra. That's right. Shinra Kishitani.

Izaya Orihara had any number of pawns to do his bidding, but she remembered that the only one he considered a friend was this black market doctor. But what was he doing here?

"...Why, good evening. Don't be alarmed. There's nothing wrong here," said the bloodstained man. He smiled at her and approached, dragging his foot. He was holding a mop that he'd clearly found inside the building as a crutch.

"Shinra...Kishitani."

"Huh? How do you know my name?" asked the red-eyed Shinra. So he wasn't Niekawa's cat's-paw.

Izaya Orihara's friend, Manami considered. *Would he suffer if he learned that his friend died?*

She concentrated on the ice pick she kept concealed on her person. Shinra, meanwhile, had the red eyes that were a dead giveaway of Saika's possession, but he beckoned to her just as if he was normal.

"Have I given you a checkup in the past, perhaps? If so, I've got one little request," Shinra said, approaching her.

Manami wasn't sure whether she should pull out the ice pick yet and kept her hand on it. "Mr. Kishitani, do you know Izaya Orihara?"

"Hmm? Well, he is my friend. And?"

"I don't know much about having friends, you see... What did you think when he got stabbed a little while back?"

It wasn't the kind of thing you asked a man in bloodied pajamas. She seemed to be plenty abnormal herself—but Shinra considered the question seriously.

"Let's see... I think I figured, *He must have earned it.*"

"..."

"When he called to tell me about it, I said, 'Oh, cool,' and hung up. Was that mean of me?"

"No. It's all his fault. I think that's a perfectly reasonable response," said Manami. She exhaled and let go of the ice pick she was keeping concealed.

Everything Shinra said was indeed true, but it was so far from the typical concept of a "friend" that she saw no value in killing him. Plus, Izaya was the kind of person who would watch a friend die with a smile on his face.

It was why he filled her with such hatred, Manami knew. She asked the man in front of her, "Are you hurt badly?"

"Oh, this? I'm all right. Thanks. It hurts a whole lot, but I'll manage," Shinra said, not realizing that the girl whose concern he appreciated was the very person who threw Celty's head before the eyes of the world. "Actually, this might be a strange thing to ask, but...can I borrow your phone?"

"...Pardon me?"

"I need to go somewhere, but I don't have a phone to arrange a ride... I need to call a taxi and then either my mother-in-law or my dad... Actually, not my dad," Shinra muttered to himself, eyeballs bright red.

Manami thought it over and decided to offer Shinra her shoulder.

"Oh no, it's fine; I can walk on my own."

"But it must be painful."

"You know, a girl shouldn't be giving suspicious people a shoulder to lean on in the middle of the night," the red-eyed man said, which was a strangely specific piece of advice, but Manami's expression did not change.

"No, it's fine. All you have to do is answer something for me."

"?"

"About Izaya Orihara," she said, her voice flat and mechanical. "Tell me if you know anything that he really, really hates to have happen."

"Why?"

"Because I want to kill him, and I want it to be awful for him," she admitted freely.

Shinra smiled as he dragged his leg along. "What is that, jealousy? Or one of those emotions? No, that's love."

"You're wrong," Manami said flatly, neither angry nor pleased.

"Let's see… Something he would hate… *Ah! Ah!*"

Shinra winced occasionally from the pain in his joint as he walked. But otherwise he maintained a thin smile that, combined with the red eyes, made him look like a creepy clown.

He decided to go to the main street to catch a taxi, and as they walked together, he reminisced about the past as a means of answering the girl's question.

"Let's see… Izaya is never disappointed or disgusted by people. So anything involving human relationships or the ugly side of people, like betrayal or death, isn't going to bother him."

"…"

"But actually, I don't think that's because he's mentally strong or anything. Just the opposite, in fact."

"?"

Manami gave him a questioning look. He leaned onto her shoulder for support as he made his way slowly down the street.

"People think of him like some cold-blooded monster, but he's more human than anyone I know; he's so fragile inside. If you pumped him full of love and betrayal and such, I think he'd fall apart. I think that's why he decided to love humanity by letting everything wash over him. Do you see what I'm saying? He accepts everything, but he doesn't take it *in*. He lets it wash over him."

"Wash over…?"

"Yes. Think of those *koinobori* poles, with the carp streamers that blow in the wind. At first glance, they appear to have wide mouths and insides that happily swallow everything into them…but there's no bottom to that container. It's just a hollow tube. So of course they can accept everything into their mouths; they don't actually hold it. Of course he can love everything."

It was hard to tell exactly what Shinra thought of his friend's disposition. But the little smile never left his lips.

"Oh, sorry," he said to Manami. "You didn't want to know his nature, just the things that he hates."

He closed his eyes and exhaled quietly.

"I think…simple pain, heat, agony… He hates those things."

♂♀

Ikebukuro—inside an office building

"*Kahk…*"

Breath returned to Izaya in the form of a cough.

The air he expelled contained flecks of blood.

His attempt to seize understanding was besieged by ferocious pain.

"…!"

For an instant, he forgot who he was and why he was here.

The awful pain was inseparable from heat in his mind, creating the brief illusion that his entire body was on fire. Agony tore through his being, preventing him from even passing out.

I'm still alive.

Izaya was not the type of person to argue about guts and willpower overcoming flesh. But he didn't rule it out, either.

He summoned all his mental strength, forcing the pain aside so his brain could work unimpeded.

What happened? I was atop the beams, and…I fell…

The shock was so strong that even memories ten seconds old felt vague. He reached back what felt like ten years to arrive at last at an answer.

That's right. He hit me. The monster used a metal beam like a bat and hit me like a ball.

"…Monster," he spat.

If his opponent had been a human, Izaya would have praised the strength of the man who hit him, near-lethal blow or not. But Izaya no longer recognized Shizuo Heiwajima as human.

All he felt was horrible, detestable pain, his entire body being devoured by seething agony.

Apparently, he was inside a building. After being struck, there had been a shock against his back and a sound like glass breaking, as he recalled it.

"..."

He looked around, his back against the ground, and saw a number of office desks. So he was inside of an office of some kind.

I was lucky.

After Shizuo struck him, he'd flown into the building across the street and crashed through a window. Perhaps the glass of the window had cushioned him, because aside from a number of lacerations on his clothes from shards of glass, his arteries were miraculously intact.

Instead, the blood oozed from a myriad of smaller cuts all over him. Izaya looked to the broken window.

He couldn't tell what was happening outside. There was only one thing he could say for certain.

He's going to come here to finish the job.

But the death sentence that was the truth also sent Izaya's heart trembling.

That means it's not over yet.

And when he'd reached that point, there was a sound of breaking glass up above. It could mean only one thing.

Shizuo Heiwajima had jumped here from the building across the way.

With legs powerful enough to kick a car like a soccer ball, a narrow alley was an easy gap to cross in a single leap. But few people, even if they had the same leg strength, would jump from such a tall building to another, knowing that a fall would be fatal.

If only he'd fallen, Izaya thought briefly, but then he remembered how Shizuo had kicked aside the forklift that had fallen from that height. *No...maybe a fall of that distance wouldn't kill him. And why would I hope that he went to his own demise? The entire point is that I've got to purge the monster from existence.*

He chided himself for indulging in such a naive thought and smirked.

"Yes, that's right."

He clenched his fists, telling himself that at least the nerves there still worked. And then, withstanding withering pain all over, he got steadily to his feet.

"I'm here to vanquish a monster."

Perhaps it was his one-sided, selfish love for humanity that brought his willpower back to him. And yet, not a single "beloved" human face came into his mind's eye.

Not the parents who raised him.

Not the sisters who looked up to him.

Not the brother-loving woman who made for such a capable, unquestioning secretary.

Not the crazy friend who was the first to see his true nature.

Not the many unfortunate, despairing people he'd sent into ruin.

Not the naive fools who thanked him for sparing them on an idle whim.

Not even the boys on the border between normalcy and ruin.

Not a single face came to mind.

But still, he loved humanity.

Izaya Orihara, possessing a view of humanity that was as blank as the void, got to his feet.

"It's not to run away."

When Shizuo Heiwajima descended the stairs, the door to the office was still open.

"…" He watched carefully, saying nothing. Normally he would be shouting something like "Where did you go, fleabrain?!" But this situation was anything but normal.

He held everything inside, even his voice, conserving and converting all his energy to the purpose of eradicating Izaya Orihara from the earth.

Shizuo made his way slowly into the office, until he noticed a bloodstain on the floor near the center of the room.

Despite all his fury and hatred being turned solely on Izaya, Shizuo was not yet a raging, berserk animal. That might have been the benefit of all the time he had spent waiting and perhaps even what he yearned for.

Shizuo had misjudged his jump and crashed through the glass an entire story above where Izaya had landed, but he did not simply stomp his way through the floor to get down there.

The lights were out, so he wasn't worried that some innocent person might get hurt. But even still, Shizuo's furious instincts gave him a warning. He'd clashed with Izaya Orihara so many, many times before that he knew one solid fact.

Unless he watched himself kill the man, Izaya would not be dead.

It didn't matter if he was buried under rubble. There could be no rest until Shizuo saw the body. And when you couldn't see him, that was when you were in Izaya's danger zone.

That wasn't a rational, known fact that he kept in his brain. It was something that Shizuo had come to understand innately, through years of near-fatal brawling with Izaya.

There was no point to it unless he finished Izaya off visibly.

He could pack the man in concrete and dump him into the sea—and as long as Izaya was still alive when he disappeared under the waves, there could be no rest.

And even if he *was* dead, the unease would still live on in the city. His dead body could turn up in the rubble of the building, and people would still think, *Does that body really belong to Izaya Orihara?*

Among those who knew Izaya Orihara, the unease would live on, like a swelling that would not subside. And that was why Shizuo Heiwajima was here, to ensure that it did not happen.

He had to witness the sight of Izaya Orihara being eliminated from the earth.

However much rational sense Shizuo still had now, if he was his normal self, he would say something like this: *I'm not here for the sake of all the people Izaya's harmed. It's all for my own selfish reasons.*

On the other hand, if he were the sole target of all of Izaya's malice, it would not have come to this situation, either. It was the way the malice was entangling all those around him, like Vorona, like Akane Awakusu, Shinra, Celty, and Tom, that had Shizuo so cornered and furious.

In a sense, it was ironic.

If he were the Shizuo from before he fought the crowd of Saikas and began to feel differently about his own strength…

If he were the Shizuo from before he met Akane Awakusu and learned how to use his strength to protect...

If he were the Shizuo who'd become trapped by his own violence and chosen to place himself at a distance from his surroundings...

...then he might not be in this position now.

Or if he was, then maybe he'd be screaming and chasing his opponent around like he so often did before.

But he did not this time.

Shizuo Heiwajima accepted people, connected to people—and because of that, he was tormented when they were hurt, and he trapped his unprecedented anger within himself, so that now it exploded.

It might lead to nothing but tragedy, but there was no stopping him now.

In a sense, it was his connections to others that created the single devastating weakness of the demon that was Shizuo Heiwajima.

And now Shizuo was falling into his least favorite development.

Izaya Orihara was nowhere to be seen.

He was gone, leaving behind only a bloodstain in the office.

Perhaps he was setting up an ambush. Shizuo stared around, then began lifting up the office desks one-handed, one after the other. But there was no sign of him hiding anywhere.

He couldn't have had time to set up some flaming gas trap, like he did earlier.

"..."

Shizuo headed out of the office and glanced around the building. Aside from the green emergency exit panel, there was just one illumination glowing.

The elevator light.

He approached without making a sound and confirmed that the light was moving. It was indicating that the elevator was traveling downward from this floor. Of course, it was possible that the elevator was just a feint and that Izaya was still hiding on this floor.

But that, too, was merely another facet of escape.

"It's not to run away," Izaya had told himself, and yet mysteriously, he had vanished from the building.

Shizuo hadn't heard him say that, but he could sense that the man truly intended to kill him. He gave not a single thought to what Izaya might actually be plotting and sneaked back to the office area.

Then he stuck his head through the broken window.

Izaya could pop up behind him and push him through it. He could have gone up a floor during the elevator distraction and prepared a rope or something to hook around Shizuo's throat.

But Izaya knew full well that these things would mean nothing.

So instead, he chose to allow Shizuo to catch sight of him.

The elevator hadn't been a distraction at all, merely a straightforward means of exiting the building.

When Shizuo saw Izaya, dressed in his usual black clothing, running down the dimly lit alley, his expression did not change one iota.

Instead, he placed his foot upon the frame of the broken window, as though this were a perfectly ordinary thing to do—and stepped out into the open air the way a person would walk down a staircase.

♂♀

Alley

"Why, hello there, young Orihara. What has you in such a hurry?"

"…"

Shingen, wearing a gas mask like always, spotted Izaya leaving the building, but Izaya gave him no more than a glance before scampering away.

"Hrm… Well, how about that, Egor? I've just discovered that being totally ignored by a person younger than myself hurts more than I realized it would."

"Are you saying you've never been ignored before this?"

"Why did you phrase that question as though it seems only natural that I would be ignored? Not only that, he was one of my son's few friends, and—whether he did it or not—he was brought in by the police for stabbing my son years ago! Surely my presence would earn *some* kind of reaction…"

Egor ignored Shingen, who then launched into a pointless speech about nothing important. Instead, Egor focused on the building above them.

"…What?! Egor, are you ignoring me, too?! Don't forget that not only are you younger than me, you are also a pawn I hired with money! But do not worry! I am a man of generous and forgiving spirit! I can be friends with a man I hired with money and be close enough to send him a holiday card containing a photograph of me and my new wife being disgustingly sappy togeth— *Whoaaa!!*"

Egor grabbed him by the collar midsentence and yanked him closer with one hand. The force of it caused Shingen to smack against the wall next to them.

"Gwah! What was that for?! Was all that bragging about my new wife making you jealous?!" spluttered Shingen.

"I'm sorry. It was because—," Egor started to say, but then a human being came plummeting down on the spot where Shingen had stood seconds ago.

"…?!"

"—you were in danger there."

The man who descended just feet in front of the shocked Shingen silently glanced toward where Izaya's shadow fled the scene.

"…"

And without blinking an eye, he began to race after him. Egor watched him go, then shrugged.

"…He's like the Terminator."

"Yes. And while this is exceedingly awkward for me to admit, I suppose that I owe you an…apology?"

"No, you don't. Besides, it's true that I'm jealous of how hot your wife is," Egor said with a dashing smile. Then he eyed the middle-aged man slumped over lifelessly at the side of the alley. "What should we do with him?"

"Hmm?"

Shingen followed Egor's head bob and saw Seitarou Yagiri muttering to himself.

"It's gone… My…head… Dullahan… My…head…head…"

He approached his old friend, who seemed to be in the midst of a dissociative episode, and waved. But Seitarou gave no reaction. Shingen sighed through the mask.

"So this is what becomes of one whose heart is stolen by that which lives on the flip side of reality. What a pitiable shame."

"Yeah, it's like seeing your own son's future, right here," Egor noted archly.

But Shingen just shook his head. "No, Shinra would not break down over a little trifle like this. If anything, he would say something like 'Adversity is but a trial on the path to love' and become even more hyperactive and tunnel-visioned."

"That's not much of an improvement, though. Um…what are you doing?"

Shingen had pulled a felt-tipped pen out of his pocket. "I found this pen by rifling through my pockets. It seems like a good opportunity to scribble something mischievous on Seitarou before he comes to his senses. Hmm…is it still valid to draw the kanji for *meat* on someone's forehead, or is that passé now? What do you think, Egor? Have you got any brilliant avant-garde ideas…?"

Shingen turned and stopped in the middle of his sentence when he saw the look on Egor's face. "Ooh," he murmured with fascination.

Egor's face looked just the same as it had moments ago. But with one very distinct difference.

The whites of his eyes were now red and bloodshot as they gazed into the distance. Shingen reacted to this eerie sight by remarking, "So I suppose you got cut by Saika at some point. Your possession doesn't seem too strong, however. I'm guessing it was Sonohara."

He nodded, reassuring himself of this supposition, and continued, "So has something changed with the Saikas?"

"I've been noticing for the past few hours…that another mother and her children and grandchildren are spreading their aura rather thickly."

Shingen nodded a few more times. Then, resigned, he shook his head.

"…Ah. Well, it certainly can't get much more troublesome than this."

♂♀

Inside the van

"So this is…um, Saika."

By means of demonstration, Anri allowed the tip of the katana to protrude just a bit from her palm.

"Ooh, that's amazing. How does it work?" asked Saki, who was sitting next to her and staring with interest. Togusa peeked through the rearview mirror at the exhibition, and his jaw dropped with shock.

"Huh. That's real strange," said Seiji, without much apparent interest. True to character, Namie followed that up with "You don't need to pay attention to her, Seiji" as she brushed her fingers through his hair.

But the most dramatic reaction by far belonged to Yumasaki, who first trembled when he saw the blade emerge from Anri's hand. Then he began to emit an eerie moaning sound: "Ooh…ooooooooo…"

Lastly, he grabbed Anri's wrist, staring at the blade closely. Tears began to drip from his eyes.

"Um, what…?" she stammered.

"The promised day has arrived at last!" he shouted. "I always knew that I would one day get the chance to earn supernatural powers of my own! And now…and now! Will I be able to have a Saika of my own?! If so, then I am not opposed to taking lessons from an *iai* dojo every day to prepare for the coming battle against the all-powerful enemy!"

His excitement flustered Anri. "Um…er… First, when you have the sword, Saika sends a curse seeping through you, trying to love humanity."

Yumasaki abruptly came to a standstill. "Humanity? Like…three-dimensional humanity?"

"Three-dimensional…?" Anri repeated.

Kadota threw her a lifeline. "He's asking if you mean actual living people, not just anime characters and whatnot."

"Um…Saika has never shown an interest in manga or novels…as far as I know…"

Instantly, the boy deflated and let go of Anri's hand. "Oh…I see… Then I respectfully decline my suggestion of having a cursed blade."

"Huh?"

Anri was surprised to learn that he was being serious about "having" a cursed blade at all and failed to grasp where he was going with this. He looked at her apologetically and explained, "I would do almost anything to build a bridge to two-dimensional characters, but I've got better things to do with my time than help facilitate three-dimensional romance."

Annoyed, Togusa turned to Yumasaki and said, "In that case, why couldn't you use that cursed blade to make some hot woman your girlfriend?"

"Huh? Do I stand to benefit in some way by making a three-dimensional girl my girlfriend?"

"Honestly, I'm kind of amazed at how firm you are on your standards," Togusa said, half in admiration.

"But all of that aside! I can't wait to see Karisawa again so we can share in the joy of knowing that the cursed blade is the pathway to two dimensions! Let's go rescue her as soon as we can! What are we doing, Togusa? Hurry up, hurry up, run, run, run!" He smacked the window.

"Shuddup!" Togusa bellowed. "Don't get fingerprints on the window! I'm driving as fast as I can, but I can't change a red light!"

While the driver and back seat passenger argued, Kadota glanced over his shoulder and said to Anri, "Just checking, but…if Karisawa turns out to be under that Saika thing's control, can you do something about that?"

"…Yes. If I find the mother of Karisawa or the other people afflicted by Saika in town—in other words, the source of the possession—and I use my Saika to overwrite their curse and set them free, then they should return to normal."

"Okay…well, on the rare chance that it's actually the case, we'd appreciate your help with that. I'm sorry about this," Kadota said, tilting his head forward into a bow from his awkward position.

Anri quickly waved him off. "Oh no…I was the one who got her involved."

"What do you mean? You didn't do anything. I don't know whose fault this is, but you shouldn't trouble yourself over it."

"But," she said sadly, lowering her face, "if we can't find her Saika mother, then I'll have to hurt Karisawa a bit…"

She looked forlornly at the blade protruding from her palm. Kadota asked, "Do you, uh…have to cut 'em to a point where it becomes life-and-death?"

"N-no, just the tip of the finger would work, I think."

"Then there's no problem. Karisawa isn't going to be upset about something like that." Kadota chuckled, trying to cheer her up. "I'm telling you it's fine. You have my permission. I'll take responsibility."

Feeling the warmth of his words, Anri looked at Kadota through the mirror and said, "Um…"

"Hmm?"

"Thank you."

"What did I just say? We're the ones who need to thank you," Kadota said with a smile. The image of Karisawa's face floated into Anri's mind. It was the same kind of warmth she felt when Karisawa said, "I can forgive you of everything." Maybe Kadota and Karisawa were rubbing off on each other because they spent so much time together.

And then there's me… I spent all that time with Ryuugamine and Kida, and I couldn't do anything… I didn't try to change myself…

And that was why she had to do something now. It was that resolution that led her to reveal the situation to everyone here in the van—but their reactions were far from what she feared might happen.

She imagined that when they learned her secret, they'd treat her like a monster, or suspect her of being the actual street slasher, or perhaps even subject her to some kind of medieval witch hunt.

But their reactions were so *normal* that it actually left her confused and shaken.

"Um, aren't you…afraid of me?" she said, to her own surprise.

Yumasaki tilted his head, as though he couldn't fathom why she would ask such a thing. Namie snorted and said, "I might look down on you for it, but I certainly don't have a reason to feel *afraid* of someone as meaningless as you."

"You don't have a reason to look down on her, either, Sister."

"Oh…I-I'm sorry, Seiji! That was just a saying—it wasn't what I really feel!" she stammered when she caught the whiff of criticism in her brother's stare.

Saki smiled and said, "It was a surprise, but I'm not afraid of you," as simply as if they were talking about any ordinary topic.

Anri replied, "But I'm…I'm not human…"

Kadota butted in to say, "Listen, young lady."

"Y-yes?"

"Would you dare say that around Celty?" he asked in all seriousness.

"…!"

She had no answer.

"She's far less human than you are, but nobody in this group dislikes her."

Namie looked displeased with that. "Well, I don't—"

"Read the room, Sister."

"...F-fine, Seiji. Don't worry, your big sis is more than capable of being tactful."

Kadota ignored their banter and continued addressing Anri: "Whatever it was like the first time, none of us are afraid of Celty now, because we know her. We know what she's been doing, what makes her happy, and what makes her sad. Just maybe not as well as Shinra does."

"..."

"When people are afraid of something, it's because they can't see the inside of what that is. Even a walking explosive like Shizuo Heiwajima doesn't have to be scary to someone who understands exactly what it is that gets him pissed off," he continued, drawing on another example. "So we're all able to accept you because we know what kind of a person you are."

"Uh..."

"Whether you were being sincere or polite, that accumulation of your interactions with others led to this result. Do you get that? So be confident in who you are," he said, keeping his tone light. But even so, the words permeated her heart deep down.

Mika, who had held her silence in the seat ahead of her, suddenly turned around and bowed. "Anri...I'm sorry!"

"Huh? Huh? H...Harima?"

"The truth is, I knew. I knew you were possessed by that sword..."

"?!"

Anri's mind went blank at the revelation.

"I don't want to go into why, because it's a long story...but in the end, I chose to go with Seiji over you... I knew that you were struggling with personal problems, but I never cared about anything but Seiji!"

That explanation didn't actually explain anything exactly, and the mood in the car turned to awkward silence.

Namie and Seiji knew about Mika's situation, but neither of them made much of an effort to argue for her. In fact, Namie saw it as an opportunity to kick a downed rival.

"Seiji, any woman who would abandon her friends is trash. Especially if she chooses a moment like this to admit it, hoping that she'll get an easy chance at forgiveness. You should break up with her soon."

"What about you, Sis?"

"I don't have to worry about that, because I don't have friends!"

"Well, at least you're thinking positively."

As she listened to the others talk, Anri found that she accepted their arguments much easier than she'd expected.

Anri's image of Mika Harima was of a person who could do just about anything. If you took away the stalkerish side of her personality, she really did fit Anri's mental image of a perfect human being.

The revelation that she also knew about Saika did not produce a particularly powerful shock to Anri. Nor was she stunned that Mika knew about Saika and had chosen to put herself at a distance.

She chose Seiji Yagiri, not Anri Sonohara.

That was an honest statement.

Anri knew that if it came down to it, Mika would prioritize Seiji's life over her own. So it wasn't Anri's call whether to forgive her or not. That just didn't matter.

There was only one worry on Anri's mind.

She looked at Mika, her red eyes flashing, and asked, "Um…are you sure…you're not afraid of me?"

Mika beamed at her and said firmly, "Listen, Anri."

"Yes?"

"The next time you ask me that, I'm going to get angry."

That was enough for Anri.

This was the girl who'd saved her in the past when she was being bullied. The arrival of Seiji had made it seem as if that girl had gone for good, but here she was in the van right now.

The world within the picture frame in Anri's mind suddenly shook. She realized with a start that the van was with her, on *this* side of the frame. Or perhaps it was the size of the frame itself that had just widened.

"Thank you… Thank you…so much…!" she said to the group of them. Big drops began to fall from her glowing red eyes.

"Now, now, don't cry. You've got to save those happy tears for Mikado and Kida," Mika joked warmly. "If some other car looks at us, they'll think that Togusa's band of thugs have kidnapped a couple of girls."

"You know, I don't appreciate that you only think of me as the ringleader in *those* situations, rather than Kadota…," Togusa said.

The rest of the car laughed awkwardly at that. Anri smiled, too, and felt a resolve form within her.

She would find a way to bring Mikado Ryuugamine and Masaomi Kida within this ring of friendly connections she had now.

Maybe neither of the two boys wanted that. Maybe it was only her own selfish desire.

But this time, she was going to be selfish.

And with that honest admission to herself, she retracted the Saika blade into her palm.

But in that moment, she felt as if she heard Saika's voice again.

"You're going to discard me? No matter how you struggle, you will never escape from me. Don't forget, it's my role to love people."

Anri smiled to herself and treated these words, mixed among the sea of love curses, as nothing more than a misheard statement at the worst.

Someday, I hope to love people with you. Me and you…learning to love in the truest sense.

The curses of love stopped for just an instant, then Saika's voice resumed.

"I keep telling you. Humanity belongs to me."

The tone was sulking, but Anri didn't detect any force behind it.

As usual, Saika's curses reverberated throughout her mind.

Saika's intelligent words. Were they just an illusion that Anri's own mind was creating? Or were they Saika's true personality speaking to her? She did not know.

But it was odd that, even before Anri got into the van and admitted her secret to these people, she had felt the distance between herself and Saika was smaller than before.

It seemed that Saika was happy that more people had accepted the existence of the cursed blade without having to use those accursed words of love—but again, Anri would never know whether that was just a trick of her own mind or not.

*   *   *

The hollow sound of hands clapping brought Anri's consciousness back to the interior of the van.

Yumasaki had struck his hands together and did a wriggling little dance with his upper half. He said to her, "At any rate, now this means that Anri has officially become a member of the guild!"

"…'Gild'?"

"The Adventurers Guild. That's the group that Dr. Kishitani put together to solve this problem!"

"Oh…"

Anri wasn't very familiar with the English word *guild*, but she was definitely on board with solving the problem, so she let it slide in this case.

"The problem is that the founder, Dr. Kishitani himself, was abducted by a mysterious woman in glasses who produced wires from her hands. Let me tell you, though, those wires were really cool."

"Huh?" That sounded to Anri as if it could refer only to one woman. "Do you mean…Miss Kujiragi?"

Suddenly, the inside of the van stirred, and all the attention gathered on Anri again.

"You know Kasane Kujiragi?" demanded Namie.

Anri nodded. "Yes, I got her business card. It only has her phone number, though…"

"Card?!"

The others murmured even more, but Anri remembered something else about that meeting and added, "Oh…I'm sorry. The card is still in my schoolbag, so…it's at home."

There was no saying whether Kujiragi would answer the phone, but given the circumstances, that was valuable information.

"What do you think? Should we go get it?" Togusa asked.

"Nah, let's pick up Karisawa first. It won't be too late after that," Kadota suggested.

It was then that Anri remembered another tidbit. "Oh! Karisawa has one, too!"

"Has one what?"

"Karisawa-san got a business card, too, because she was going to join the cosplay club. Miss Kujiragi, I mean."

Even Kadota looked shocked by this. His eyebrows rose. Now it was the turn of everyone else in the van to look bewildered.

"Cosplay...club?"

♂♀

Near Russia Sushi

"..."

In the chaos of the night district, a red-eyed Karisawa walked slowly onward.

But she hadn't been sliced by Saika.

No, she was just *pretending* to be a child of Saika and walking right through the town, out in the open.

Fifteen minutes ago, feeling that she would soon be caught, Karisawa decided to take a gamble.

She went into the cosmetics she carried around in her usual backpack for cosplay purposes, pulled out red contact lenses for cosplaying, and stuck them in her eyes. They didn't cover the white of her eyes, so if you paid attention, it would be obvious right away.

But she cleverly narrowed her eyes to keep them showing only the red irises and walked nice and slow. Thankfully, the other red-eyed people around only briefly glanced her way from time to time but otherwise passed without reaction.

Karisawa was very lucky.

The children and grandchildren of Saika could sense the presence of other instances of Saika, if not as strongly as their parents could. But in the midst of a crowd of Saikas like this, the haze of all that aura made it much harder to pick out the negative space of one ordinary human.

A Saika mother—the original one from which the others stemmed—might have finer control of the senses, but to the grandchildren whom Nasujima and Haruna had ordered to cut any human entering this area, the ultimate means of detecting Saika spawn from humans was essentially just the color of the eyes.

And though Karisawa wasn't aware of it, she was also lucky that the Blue Squares had shown up and drawn much of the overall group's attention. She kept walking down Otowa Street beneath the raised expressway toward the Sunshine area when she noticed something new.

Whoa, there's a ton of people right outside Russia Sushi. Are Simon and the boss okay in there?

Despite her concern, however, she attempted to pass by it—until she spotted a familiar face and came to a stop.

It was Anri Sonohara's friend, the one she had met in the hospital cafeteria earlier in the day. She was crouched down on the street outside of Russia Sushi and seemed to be acting differently than the other red-eyed people.

I wonder what the matter is. Maybe she's still in her right mind?

It was hard to tell from this distance, so Karisawa tried her best to approach slowly, avoiding notice. If the girl wasn't affected, there might be a way to sneak over and help her get away, she thought considerately.

As she approached, she noticed a man talking very excitedly next to the girl. On the other side of him was a boy with normal eyes, looking terrified at the scene around him. The trio clearly stuck out amid the crowd.

What…is that?

Karisawa approached from their blind spot. About half of the group around was focused on Russia Sushi, and the other half was looking at the exterior of Tokyu Hands for some reason. She didn't have to worry about them spotting her.

Keeping her eyes narrowed, Karisawa got close enough to hear the man speaking. That was when she heard a name she recognized come out of his mouth.

"So the blue guys are here now… Shijima, which of them is Mikado Ryuugamine?" Nasujima demanded.

At his side, Shijima glanced through binoculars and reported, "Everyone who had Mikado Ryuugamine's build is wearing those masks with the cut-out eyes… So he might be one of them. Shall we call the Blue Square lookout you took over and have him figure it out for us?"

"That's going to be our only option in the end. But they'll be suspicious if we straight-out ask for his location. If he hasn't actually come to this street, that'll only give him the chance to scamper away," Nasujima said carefully. Then he added, "On the other hand, if we can get the Dollars under control, they'll be all the muscle we need. Then I'll have the Dollars find Jinnai Yodogiri's location for me. And his secretary, Kasane Kujiragi, too."

"Even the secretary?"

"Yeah…she's the one who made me Saika-possessed to begin with. She's like old Yodogiri's secret backup weapon."

"You're right… It was the secretary who first suggested investigating the Dollars," Shijima recalled. It reminded him of just what a twisted position he was currently in and how he'd gotten here. It was depressing.

In fact, it was Yodogiri who had ordered him to infiltrate the Dollars and "make contact with the Headless Rider," but Nasujima had added one instruction on top of that.

Now that it was clear that Nasujima's goal was to take over the Dollars, he realized exactly how completely up shit creek he was. He had accepted Nasujima's invitation thinking that it might be the ticket out of Izaya and Yodogiri's control, but now he regretted that choice.

Escape seemed impossible now. The only thing Shijima could tell himself was that he was wandering around a nightmare and that he should try to drag down as many others as he could.

"So what are we doing about Yodogiri and Kujiragi?"

"We can overpower them with enough numbers. But it's not clear whether either Yodogiri or Kujiragi is capable of being controlled with Saika. So let's just bury them somewhere."

Bury them—i.e., kill them. Shijima felt a chill go down his back.

He had operated a drug-dealing organization and should have been used to cold, hard talk like this. But that kind of brutality coming from someone with the power to overrun the shopping area with zombie-like pawns terrified him.

Nasujima snickered to himself, whether aware or not of Shijima's fear, and said, "But before you bury that Kujiragi woman, I'd like to have some fun with her."

*   *   *

Nearby, Karisawa overheard this suggestion and felt both disgust for the man who said it and a powerful unease.

Mikado Ryuugamine and Kasane Kujiragi. Both distinctive names, the kind that you would never hear by mistake.

Why is he talking about Mikarun and Miss Kujiragi?

Whatever the reasons, it was clear that this man was attempting to go after them. If he was the leader of these red-eyed people, then whoever was his target didn't stand a chance, unless it was a military battalion or his name was Shizuo Heiwajima.

Karisawa swallowed hard and made to leave the scene, keeping her eyes narrowed.

In the midst of that motion, Haruna Niekawa turned in her direction, and their eyes met. The other girl's eyes were red, too, just like the people around them.

Aw, darn. Already infected by the slasher. Oh, well. I'll come back with Dotachin and the gang to save you. Hang on until then, Karisawa thought. Niekawa kept staring at her. *Uh-oh… Am I in trouble? Did she spot me?*

Karisawa quickly turned away but not before she saw Haruna's mouth move—and suddenly a cell phone ringtone cut through the scene before she could say anything.

"What's that?"

The man and the boy next to Haruna turned toward the sound. But it wasn't coming from Karisawa's phone. It was coming from the phone in Haruna's hand.

"What's up? You hardly ever get any calls. I mean, you didn't even give your old man the number," the man said, mystified. Then he demanded she give it to him.

"…Yes, Mother."

Karisawa heard this unnatural back-and-forth as she made her way out of the area as nonchalantly as she could. She needed to tell Kujiragi and Mikado about the danger encroaching upon them.

But because she did, she failed to learn that the phone call Haruna Niekawa received was actually from a girl that she knew quite well.

"What does this mean? Why is her contact info saved in your phone?"

The name on the screen was Anri Sonohara, a former pupil he'd tried to assault. But his shock soon turned to sick glee, and he licked his lips.

"Well, that doesn't matter. I've come up with a good idea."

♂♀

Within the van

"She's not picking up," Anri announced sadly to the passengers of the van.

She'd called Haruna's phone, hoping her friend might know something that could help them, especially since they'd recently traded contact info, but all she got was an endless ringtone.

"Well, it's pretty late. Almost morning, in fact. Most people wouldn't pick up," Mika offered.

"And if she were actually the ringleader, she wouldn't pick up regardless," Saki suggested.

Anri considered these things and said, "But when I met her yesterday, she didn't seem like she was about to do something like—"

Abruptly, the ringing of her call paused, replaced by the sound of wind.

"Hello? Is that you, Niekawa? Um, I'm sorry to bother you in the middle of the night...," Anri said, thinking she'd gotten through.

Instead, the voice she heard was one she could never have expected.

"It's been so long, Sonohara."
"...Huh?"
The man's voice caused Anri's body to tense up.
"You're a very bad girl to be awake at this hour of night. Have you turned to a life of delinquency? Your teacher is very sad."

It was an unctuous voice, practically clinging to the skin of her shoulders through the phone. She hadn't heard that voice in half a year, but it was very familiar to her.

"M...Mr....Nasujima?"
Mika and Seiji looked up when they heard that name. It belonged to a teacher at Raira Academy who had been hospitalized in February

and then went missing. Why would Anri be talking to him all of a sudden, when she had been calling Haruna Niekawa's phone?

Even Mika, who knew some of the backstory, was surprised by this. She stared at Anri's phone in wonder.

"Wh-why would you be picking up…?"

"That doesn't matter. Ah, it's really wonderful to be hearing your voice again, Sonohara."

On the Night of the Ripper, Nasujima had seen her holding a katana, and then he ran, screaming in fear. It was the last memory she had of him. But now he was gloating through the phone, as though he were completely in control of her fate.

"Oh, how I wish to see you. Can you make it here now? I can help you with any problems you're having."

"Um, what happened to Haruna?!"

"Oh, Niekawa? She's sitting right next to me. She keeps calling me 'Mother, Mother.' It's very sweet, really."

"…!"

That told Anri quite a lot. Through circumstances she did not yet know, Nasujima had become a Saika carrier. Whether he had an original or was someone else's child was unclear. All she knew was that he had cut Haruna Niekawa and now controlled her.

"Where…are you?"

"Now, now, no rush. You know where Tokyu Hands is? Right outside of the Sunshine building. We're just hanging around that area until morning, so if you've got some time, swing by. If I see you, I'll call out to you."

"Haruna is safe, I assume?" Anri said, her voice tense. This seemed to catch Nasujima by surprise.

"Wait, are you worried about her? When did you two make up? I seem to remember you turning blades on each other because you were fighting over me."

"Answer the question!"

"Don't worry—I haven't messed with her yet. Once tonight's party is over, we'll be taking our time with a very special private lesson."

"Release Haruna at once…or else…"

She had to fight to ensure that the blade didn't rip right through her hand and the phone she held in it.

That wasn't the way that someone being ruled by another's curse talked. Like Haruna once had, Nasujima had somehow overcome Saika's control. Anri knew that Niekawa was in great danger. Her mind raced, trying to pin down where they were.

Only half a day ago, Haruna had declared that she would kill Anri in the same breath that she suggested they be friends. But Anri felt an odd kind of empathy for her. Perhaps it was because they were both possessed by Saika, or perhaps there was something about them being girls of the same generation; she didn't know for sure.

Unlike the people in the van, Haruna was more of an enemy than a friend—but Anri still felt a terrible shock when she realized that the girl was under Nasujima's control.

And the shock didn't end there.

After he'd enjoyed the panic in Anri's voice for several moments, Nasujima chuckled slimily and added, "There are two other people you know coming to the party, too."

"Huh…?"

"Mikado Ryuugamine and Masaomi Kida. You were close with them, weren't you?"

"_____"

Her mind froze. She nearly dropped the phone.

At first, she didn't understand what he was saying to her. But then Nasujima continued, driving home her despair.

"If you want to tell the cops about this, be my guest. I'll just play dumb, and Ryuugamine and Kida will back me up with statements that support my story."

"No! Wait! What…what have you done to them?!"

"Nothing…*yet*. I just invited them to the party."

And with a chuckle, he hung up the phone.

♂♀

Outside Russia Sushi

"Now, Shijima, I want you to keep an eye on them for a while. I'll give orders to the Saika-possessed, too, though."

"Keep an eye on them?" Shijima asked.

Gleefully, Nasujima explained, "Knowing Sonohara's personality, she'll probably rush to call Ryuugamine about this."

"So if he's one of the guys in the ski caps outside of Tokyu Hands, then we'll know that whoever answers a phone next is him."

♂♀

Inside the van

After Anri hung up, she told the others what the call had been about.

"No way, man...," marveled Togusa. "Why would he bring up Ryuugamine and Kida out of the blue?"

With a frown, Kadota offered, "Dunno. But there's definitely been some bad business going on in Ikebukuro lately. There's no telling what might happen."

"And there's Karisawa to worry about, too... Let's rush over to Tokyu Hands! Speaking of which, what's up with all the red lights?!"

The trip from Shinra's apartment to Otowa Street wasn't that far in terms of distance. Even during rush hour, this should be about the time they would finish the trip. But for some reason, the van was barely halfway to its destination.

"No, it's not reds, it's just plain old traffic. Shit, why is it like this so late at night?" Togusa swore. He turned on the car radio to see if he could pick up a traffic report. Fortunately, it was right at the late-night news, five minutes past the hour.

"*...a number of traffic accidents in the Ikebukuro area, causing gridlock all over...*"

"Accidents?" Togusa repeated.

"*...and there are also multiple sightings of groups of people out on the street committing acts of violence. Perhaps that's connected to the accidents themselves...*"

And almost as if timed to the radio broadcast, there was the sound of multiple motorcycle engines roaring behind the van. A few seconds later, there was a clamor of exhaust and blaring musical horns as several loud and flashy bikes passed them.

"Meetin' up at this hour? And they've still got those obnoxious horns? Didn't they go outta fashion? That stuff's outlawed now," Togusa grumbled.

But more and more motorcycles blazed past them. A few seconds would pass before more bikes went by, then another ten or fifteen, trickling bit by bit. All in all, quite a large number of motorcycles were heading toward Ikebukuro.

"What is this, some biker gang head honcho retiring? There's so many."

"They're not going to turn out to have red eyes, are they?" snapped Namie, who didn't care how this question might affect Anri.

But the girl shook her head. "I didn't feel even the slightest hint of Saika from the people who just passed us...so I don't think that's it."

"Damn...feels like everything's working against us," hissed Togusa in frustration.

It almost seemed as if getting out and running would be faster, but he wouldn't suggest that. If he did, Kadota would actually hop out and try to run it with them. Kadota played it off bravely, but in his present state, he could barely walk. They'd given up on trying to stop him from going with them to help Karisawa, but Togusa wasn't going to allow him to try anything beyond his means.

While the van was stuck in place, the swarm of motorcycles heading toward Ikebukuro's city center made Anri worried. She decided to take out her phone.

"I'm...going to call Ryuugamine and Kida now."

Saki turned to her from the adjacent seat and gave her a reassuring smile. "Don't worry—I'll call Masaomi for you."

"Oh...thank you. I appreciate that!"

Anri bowed to the other girl, then brought up Mikado's contact information and hit the call button.

But neither of them got an answer to their call, and the mood in the van soon turned uncomfortable.

Anri prayed that they were just at home sleeping. In the meantime, she made a resolution to herself: If the two of them had been possessed by Saika due to Takashi Nasujima, she would have to slice Nasujima herself.

*   *   *

It was ironic that she had once told her teacher that she hated him, and now she was preparing to attack him with a sword that existed to love others. But Anri's determination was quiet and crisp.

She would not hesitate. She was going to slash a man not worth slashing.

♂♀

Outside Tokyu Hands, Sixtieth Floor Street—at that moment

"So…what now?"

Down on the street, Chikage headed over to the crosswalk so he could check out the scene across the way.

This was a place where taxis often stopped to wait for riders, but for some reason, there was not a single one here today—but Chikage, not being very familiar with Ikebukuro, didn't pick up on the distinction.

Instead, his attention was drawn by the vehicles stopped at the entrance to Sixtieth Floor Street. At the spot where the expressway had been previously blocking their view, there were many more cars than he'd initially imagined. Some of the stopped cars might have belonged to ordinary drivers, but given the number of youths in blue beanies and ski masks loitering nearby, it seemed clear that nearly all of them belonged to the Blue Squares.

"Well, well! For a group started by middle and high schoolers, they got better cars than Toramaru!"

Chikage had heard that they had a number of legal adults in their gang, too. He waited at the light for the crossing signal to turn green, feeling excited.

This is nice. They're ready to rock, even though it's the middle of the city. The only problem is…

He was looking forward to the simple pleasure of a good fight with the Blue Squares, but it was the ordinary citizens wandering around that spooked Chikage.

You'd think that with a bunch of guys repping colors around, they'd be more nervous or would try to clear out. But they're just standing, wandering around, doin' nothing.

He felt an eerie kind of danger from all the people walking around without any apparent purpose.

Then again, I did tell him I'd handle this.

But when the light turned green, he stepped out into the crosswalk with a grin.

"Yo!"

When he got to the other side, he clapped a hand on the shoulder of the nearest boy with a blue beanie.

"...Huh? The hell you want?" the boy asked suspiciously.

"If I said I was a friend from Saitama whose motorcycle you guys burned up, would that ring a bell?" Chikage asked.

The boy's face paled immediately. He looked over Chikage's shoulder.

"...? Wait, are you alone?"

"Dude, I got *lots* of girlfriends. I'm not lonely. Now, you look single to me, but don't give up, buddy. You enjoying your youth?"

"...I see," said the boy with a grin and beads of sweat on his cheeks, ignoring Chikage's taunt.

"You know, being single's not all that bad."

The next moment, two more thugs approaching behind Chikage swung wooden bats at his head in succession.

There was a loud, crisp smack, and one of the two bats snapped.

"Ha! But you're gonna be all alone in your coffin, old man!" the boys laughed.

They all imagined what would happen in the next moment, when their accoster crumpled to the ground. And yet...

"...See, something's not right."

Chikage grinned at them, blood streaming from his head.

"?!"

They flinched and took a step away from him. Chikage motioned with his chin toward the "normal" people walking around Sixtieth Floor Street. "You gotta be crazy to hit a guy in the head with a bat in the middle of a crowded place like this...but it doesn't make sense, right? Nobody's watching; nobody's calling the cops... This ain't the usual bit about city folk not carin' what happens to your neighbor.

There aren't even any looky-loos whipping their phones out to take video."

"..."

The boys exchanged a glance. It must have occurred to them, too.

Chikage took a step closer to them, smiling.

"But all that aside..."

"?"

"That kinda hurt, you sons of bitches!"

He swung a majestic hook punch at the boy holding the still-unbroken bat.

"*Gbya—?!*" the boy shrieked and spun himself sideways. He was about Chikage's size, but the difference in strength between them was vast.

On that signal, a number of other youths wearing blue who hadn't noticed Chikage up to this point suddenly grasped the situation. On top of that, even more boys emerged from the vans parked in the street—and some adults, too. And still, the ordinary people on Sixtieth Floor Street did no more than occasionally glance over and resume their wandering.

Yeah, something about that is creepy, Chikage thought, a shiver running down his back. He cracked his neck to warm up and focused on the approaching opponents instead. *Whatever. I can whup all these fools before I worry about them.*

"Hang on—do any of you even care what happens to Masaomi Kida?!" he shouted in the midst of countering a kid who came swinging at him.

Another kid in a ski mask answered, "Yeah, it *doesn't matter what happens* to Mr. Kida."

"Wha...?"

Aoba Kuronuma pulled off his mask, smirking and cackling with glee. "I already know everything."

♂♀

The rooftop of a mixed-use building—a few minutes earlier

"Damn, you really can't see anything from here..."

Masaomi was still on the roof, watching, as Chikage instructed him to do. His cell ringtone went off loud and clear from his pocket.

"Whoa!"

He'd been so focused on lying low that the sound made him panic before he realized that it was probably inaudible from the ground, and he took out his phone with relief.

But at the same time, he got an odd feeling of wrongness.

As if he'd sensed some other sound, not the ringtone, echoing behind him.

"..."

A clammy sweat broke out all over Masaomi's body. He turned on the spot, slowly.

Slowly, slowly, so slowly...

He didn't know why he felt this way, but he had a strong premonition that he shouldn't turn around. That he might lose something precious to him.

A variety of worries racked Masaomi within the span of just a second or two. He almost felt as if the moment he spun around, he would witness some horrid, unrecognizable monster that would twist his head right off his shoulders.

But once he started, he couldn't stop. He had to turn the whole way.

There ended up not being a monster, so Masaomi's fears were unfounded.

He was not, however, relieved by what he saw.

Because the other sound he heard was most definitely the ringtone of a cell phone that didn't belong to him—and he understood what it was that had caused the anxiety within him to explode.

He recognized that ringtone.

"..."

At first, he thought that he was completely alone on the rooftop. But eventually he saw, within the darkness, a little light flash on behind the large external air-conditioning unit.

"...Who's there?"

Masaomi's phone continued to go off. The screen said "Saki Mikajima" on it, but he didn't have the frame of mind to even look at it.

Across the roof, the person staring into the little light of the other phone read out the name of the person listed for that incoming call.

*   *   *

"It's from Sonohara."

It was a familiar voice.

But even though he was looking right at his ringing phone, he did not answer it.

"I wonder why she's calling now. It's nearly morning."

It was a voice Masaomi didn't want to hear out of nowhere like this. He was here specifically *to* hear that voice, but this was a sneak attack. It felt as if he were climbing the stairs to a bungee-jumping platform only to lose his footing and fall all on his own.

The boy stood there, wearing a smile.

A rather troubled smile on his childish features.

It was so typical. The very face that Masaomi remembered when he thought of him.

"Hi, Masaomi."

"Mikado...?"

"It feels like it's been forever."

Now that he was faced by Mikado Ryuugamine wearing that same old smile, Masaomi found that he couldn't say anything.

The ringtones of the two phones mingled, turning into one mangled sound, echoing across the darkened rooftop.

The sky was devoid of even the stars.

Only the writhing shadow above them watched the two.

Silently, secretly.

Enveloping all below it.

Chat room

Kuru: It would seem this place is coming to an end.

Mai: It's sad.

Kuru: Well, perhaps it is just the changing of the times. Even if this had not happened, the very concept of the chat room itself might be fated to die out. New tools for communication evolve out of the online ether by the day, such as Mix-E and Twittia and Bodybook and FINE. It is only natural that people would trickle from chat rooms onward to new places.

Kuru: Of course, the truly good things will last beyond the ages. This chat room might be a closed place, but it was not a place everyone would call home. That is the extent of it.

Mai: I wonder.

Kuru: But the world changes with the times. Perhaps someday there will be an age when this chat room is necessary. Whether that will be in three days, or three years, or only in the moments before our death, when we reflect upon the past. Let us hope that the program still exists on the server at that point.

Mai: Let it happen.

Kuru: That is not how it works. And if it worked, it wouldn't actually revert our minds back to this state.

Kuru: Well, any more of this pontification will only muddy the waters. Rather than needlessly draw out the ending, perhaps we should simply take our leave.

Mai: You're showing off.

Mai: Ouch.

Mai: I got pinched.

Kuru: And now, my best to all of you.

Kuru: Despite the ending, it was not displeasing. In fact, I'm even grateful that I was able to see an entertaining show to round it out. I wish I could have spoken with others like Kid and Saki more, but I will have to look forward to our next meeting under different circumstances.

Kuru: One of the best parts of being online is the countless paths one can choose to form connections.

Mai: You can do that off-line, too.

Kuru: And now everyone, a very good sign-off to you.
Mai: Bye-bye.
Mai: It was fun.

Kuru has left the chat.
Mai has left the chat.

The chat room is currently empty.
The chat room is currently empty.
The chat room is currently empty.

.

.

.

CHAPTER 12
Where There's a Will, There's a Way

Shinra's apartment—several months earlier

"By the way, Celty, did those three ever make up?"

"Make up? Who are you talking about?"

Celty was watching a comedy show on TV when Shinra brought up this bit of idle chat.

"You know, the ones from Raira."

"Oh, you mean Mikado and his friends."

"Well, I only know Anri and Ryuugamine. Was just wondering if anything new had happened with them."

"I don't know... That's their problem to deal with. It's not up to us to solve it for them."

Shinra read the words off her PDA screen and shrugged. "Well, I suppose you're right about that."

"It's strange for you, of all people, to be worried about others."

"From all you've told me about them, I've started to think of my own high school days," Shinra remarked wistfully.

Annoyed, she typed out, *"Stop that. They're not as perverted as you."*

"Perverted? What a blunt assessment. It's not an issue of sexual proclivities but of human relationships. Since Anri is the girl of the bunch, I guess that she would be in your position, Celty. With Orihara and Shizuo being Mikado and, uh, Masaomi, is it? If they were us."

But Celty wasn't quite buying his comparison yet.

"Who are you?"

"The Saika possessing Anri, I suppose."

"Don't try to stretch your analogy too hard."

Undaunted by her snark, Shinra happily continued comparing his high school experience to the current-day teens.

"I think our relationship is exactly the opposite of Mikado and his friends'."

"The opposite?"

"Yeah. They've all got secrets they're keeping from one another. But they managed to make that work, and they all wanted to keep things friendly, I think."

"You could be right about that," Celty typed, shrugging. It was the closest she could get to a nodding gesture.

"But in comparison," Shinra continued, "Orihara and Shizuo never bothered with any secrets. Well, Orihara actually had plenty of secrets, but he never tried to hide what kind of a person he was. And the result was a relationship that was the exact opposite of Mikado and Masao-mi's. And unlike Anri, you were basically an observer, if anything, at that point, Celty."

"Well…at the time, I didn't really want anything to do with humanity."

"I think that's fine. But while it might have been fun, when I consider the potential future we could have had with you making four of us, all getting along, I hope that Mikado and his friends can figure this out."

"Are you jealous of them?" Celty teased.

Shinra shook his head. "Not at all. I mean, I'm perfectly happy with you, and I can't imagine a life surpassing this so much that I would be 'jealous' of it."

"…You say the most embarrassing things with the straightest face."

It should have been a dash of cold water on Shinra, but his sappy reflections didn't stop there.

"You know, I guess you could say that I'm completely the opposite of Saika, too."

"How so?"

"If Saika is a girl pining with love for all of humanity, then I'm a man who's only ever cared for something that isn't human…and only one in particular: you."

Celty's chest rose and fell as though she were inhaling and exhaling a sigh. Then she typed, *"And that's all you really wanted to say."*

"Yep. That's all I wanted to say," Shinra admitted.

Shadows stretched out from Celty's body. The solidified darkness became a black cocoon, enveloping Shinra's body within its shadow.

"Stop being so embarrassing," Celty wrote on the PDA, then realized she couldn't show it to him this way. Then she noticed that the cocoon was strangely quiet.

…? That's strange. He's not carrying on like he normally does.

By way of answering her question, Shinra's voice came out of the cocoon.

"Lately, I find that the dark makes me feel relaxed."

"…"

"I think that this shadow is a part of you, Celty. It's the color that belongs only to you in the entire world, a black that absorbs all light. As far as I know, at least."

She could sense him smiling in the darkness.

As a matter of fact, he was. "Maybe the reason that I wasn't scared of the dark, even as a child, was because I felt your presence within it. So while I can't see a thing in here, there is one thing I can say with pride.

"You are truly beautiful, Celty."

~~~!

Celty's limbs and shadow quaked, undoing the cocoon. She promptly used that shadow to hold down Shinra's hands and feet.

"I told you! Stop saying things that embarrass me! Geez!"

To hide her embarrassment, she rolled Shinra out into the hallway, then went back to focusing on her comedy show.

It was a little act of domestic happiness that happened often in Shinra's apartment.

But it was the accumulation of such trivial scenes that made Shinra Kishitani who he was.

His daily life, filled with bliss as it was, did indeed create something within Shinra.

And while Celty did not know what this was, it was something that Shinra treasured and kept safe.

Even if others would laugh at him for it or shun and fear him for being "abnormal."

♂♀

Kawagoe Highway, outside Shinra's apartment—present day

"Ah, what a beautiful sky," said a man in a white lab coat, staring up at an abnormally dark sky above his apartment building. "That's my favorite color."

Shinra Kishitani.

He was back.

He returned home while Kadota and the others ventured out. His stepmother tried to stop him, but he barreled over her with a stream of excuses and within minutes was poking his head into the entrance of his apartment again.

He was wearing his usual white coat now, not the pajamas. He had wrapped bandages all over his body and was carrying a crutch made out of a mop wrapped in aluminum foil.

"Hey, you look the part."

"Oh! You're still here?" he said to Manami Mamiya, whom he'd met only moments ago.

"I was going to ask you more about Izaya."

"That's very dedicated of you." He chuckled, plopping down the crutch and hobbling around with it. In fact, it looked exactly like a proper injured person's movement—except that both then and now, his eyes were dyed dark red.

"What...are you?"

"I'm merely a doctor."

"I've seen several people Niekawa sliced whose eyes went red like that, but you're the first one I've seen acting normally afterward."

It was the kind of question that only someone who'd seen the

Saika-possessed would ask. Shinra thought it over and said, "Ah...yes. I suppose I must have reached the same side Niekawa did. It's kind of like hypnosis, except that I forcefully undid the hypnosis and learned how to use it myself...I guess."

"You also sound livelier than you did before."

"I gave myself a painkiller."

But even Manami, who was not a professional doctor by any means, could tell that Shinra's skin tone was not good. He looked as if he ought to be in a hospital bed.

Thinking about hospital beds reminded her of the time she tried and failed to stab Izaya while he was hospitalized. She chided herself at that bitter memory and tried to get past the topic by asking, "Where are you going that you're forcing yourself to move around like this?"

"That's a good question. Where should I go?"

"What?" She drew her eyebrows together.

"Celty Sturluson," Shinra said.

"Huh?"

"That's the name of the woman I love. I want to go see her, but I'm wondering where I should go to do that," he explained, looking up at the sky.

"That's the name of the Headless Rider, right?" Manami asked.

"She's a dullahan. I don't know exactly everything that's happening... but I have a feeling that she might have recovered her head."

"..."

Manami's dull, cynical eyes darted away. She was the one responsible for taking the head from where it had been safe.

"She's probably back home by now, right? Izaya told everyone that the Headless Rider had the memories of home in her head, and her role, and all that old information."

"If that's true, then I'd make preparations right now to leave for Ireland." Shinra tottered along, gazing up at the sky, bliss making his features slack. "But Celty is still in this city. I can tell."

"How?"

"The sky...it's the same color as Celty."

"Huh?"

Manami looked up with him.

There was nothing there.

No starlight.

No moon.

Not even the atmosphere reflecting back the dull glow of the surface lights, that feature unique to large cities.

Manami was used to that light, so the abnormal darkness of the sky was eerie to her.

Shinra looked up at it with eyes like a boy talking about his dreams for the future. "Just knowing that Celty's somewhere up in that sky means that I have no reason to stay locked up in my house."

"…"

"I don't even care if she never comes home. I'll go to her instead."

It was the kind of thing that a stalker might say, but Shinra's red eyes sparkled crisp and clear as he said it. Manami found herself ever so slightly jealous.

"…I envy you a bit."

"?"

"I don't have any forward-looking dreams like that. I only want to torment Izaya Orihara," she said, admitting her hesitation for the first time.

But to her surprise, Shinra said, "Really? That sounds like a wonderful dream."

"Huh?"

"I mean, of all things, 'tormenting Izaya' is a huge dream. It's quite forward-looking. In fact, making him absolutely regret doing something might be a more difficult dream than getting elected to the Diet."

She didn't know how seriously to take the man's statement. "Aren't you normally supposed to stop someone when they say something like that?" she asked him.

"Did you want the normal answer? For one thing, whatever humanity does to Izaya, he's earned every last bit of it. I guess Celty might say something like *'It's a waste to become a murderer for someone like him. Just half kill him instead.'*"

Shinra was so smitten, he could inject Celty into his answer to a completely unrelated question from a stranger. He gazed up at the starless sky like an innocent child.

"My dream is very simple. I want to continue to love the person I love forever. I want to be with her forever. That's all. I'd like for my beloved to be happy forever, too, of course, but that will always be second place for me."

"…Sounds obsessive, like something a stalker or abuser would say."

"I agree. But if anything, I'm the recipient of domestic violence in this relationship," Shinra said, his cheeks dimpling as he thought back fondly on the times that she'd hit him. "But what I'm about to do might be far worse than any punching or kicking you could imagine. Still, I have to do it. Otherwise everything I've said to Celty up to this point will be a lie."

He looked mournful about this but turned it around into a smile again as he looked up once more at the sky.

"Even if it means Celty with her memory back is going to kill me."

♂♀

Interior of building under construction

Kujiragi kept her distance as Vorona and Mikage Sharaku stared each other down. She felt an eerie disquiet in her breast.

It wasn't her own senses. It was something that she felt through the Saika under her command. But she wasn't holding it directly at the moment, so the sensation was dull, indirect.

"…"

In any case, the woman wearing the *dogi* was not the kind of opponent you wanted to fight barehanded.

She considered going back to retrieve the Saika she was using to restrain Celty Sturluson, but if she left Vorona to fend for herself, there was a very real possibility that she would lose.

And just when she thought about suggesting retreat to Vorona, she felt a subtle vibration in her suit pocket. Recognizing the rhythm of an incoming call to her cell phone, Kujiragi took it out and looked at the screen without emotion.

When she saw that it said "Karisawa (Cosplayer ♥)," she inclined her head in curiosity. When they'd traded numbers, she hadn't thought the girl was the kind of person to insensitively call in the middle of the night, and she couldn't imagine what kind of emergency would necessitate it.

"Don't you want to answer your phone? We can wait, if you want," said Mikage, blocking the way to the stairs with a confident smile.

Kujiragi ignored her and put the phone to her ear. "Kujiragi speaking."

"Oh, Miss Kujiragi?! Thank goodness... You're all right!"

"?"

Why would she need to be "all right"? Kujiragi wondered.

The voice on the phone continued, *"Listen, Miss Kujiragi! I just managed to escape myself. Stay away from the Ikebukuro Station area! If you can, flee to Saitama or Chiba!"*

"...You sound rather flustered. What is it that you escaped from?"

"More street slashers...uh, dozens of people with red eyes! No, hundreds! This guy who seems like their leader mentioned your name and was talking about burying you and attacking you and stuff!"

"..."

Kujiragi stayed calm, but this did cause her look to darken.

The Saika-possessed? Me?

Would it be Haruna Niekawa or Anri Sonohara? But she said the leader was a "guy," and that didn't make sense.

"...What would you say this man's features were?"

"Um... He had a fancy nightclub-host-style haircut, and he was talking to that long-haired girl—you know, the one with you and Sonohara at the cafeteria in the hospital. But she was saying weird stuff to the guy, like 'Yes, Mother,' and it just didn't make any sense..."

"..."

Takashi Nasujima.

Based on that information, that was the most likely identity of the Saika-possessed. He was a pawn originally created to keep Izaya Orihara's pawn Haruna Niekawa in check or bring her over to this side.

But since Izaya had destroyed her "Jinnai Yodogiri" system and there was no longer any need to watch out for Haruna in particular, she had essentially let him go loose.

I thought I gave him some menial task to keep him occupied and out of trouble, though... Did he overturn Saika's curse somehow?

In order to break Saika's control and use it at will, one needed mental strength that surpassed the cursed words that poured in through a cut from the blade.

I would not have pegged that Nasujima man to have that kind of mental fortitude...

But Kujiragi underestimated Takashi Nasujima's powerful self-love. She wasn't able to accept that he could overcome Saika's power on his own. And yet, if Haruna Niekawa was calling Nasujima "Mother," then at the very least, he must have "overwritten" Haruna's Saika curse at some point.

And beyond that, the talk of a swarm of Saika-possessed in Ikebukuro's streets was worrying. If they were going to make a kingdom of Saikas on their own, she was content to let them do it—except that Karisawa said they were definitely talking about going after her.

"I'm sorry to have worried you. Thank you. Please get away from there at once, Karisawa."

"I will. The red-eyed people aren't surrounding me anymore, so I think I'm all right... Just be careful. I'll do whatever I can to help, so call me back if you need anything!"

"...Your concern is appreciated."

She hung up the call, then considered what her next move should be, given the arrival of this unexpected enemy. Should she break through here, or at least remain inside the building long enough to confirm the ending of her primary foe, Izaya Orihara? Or should she put off ascertaining this fight and rush to eliminate the trouble surrounding Saika?

After moments of thinking, however, the path forward made itself clear in an unexpected direction.

"Oh? What are you doing here?"

"?" "?" "!"

Three women turned in the direction of the voice and saw a freakish figure wearing a gas mask.

"Huh? You're the guy I see talking with my brother at the gym sometimes."

"Ah, then you must be Eijirou's...I mean, Shingen Kishitani Mk. III's little sister."

"Mk. III...?" Mikage asked, a question mark floating over her head.

Shingen continued talking to an audience of himself. "The first one is wise! The second is refined! And the beauteous peony, that walking lily, is Mk. III! A beauty that grows in the telling, you might say! Fortunately, unlike that dried-up husk of a young man, this sight is a much more attractive one. They often say that three women gathered together is a cacophony, but this is looking more like fisticuffs than anything else, no?"

"If you don't explain why you're here, I'm going to footsie-cuff your jaw until you drop like a stone."

"I would prefer to be kicked in the buttocks instead… But that aside, I was coming here to speak with Kujiragi. Thanks to you two, I didn't need to climb all the way up the building. Thank you for that," Shingen said, completely oblivious to everything else going on.

But rather than looking displeased, Kujiragi asked, "What did you have in mind?"

"Well, that wire you used to tie up Celty returned to its katana form and fell to the ground. I was going to ask if I could have it."

"You will need to pay an appropriate price for it."

"I'm glad you brought that up. See, if you agree to overlook my invocation of the finders-keepers rule, I am willing to neglect reporting you for illegal possession of a weapon. In fact, I'll even be willing to ignore the fact that you set that horrid stalker upon Shinra to injure him," said Shingen, choosing to give up on avenging his son.

Kujiragi replied, "While that was Jinnai Yodogiri's suggestion, I will admit I bear some fault for authorizing it. But I will not be giving up Saika at this moment."

"Listen, let's go outside and talk. You were just coming *down*, weren't you?" Shingen said, which struck the three women as odd. They shared a look.

"Your suggestion is unclear. I desire a rendezvous with Sir Shizuo. When the situation is so close at hand, the reason to descend the building is nonexistent," said Vorona, speaking for the group.

Shingen made a grandiose pantomime of looking confused, given that his face was covered by the mask. He chuckled and said, "Actually…both Shizuo and Izaya jumped down onto the street and left quite a while ago."

An unpleasant, clammy breeze blew between the three women.

"…"
…
"…"
…
"…Huh?"

Mikage stood at the center of the staircase, arms folded, head tilted to the side. Sweat trickled down her cheeks.

Shingen shook his head theatrically. "Was that Japanese too difficult for you? Shizuo! Izaya! Not here! Go back to town. Human, good-bye. Shingen, no tell a lie."

"Do I need to kick your face in?" Mikage asked, vein twitching on her temple.

Shingen waved his hands and backed away. "Now, now, not so fast. I apologize for joking around, but I'm telling the truth when I say they're not here anymore."

His breath exhaled from the exhaust port of the gas mask.

"Besides, do you think that a true battle to the end between those two could be contained within a single building?"

♂♀

Out in the city

The only way to describe the vending machine was "unlucky."

It just so happened to exist along a street that Izaya ran down and happened to be the one that Shizuo decided to pick up and throw.

It came crashing and bouncing into the darkened street. Izaya dodged it with inches to spare, but he wasn't moving as sharply as he usually did, perhaps because of his painful fall.

Normally, he might have shaken off Shizuo's pursuit by now. But while he could still hop over fences and up electric poles in parkour fashion, he simply wasn't as fast as normal. Because he was only barely succeeding at staying away, Shizuo had the occasional opportunity to strike, and a little part of the city was destroyed each time.

If it continued for long enough, it might be classified as a small-scale natural disaster, but the police had not yet showed up to curtail their chase. Not because they were sleeping on the job, however.

*   *   *

Every available officer on the Ikebukuro force was already occupied with a *different* matter.

♂♀

The rooftop of a mixed-use building, Otowa Street

"Mikado… Is that you, Mikado?!"

Of the many emotions in Masaomi's voice, joy at their reunion was overshadowed by the confusion of not yet being certain of what was happening.

While Masaomi was dazed with shock, Mikado smiled sadly. "It has to be a question?" Then something occurred to him. "If I were you, I'd say something like 'Then who am I?'"

Masaomi gasped with a start, chuckling. "Multiple-choice question. One, Mikado Ryuugamine. Two, Mikado Ryuugamine. Three, Mikado Ryuugamine…right?"

He grimaced, thinking back to the day that Mikado came to Ikebukuro.

"And you completely ignored that joke of mine."

"I still think it was a terrible, embarrassing attempt at humor."

"What was it again? $\sqrt{3}$ points?" Masaomi's grimace gradually turned into a smile. Tears bloomed in his eyes. "Mikado… It really is you, Mikado…"

"Who else would it be?"

"I dunno… I just can't believe it. I wouldn't have expected to see you right behind me, out of nowhere…!" Masaomi shook his head, finally recognizing the situation, filled with joy at their reunion. "Oh…that must be it. I guess Rokujou must have cleared it all up already, huh?!"

That was how Mikado knew to come here. He'd been told this was the place where the hostage would be handed over, Masaomi guessed.

Except that Mikado immediately proved him wrong.

"I'd guess Rokujou is over by Tokyu Hands right now, fighting with Aoba and his friends."

"…Mikado?"

"I did give them bats and stuff, but he's not going to be that easy to beat, is he?" Mikado said, with that same familiar smile. Masaomi's joy immediately flipped over into concern.

"What…what do you mean?"

Then Masaomi remembered.

He remembered when his old friend here had set fire to the man who'd tried to attack Anri. He had smiled then, too, right after he'd nearly burned a man alive.

With that same smile now, Mikado said, "Rokujou isn't the type of person who takes hostages and demands a deal. I had a hunch that he was playing up the villain role in the hope that you and I would meet."

"…"

"With the Dollars' information network, I found you and Rokujou right away. I had Aoba's friend follow you guys. And another person I sent to Tokyu Hands said that Toramaru didn't appear to be setting up an ambush around there."

"Ha-ha…wow, you Dollars really are something else. It's the middle of the night!"

"It just means that many of the people wandering around the city at night are part of the group," Mikado said.

Masaomi couldn't even take a step closer to him. Normally, if he were meeting an old friend again, he might have rushed over to share in the joy. Perhaps they'd replay a scene from some movie about the inspirational struggle of growing up, where he'd punch his friend and then say, "Hit me back!" Perhaps he'd smack his friend's shoulders, happy to see him safe and sound.

But Masaomi couldn't move.

His experience as the leader of the Yellow Scarves, the senses he'd honed by living through street battles, caused him to falter and stay away from his friend.

That was Mikado Ryuugamine over there, all right. But something about him was fundamentally different from the Mikado he knew, causing Masaomi's joy to steadily morph into doubt and suspicion.

No, this is wrong. If you run away now, it'll be exactly the same as before.

He held his ground, swearing to himself that he wouldn't flee this situation, too.

"Then I guess there was no need for me to have shown up as agreed over the phone, huh?" Masaomi said with a shrug, trying to keep the conversation going.

Mikado just shook his head. "It seemed like the perfect opportunity."

"?"

"I wanted to show you something, Kida."

"Show me...?"

Masaomi thought it odd that Mikado was switching between calling him Masaomi and Kida, but the content of his words was more pressing right now.

"Well, you didn't actually see the first meeting of the Dollars, did you?"

"...True. I heard the stories, though. In fact," Masaomi said self-deprecatingly, "considering it now, I must have looked like a real clown when I came to all excited, saying, 'Hey, Mikado, did you hear about this?'"

"Yeah... Sorry, Kida."

"?"

"I know it's a little late to be saying this, but I'm technically the founder of the Dollars."

"...Wow, that is *really* late."

It was something that Masaomi had known for quite a while now, but when he heard it from Mikado's lips, the truth took on a heavy mental weight.

"I told myself that I'd only say it when Sonohara was here, too..."

"So why don't we call Anri up? She called you, didn't she?" Masaomi asked. He looked at his own phone. The call he'd gotten was long expired. There was a message on the screen saying, "Call received: Saki Mikajima."

Saki?

At the exact moment that Anri was calling Mikado, Saki had tried to call Masaomi. While he wondered what this could possibly mean, his friend said, "I would have liked to call Sonohara here so I could show her what I'm about to show you, but...I just think it would be too dangerous."

"What is it that you're gonna show me? I'll happily check it out if it's a dirty mag," Masaomi joked with a shrug. But that was not Mikado's answer.

*   *   *

"A meeting of the Dollars."

♂♀

Outside of Tokyu Hands

"Hey, you got a moment?"

Chikage turned to face Aoba, his face red from the blood streaming down it from his skull.

"As far as I can tell, you seem to be the leader of these guys."

At his feet were about a half dozen Blue Squares, victims of his fighting prowess.

"Don't you find all those looky-loos out there kinda strange?"

"..."

Aoba returned his question with silence.

He had noticed it, too, by the time he arrived outside of Tokyu Hands. The pedestrians around them were acting strangely. And unlike what his friend said over the phone, it did not look like "fans excited about a secret pop idol concert."

But they weren't interfering with his business, so he largely ignored them—except that now the brawl had broken out, they weren't running or making noise or recording videos with their phones at all. That part was eerie.

Aoba was curious about the mob that was literally "merely observing," but in all honesty, the eeriness of that was far outshone by Rokujou's abnormal strength.

"What are we gonna do, Aoba?" asked one of his friends in a blue cap. "This guy's crazy!"

"We'll call for Yoshikiri from the van," Aoba replied. "Oh, and wake Houjou up, too."

Chikage looked lonely. "What, are you just gonna ignore my question?"

"I'm sorry. You're so tough—I've got bigger problems to worry about."

"Actually, I'm goin' easy on you kids. After all, I don't wanna accidentally beat Mikado Ryuugamine to death."

There was no way for Aoba to tell whether he was bluffing or not about going easy on them. All he knew for certain was that the man before him had instantly incapacitated five of his followers.

"...I'll admit it. I didn't realize what we were up against with a Saitama gang."

Chikage, for his part, greeted the gang leader's words with a shrug.

"Look, I'm not hoping to keep up this fight forever, y'know. If you could pay me back the money for the bikes you burned up as an apology, I'd appreciate it. And as far as the number of my guys you beat up, we can ante up the guys I've just beaten and call it even."

"I get the feeling that you've already gotten us back twice over for what we did."

"You took out ten of mine. So I'm only halfway there, but out of respect for Kadota..."

Chikage paused. He had heard a sound that any motorcycle gang member would recognize. It was the sound of engines revving, exhaust, and the obnoxious clamor of the musical horns that had long been outlawed.

Chikage didn't make that kind of racket when he rode, because one of his girlfriends said she hated loud noises—but there were plenty of rival gangs who had a very strict code when it came to motorcycle noise: Bright makes right. They did everything they could to be obnoxious.

That sounds like...Gozumezu Guns from Nerima, maybe? No...I can hear the guys from Poliseum as well.

The sounds being played by the approaching horns were familiar to Chikage, who had to wonder what this was about. Would there really be a gang ride at this exact moment?

Chikage was an optimist at heart, but he wasn't naive. This was not just a coincidence. Alarms were going off in his head.

But before he could do anything about it, they reached his view.

A number of bikes that even from a distance obviously belonged to a gang rounded onto Sixtieth Floor Street. Once he could make out some of their faces, Chikage was aghast.

"Wait a minute, it really *is* Gozumezu Guns and Poliseum together."

*   *   *

"Not quite, Mr. Rokujou."

The clamor of the motorcycles was loud enough that Aoba could barely hear any of what Chikage said, but he understood the gist of it. Amid the noise, he murmured, "They're not together until *after* this."

And then, just to prove him correct, more and more bikes, dozens of them, and even some cars and vans, came into formation along the road. It was clear at a glance that this was more than merely one or two gangs.

"Plus, they're not motorcycle gangs anymore."

His face twisted in a dark smirk, Aoba spoke words that no ear could hear.

"They're Dollars now."

♂♀

Outside of Russia Sushi

"What's this? What's happening?"

The roar of the motorcycles was enough to draw Nasujima's attention at last.

The Blue Squares he'd infected with Saika hadn't said anything about this. Either they hadn't been informed, or something major had happened out of the blue.

It wasn't only the biker gangs. Some street-thug types were prowling over on foot as well, and some of them were among the Saika-possessed, but the rest of them were clearly taking part in whatever this was reluctantly, as though they'd been invited by their friends or forced to attend by senior members.

The one thing they all shared in common was that they were the kind of people who would threaten others for money any day of the week.

"Yeah, whatever. The common rabble are easy to deal with," Nasujima said to himself with a leer, conveniently describing his own army of Saika-possessed as well.

*   *   *

"Either way, they'll all be my pawns in the end."

♂♀

Tokyo

"Got it. Keep an eye on it from a distance."

Akabayashi was in the process of traveling when he got a report over the phone from the motorcycle gang Jan-Jaka-Jan, who were working directly for him.

"Now, you said you saw thirteen gangs and that was only what you could confirm? This isn't some big regional alliance thing; cut us some slack, people."

After hearing more from the other end of the call, he narrowed his eyes and ordered, "Don't you get involved in the festivities. Keep your distance from the red-eyed folks. No point in having a zombie hunter turned into a zombie."

With that warning, he ended the call. Akabayashi sighed heavily, the smile gone from his face.

"You're getting a little too rambunctious, young Ryuugamine."

♂♀

The rooftop of a mixed-use building

"Hey…what is all that?"

Masaomi peered over the edge of the roof to ascertain what all the motorcycle roaring was about in the streets below. As usual, the expressway blocked the view of the main street, but based on the sound, it was clear that whatever was happening, it was abnormal.

"Shit…can't see. Damn, how many bikers they got down there? Sheesh…"

Over his shoulder, Mikado clarified, "It's not just bikers."

"…Mikado?"

"There are others from Chiba and Saitama. I guess you'd call them street thugs?"

It was a simple enough statement, but there was a whiff of disdain in Mikado's voice, along with no small measure of hatred.

"So…you brought them here?" Masaomi asked, turning around to face his friend. "How did you…? No, forget that—this is crazy! I mean, Mikado…you hate those kinds of people, and that's why…"

"That's why I went around with Aoba's group eliminating them, yes. But in fact, I personally could barely do any of it," Mikado said with a self-deprecating snort. "I was keeping busy with kicking them out of the Dollars…but then I realized that doing that wasn't enough."

"…You realized?" Masaomi repeated.

Mikado continued, "Well, I was researching them."

"?"

"It's very strange. They'll beat people up, almost for fun, but the moment you bring up information about their family, they freak out. But if you 'request' the cooperation of their leaders, the rest will happily go along with it as a group activity. In other words…they'll fight and commit violence just to go along with the group."

"Uh, dude…what are you talking about?"

Masaomi couldn't understand what Mikado meant by all this. Or to be truthful, he half expected it, but he didn't want to admit it might be true.

Essentially, Mikado had obtained the sensitive secrets of people that he hated and had manipulated them into coming here. He didn't need to do it for all of them, just one, and the rest would willingly come along for the spectacle. That was all the reason they needed to commit violence.

There were two things Masaomi didn't want to accept about this.

One was that he didn't want to think Mikado would do such a devious thing.

The other was that he didn't have a reason to do it.

"This is crazy… Even if every last member of Toramaru was here, there's no reason to gather such a huge group…"

"Oh, you've got it wrong. Rokujou and Toramaru have nothing to do with this. I feel a bit bad that he's gotten wrapped up in it, but technically, I am the one calling the shots for the Blue Squares, so…"

"What are you talking about, Mikado?!"

He wasn't acting right. Masaomi felt that he had to hit him, if that was what it took to make him see sense. He stared at his friend—and then noticed something.

An object clutched in Mikado's dangling right hand.

The pistol Mikado got from Ran Izumii was already in his hand. His finger wasn't on the trigger yet. It was pointed at the ground.

He didn't have it raised with both hands, so there was only so much an amateur like Mikado could do with it in this situation. But if he felt like it, he could shoot it at any moment.

And because he was an amateur, there was no telling where it might go.

"Mikado...?"

Masaomi immediately recognized that it was a gun.

And instantly, he knew that Mikado was not the type of person who would bring out a realistic model gun to use as a bluff. Even now, in his broken state, that was an unchanging part of Mikado's nature.

Given the many facets of the situation, Masaomi's guess that the gun was real quickly evolved into certainty.

"Where...did you get that...?"

"Oh, you know."

But Masaomi didn't turn his back to his friend. His righteous indignation was outweighing his fear of the gun for now.

"Mikado, what are you trying to do? Setting up this ridiculous gathering, carrying that thing around... What is your plan for the Dollars?!"

"..."

"I feel pathetic! I thought I was your friend, and now I can't even figure out what is going through your head..." Masaomi despaired, venting anger at himself.

Mikado just shook his head. "It's all right; it's not your fault. I planted the seeds for all this myself." He smiled sadly, still holding the gun. "And if I can't restart it, then it's better for the Dollars not to exist at all."

"Huh...?"

At last, he spoke aloud the answer that he had reached for himself.

"As of today, the Dollars will be no more."

♂♀

Shortly before Masaomi and Mikado faced off, there was a post on the largest message board within the Dollars' online community.

It was a single line.

Just one very simple sentence.

A lone individual post that barely anyone would even notice.

Probably mistyped, or some lame bit of trolling, trying to get attention.

Nobody even responded to the message, and any who saw it forgot it just as quickly.

But this message, in fact, was announcing the future of the Dollars' entire organization.

"The Dollars will disappear."

That lone sentence, posted by an unknown individual, was quickly swept along by the vast, ceaseless flood of activity on the board, lost in the depths of a sea of information.

Symbolizing the fate of the Dollars group itself.

♂♀

Sunshine building—rooftop

Upon the stage of Ikebukuro, many players with varying desires began to dance.

Driven by desire, hatred, obligation, honor, fear, and other such forces, they made their way into the open, wriggling and butting up against one another.

There was one impartial observer of the chaos unfolding.

To be more precise, there was one impartial *head* that observed the city below it.

A severed head, with a beautiful face and hair, being held by a body astride a headless horse.

Celty Sturluson.

With her head recovered now, she sent her shadow streaming far and wide, silently observing the city she presided over. The shadow blanketed the sky itself, covering the entirety of the city of Ikebukuro.

There was no visible emotion on her severed head, but its eyes were open, and it moved and reacted in a way that suggested it was part of one organism with the body that held it under its arm.

It was impossible to guess as to what she was thinking, and there were no humans present who might attempt to do such a thing. The only being that understood her thoughts was the headless horse, which Celty had called Shooter before she got her head back. It brayed to the sky.

QRRRRRRRRRRRRRRrrrrrrrrrrrrrrrrrrrrrr...

It sounded like a scream, like a roar, like the sound of the wind blowing past, all at once. The sound vibrated the vast expanse of shadow, extending far across the sky of Ikebukuro.

Celty did not react in any way to the horse's call. She simply observed the city below.

And more specifically, the clearly visible figures of Mikado and Masaomi.

♂♀

Kawagoe Highway

"Whew, I think I should be safe at this distance...but on the other hand, what's up with all the motorcycle gangs? Is someone having a retirement ride?"

Karisawa had escaped the area where all the red-eyed people were and, following the instructions in Yumasaki's text message, was now heading for Shinra's apartment.

"At least I was able to give Miss Kujiragi the message. Now I just have to get in touch with Mikarun. Did we ever trade numbers…?"

She was looking through her phone book for Mikado's information as she walked, when a car passing by her in the street suddenly sidled over and stopped right next to her.

"Huh?" She looked over and saw a very familiar van. "Ahhh!"

She raced over toward it. When she saw the face in the window, there were already tears in her eyes. "Dotachin! You're all right!"

But then…

"Oh no! We weren't in time! We're too late!"

"Huh?"

Yumasaki opened the back door and jumped out, and as soon as he saw Karisawa's eyes, he promptly pinned her arms behind her back.

"What?! Yumacchi! What?! What are you doing?!"

"Calm yourself down, Karisawa! We'll give you an exorcism now! Take it away, Shakugan no Anri!"

"Huh?! What the—?! Why is Anri here?!"

"I-I'm sorry, Karisawa…! I'm going to scrape your fingertip a little bit!" Anri got out of the vehicle next, her katana in her hand.

"Wh-what?! Wait—what's going on?!"

"Listen to me, Karisawa," said Yumasaki. "You might not realize it, but you've been infected by a blade-shaped alien parasite, and now you're its earthling puppet body!"

"What are you talking about?!" she snapped, baffled, but he held on hard.

"Don't even try to talk your way out of this! Those red eyes of yours are all the evidence we need to identify the problem!"

That was when Karisawa finally remembered: In order to fool the slashers, she'd popped in those red contact lenses.

"Huh?! Ohhh! No, no, no! It's not what you think!"

A few minutes later, Karisawa slumped exhaustedly in the back seat of the van. It was only when Anri, sword in hand, saw her and realized that her red eyes were not those of a Saika-possessed that she was fully out of trouble.

"Good grief. Totally ruined my emotional reunion with Dotachin."

"Sorry about that, Karisawa," Kadota said from the front passenger seat.

She waved him off. "Oh, it's fine. I'm over it. Besides, Azusa's the one who should be clinging to you in tears, not me. Let that be the fore-shadowing for your eventual marriage to her."

The brief confusion had actually jolted her out of her funk and back into her usual state. She breathed deep, in and out, and looked around the van again.

"So I'm kind of in the dark here. What's with the festivities?"

Not only were the people in the van different from the usual lineup, there were more than could safely fit inside. Because traffic was barely moving, Yumasaki trotted alongside the car and kept tabs on the sur-rounding environs.

There was a distant roar of what sounded like an endless gang of bik-ers somewhere up ahead, and every now and then, a few more of them wove through the lanes past Togusa's van.

"Where do we even begin...?" Kadota wondered. Before he could launch into an explanation, new information came in over the car radio.

"As for today's forecast, we've got... Excuse me, folks, there's been a breaking news bulletin just now."

The DJ's voice was followed by the sound of a piece of paper being flipped over. If they were postponing the usual weather forecast, it had to be pretty urgent news indeed. Everyone in the van listened intently, all their faces serious.

The contents of the report were far more serious than they could have imagined.

♂♀

The rooftop of a mixed-use building

"What do you mean...the Dollars will be no more?" Masaomi asked.

"Exactly what it sounds like," Mikado answered. "As of today, the Dollars will vanish."

"You mean break up? And this obnoxious biker gathering is just to commemorate the occasion?"

"Not exactly...but I suppose you might consider it something like that. It's going to be the final in-person gathering, basically. It's just that I want to show you and Sonohara what happens when people gather under the Dollars' name... What the Dollars really are," Mikado said mournfully, standing in the middle of the rooftop. "So you can see *what I created*."

From the edge of the roof, Masaomi said, "You said you started the Dollars ages ago, because you were bored... Is *this* what you wanted?"

"I know... At the start, it was more exciting. I thought I was finally about to get what I was hoping for," Mikado said, grinning like a schoolboy. He shook his head. "But now it's different. So I thought I should make it a place where I could actually welcome you and Sonohara. I want to usher you into a Dollars that I feel proud of."

"That makes sense. So why is it vanishing?"

"After the first meetup, Izaya said something to me."

"...?!"

Izaya. The mention of that name froze Masaomi solid. He choked on his words, flashing back to all kinds of memories from the past.

Mikado reminisced about just one, however.

"After the Dollars' meetup, Izaya said...you want to escape ordinary life, but you'll get used to the extraordinary right away."

"..."

"He also said, if you really want to escape the ordinary, you have to keep evolving. I thought I understood what he meant at the time, but I don't think that the lesson really sank in until it came to this," Mikado said, smirking at himself. He looked at the gun in his hand. "The Dollars became very ordinary to me...and I hit a block. Izaya was right."

"Stop it!" Masaomi shouted. "That's all his usual bullshit! He's manipulating you! That son of a bitch tells you one thing, then goes to someone else and tells them the polar opposite, just to enjoy seeing what happens!"

"You might be right about that," Mikado said, not denying Masaomi's words. "But I think I would have noticed it even if Izaya hadn't told me."

"He made you think that! That's what he does! Listen, no matter what kind of group the Dollars are, you're still you! Did you think that me and Anri would change our minds and hate you, whether you're just high school Mikado or the boss of a gang of stupid thugs?! Don't insult us like that!"

He made to rush over to his friend. The young man couldn't be right. Either he was full of himself, or as had been the case before, he was still under Izaya Orihara's spell. Whatever the case, Masaomi knew he had to wake Mikado up.

He would grab his shoulder and shake him, and if that didn't do the trick, he'd punch him in the mouth—except that he had to pause when he saw Mikado pointing the pistol at him.

"...Are you seriously pointing that gun at me?"

The answer was obvious; he didn't need to ask. But the boy was holding it with one hand, the weight making its aim uncertain. He also didn't have his finger over the trigger, so it was hard to tell what Mikado intended to do.

On the other hand, the fact that Masaomi might not know where the bullet was going made the situation that much more erratic and dangerous.

Masaomi stopped in his tracks, but he didn't shy away in fear. Mikado kept the gun pointed at his old friend and said, "I thought you might come and try to hit me regardless of the gun...but I guess even you're afraid of it."

He wasn't making fun of Masaomi; he was asking out of honest curiosity.

Masaomi clenched his jaws, stared Mikado straight in the eyes, and said, "Yeah, I'm afraid of it."

But there was no fear in his eyes. They began to smolder with quiet anger.

"Obviously I'm going to be scared when I see something like that pop up out of nowhere."

"Ah...yeah, that makes sense."

"But."

"Huh?"

Masaomi finally let all his pent-up anger explode into a howl of indignance.

"What scares me the most is this whole *situation* that would put the nicest guy I know in possession of *something like that*!"

"Masaomi…"

"Screw this! What the hell happened to make a kindhearted guy like you carry a gun?! It makes no sense! It's not right! How did it get to this?!" he demanded, clenching his fists so tight the nails dug into his palms. Then, lowering his tone of voice, he continued, "Was it…my fault?"

"…"

"Yeah, I guess so… I mean, Rokujou just said as much to me."

Now it was Masaomi's turn to smirk self-deprecatingly, if only for a brief moment. He stared back into Mikado's eyes.

"If I was putting that much pressure on you, then go ahead. I can't complain if you shoot me," he said.

"You shouldn't get desperate, Masaomi. I was the one who chose to become this way. It's not your fault."

"Then why are you pointing that at me?" Masaomi asked him, the question of the moment.

Mikado was at a loss. "I'm…not really sure."

"…About what?"

"About *who I should point this at next.*"

For a moment, Masaomi's face went slack—and when the meaning of this statement sank in, he shouted, "If that's the most commitment you can summon, then you don't need that damn thing! Go and dump it in a river somewhere before you end up firing it! Or hell, I'll go and get rid of it for you! You don't need to be putting yourself in danger like this! At worst, as long as you don't shoot it, you can always say you just 'found it somewhere'! You know?"

Without pointing the gun away, Mikado said happily, "That's the part that will always make you Masaomi. You're so much kinder at heart than I am." He shook his head, still not moving the gun. "I've already fired it."

"…Huh?"

For an instant, it didn't make sense to Masaomi. His brows creased.

So Mikado told him the simple truth.

"I already shot it twice. On the way here."

♂♀

Inside the van

"*We have details about a string of shootings within the city,*" said the voice over the radio player in Togusa's van. "*One shooting happened at the entrance to the Ikebukuro Police Department and the other at the entryway of the personal home of Chairman Dougen Awakusu of the Awakusu-kai, an organized crime operation affiliated with the Medei-gumi Syndicate.*"

The newscaster continued, crisply elocuting, detailing the unfolding situation.

"*At the scene of the shootings were acts of spray-painted graffiti, put down before the guns were fired, with the police saying that the words written correspond to the name of a delinquent group active around the Ikebukuro area, which they are investigating now...*"

"...What does that mean? 'Delinquent group active around the Ikebukuro area,'" Togusa wondered. But he already had a very good idea of what it meant.

Kadota spoke that idea out loud for him, his expression grave. "I'm guessing...it must be referring to the Dollars."

"So...what's gonna happen, then?" Karisawa asked from the back. Kadota could only give her his best guess.

"It means the Dollars just picked a fight...with both the law and the outlaws of this city."

♂♀

Tokyo—office

"...I'll be damned. He's cracked even worse than I imagined." Aozaki, the Awakusu lieutenant, sighed after he got the report from a subordinate. He got to his feet from the leather chair and pulled his jacket off the hook.

"Wh-where are you going?" the other man asked.

"To the old man's place. I've got to apologize for what just happened." When he heard about shots being fired at Dougen Awakusu's home and the police department, the first thing to pop into Aozaki's mind was the face of Mikado Ryuugamine. It should have been obvious, since he'd handed over the gun mere hours before, but even putting aside the matter of the firearm, only Mikado would come to mind so quickly as a suspect in such a self-destructive act.

Aozaki didn't expect that after passing him the gun through Izumii, Mikado would cause an incident before a single night had passed. But he was experienced in the ways of combat and precarious situations, so this did not faze him.

"The front porch of the boss's house might as well be the very face of the Awakusu. It was my action that led to this insult, so I need to be ready to sacrifice a finger or two," he said. But part of the threat he represented was that in the same breath, he could order, "Seize Mikado Ryuugamine and bring him in."

"Yes, sir."

"Personally, I'm not against that kind of wildness…but all that's out the window if you go after the head of the organization. He might be a kid, but depending on circumstances, he could end up sleeping with the fishes."

With his orders in place, Aozaki headed for the door of the office to make his way to his boss—until one of his men rushed through said door.

"Hey, what's all the commotion?" he demanded.

The out-of-breath subordinate delivered his message, and the name he mentioned caused the otherwise calm Aozaki to furrow his brow.

"Mr. Akabayashi came here alone, says he wants to talk to you…"

The rooftop of a mixed-use building

"Hey…what are you thinking?! You really are gonna destroy the Dollars…and more importantly, you're going to get yourself killed!" Masaomi shouted after hearing exactly where Mikado had shot the gun. He prayed it was just a bad joke.

But Mikado only agreed with him. "Yeah, you're probably right."

"That's all you have to say about it?!"

"But it does mean that the Dollars will cease to exist as a real thing."

"What...?" Masaomi gasped.

Mikado explained, "When word of this gets around, nobody's going to want to join the Dollars, and the people who have been part of it will all want to hide their pasts."

This was true, of course. Nobody would want to be associated with a group considered an enemy of both the police and the yakuza, especially when there was no actual benefit to being a member.

The only people you could imagine doing so would be tried-and-true rebels full of spite and attention-seeking idiots with no ability to foresee consequences, and both of those groups would earn what was coming to them.

At the very least, the people taking part for entertainment or out of a sense of obligation and the people who thought the Dollars were just some fun, harmless college-club type of gathering were going to be the first to distance themselves.

Like rats fleeing a sinking ship, they'd jump into the sea, withdrawing into anonymity and keeping their heads low for quite a while.

And then, perhaps inappropriately, Mikado said, "The Dollars will become an urban legend."

"Urban...legend?"

"Yes. Just a stupid urban legend," he repeated, eyes sparkling like a child. Masaomi recalled where he had seen that look before: when Mikado was new to Ikebukuro and watched the Headless Rider go past. It was a look of awe and horror, buoyed by overwhelming joy.

"But the thing is, urban legends evolve over time. They turn into rumors and take on more rumors as they go, spreading throughout the city," Mikado said, elaborating on his theory with some of what Izaya told him mixed in. "When the actual body is gone, only the name stays behind, continuously giving birth to false legends."

And with full self-assurance and pure delight, Mikado made his declaration.

"That is my ideal for the Dollars, I realized."

Masaomi felt like the background in the distance was warping, stretching.

"You mean...you shot a gun at a yakuza office and the police station...for *that* nonsensical reason?"

"Yup. The Dollars itself is a nonsensical idea. But if they were born from nonsense, then it makes sense that they'd disappear into nonsense," Mikado said with resignation.

"Even then, people will use the name for mischief," Masaomi argued.

"That's fine. Those people aren't Dollars anyway. They're just people using the Dollars' name. I figure, if anything, they'll help fuel the urban legend, hopefully," his friend said, smiling. Masaomi felt a chill run down his back.

Was this boy across from him really Mikado Ryuugamine?

Gun pointed in Masaomi's direction, Mikado said casually, "So... what are you going to do? Stop me?"

"Or are you here...to settle the Blue Squares versus the Yellow Scarves?"

♂♀

Outside Tokyu Hands

"I'm grateful to you, Mr. Rokujou," said Aoba, still wearing his ski mask.

The motorcycles were coming to a stop at the start of the street, keeping the sound of all that engine noise distant, so that it was quiet enough for them to have a conversation.

Chikage Rokujou stood in the middle of a semicircle of motorcycles. The bikers around him realized very quickly that it was the leader of Toramaru, and they began to buzz among themselves but didn't immediately pick a fight or start taunting him. For one thing, given that they'd all been coerced by force or by dirty tricks into taking part in the Dollars' group, none of them could say for sure that Toramaru wasn't *also* among their number.

Chikage glanced at the punks surrounding the end of the street around him and shrugged. "Well, well, another bunch of nobodies showin' up. I don't even see anyone on the level of Dragon Zombie or Jan-Jaka-Jan."

"With enough time, we might have gotten them in the group, too."

"That's a big play. Who else…? I don't see Nuimura from Big Dog Stars here. If you had an idiot like him around, I'd have to start expecting trucks to come roaring through here," Chikage said, mentioning names of other notable bikers as he surveyed the scene.

Then he turned back to Aoba, who seemed to be the one calling the shots for the guys in the blue caps.

"What does your boss think he's gonna do with all these people?"

"I don't think he means to do anything," Aoba admitted, to Chikage's confusion.

"Uh…meaning, let the chips fall where they may?"

"Our boss has no ideals. No beliefs. All he's got is sentimentality and curiosity. And he'll do stuff like this based on those things alone. When you factor in luck, this is why I have such respect for him."

It was as though he was happy to be a supportive victim of Mikado Ryuugamine's wild rampage. Then, like a child excited to show his friend the latest toy, he explained, "You need guts to have ideals and beliefs and even dreams. But he doesn't have that. His group just ballooned up on him, and he got puffed up with some empty 'conviction' with nothing behind it. Mr. Mikado had nothing to put his feet against, but he spun and spun and spun those legs, until he finally reached this point."

Aoba shrugged, and when Chikage said nothing, he continued, "Maybe that's something that you wouldn't understand, if you've always had these things."

Chikage had been silently listening to this speech. At last, he cracked his neck and said, "I don't like it when people try to cover up the truth with some embarrassing poetry shit like that. Though I do have a girlfriend who likes that stuff, so I'm not gonna say it doesn't have its place."

Rokujou glanced over in the direction of the mixed-use building, then smirked. "I just heard that Kida wanted to save his friend who went crazy, and so I decided to help him out on a whim."

"Oh, come on, that's a gross oversimplification." Aoba chuckled, his eyes shining with mirth. "There are some things only a crazy kid can pull off."

"Yeah, whether you've got some big, fancy reason behind it or not,"

Chikage said with annoyance. But as a matter of fact, he'd heard the general version of events from Masaomi already.

Even knowing that this was just the result of a kid named Mikado pushing himself into a corner with no better way out, Chikage said to Aoba, "I'll tell you one thing."

"?"

"It doesn't matter your reason. At the point you rustle up the night like this, the point you cause hell for other people, there's no difference. Everyone who does it is scum. And that includes me. And you guys," he said, coming clean. "Are you gonna go around to all the people you've fought and the folks whose sleep you disturbed and state your case for them? 'Look, these are the tragic reasons we're doing this!'"

"..."

"Whether you're mugging people to get cash to blow or mugging them to buy medicine for your sick parents..."

Behind Chikage, a Blue Square approached, brandishing a bat. But Chikage merely twisted a few inches and smashed the other guy in the face with a backhand. He looked over to see the thug crumple to the ground, then sighed and finished his sentence.

"...there's no difference to the innocent people you're beatin' up and robbing. It's ridiculous to suggest otherwise."

He turned on his heel and began to walk, not even bothering to look in Aoba's direction. "I've lost interest here... If he already knows everything that's goin' on, then I guess Mikado Ryuugamine must have gone to Kida by now." He headed back for the mixed-use building he'd come from.

Aoba was not in any particular rush. "Sorry to tell you this after your moving speech, but we can't have you going back there."

"Oh yeah?"

"Yes, Mr. Mikado and Masaomi Kida are back there. But it's only the two of them," Aoba said with a cocky smile, typing something into his phone. "It's not for any of the rest of us to interfere. Including me and you."

Two large shadows loomed in Chikage's path. They belonged to Houjou and Yoshikiri, well-known for being the two biggest and burliest of the Blue Squares' fighters. Chikage looked up at them, one a man yawning as he approached, the other a very tall boy with squinty eyes, and smiled.

"Oh, so you finally brought out someone worth my time. That's much better."

But those two were not the only ones in his way. Suddenly the guys sitting on their bikes began to pull out their phones. While the engine noise largely drowned it out, Chikage could faintly hear their ring-tones going off.

"...Is that a notification of a mass text message?"

"Well sleuthed. I just sent them a very short, simple instruction."

The bikers got down off their vehicles and turned vicious expressions toward Chikage. In the face of this malevolent aura, Aoba told Chikage what the rest of the group already knew.

"Chikage Rokujou is the enemy of the Dollars."

♂♀

Outside Russia Sushi

"...Looks like something's happening. They're taking out phones... So are we assuming that one guy in the ski mask is Mikado? Whatever the case, he seems to be the leader," Nasujima said to Haruna with a leer. They were watching the scene in front of Tokyu Hands. "If it turns into a brawl, we're gonna have our people rush them all."

"Yes...Mother."

♂♀

Inside Russia Sushi

"Is it just me, or are the motorcycles really loud outside?" Tom won-dered, his face gaunt with exhaustion. "Anyway, if we're desperate enough, I think we can jump from the roof here to the ramen place next door...but I don't think it gives us a way out of this mess—it only traps us in a different place instead."

"Oh, if pull no good, try push instead. You get discouraged, make hungry," Simon advised as he and Denis checked on some kind of equipment.

Tom didn't ask what it was for, and he was planning to pretend he never saw it, if necessary. But then Denis said to him, "We were unlucky. If Shizuo were here, he coulda flattened all those folks outside by himself."

"You might be right, but I'm also glad that's not the case."

"Oh?"

"If you take Mr. Kine's word, that's all just some kind of fancy hypnotism, right? It's one thing for people to pick a fight with him and earn what's coming to them, but I can't let him go around smashing ordinary folks who can't control themselves." Tom sighed.

Kine broke his silence to say, "Is that all you want in life? You get a guy like that on your side, you could conquer this city."

"You've got the wrong idea about me. Shizuo's an underclassman from our middle school days, and now he's a coworker," said Tom, stretching. There was a lonely look in his eyes. "Shizuo looks so sad when he's raging the way he does, but I can't even join in the carnage with him, much less stop him… It's not much to be proud of."

♂♀

The rooftop of a mixed-used building

"Well, let's see."

After Mikado asked him what he was going to do, Masaomi was silent for a while, clenching his fists.

"I couldn't do anything for you. And I guess even talking about doing things to help you is kind of condescending, huh?"

Masaomi took a step closer to the gun. Mikado's hand twitched. But Masaomi did not stop his forward progress across the rooftop.

"I might not be that smart. I'm a coward. It's pathetic to admit it, but the only thing I'm good at is fighting, to some extent…"

There were two firm acts of determination in Masaomi's mind.

One was the determination to risk his life, like he did when he stood up to Horada. Not to throw his life away but to make his friend wake up.

The other was the determination to be his best friend's enemy—again, in order to wake him up to the truth.

"So the least I can do is fight you," Masaomi said with a smile, just like he did as a child. "If you wanna go crazy, I won't stop you. But I can choose to go crazy, too."

"Masaomi…"

"I'm gonna drag you, kicking and screaming, back into the ordinary life you hate so much."

There was no hesitation in his eyes anymore.

"I'm gonna punch you, I'm gonna make you cry, and I'm gonna force you to remember."

Masaomi spoke forcefully, projecting his will, such that even if his friend had truly become something no longer human, he would deny that and will it out of existence.

"*You are not an urban legend like the Headless Rider.* You're just a guy named Mikado Ryuugamine…a normal, scrawny human being who tries to do right by everybody!"

For a moment, Mikado's expression vanished from shock. Then tears began to pool in his eyes.

"You're so strong, Masaomi."

"…"

"I was always jealous of that. It's why I really wanted to beat you," he said, summoning up not hatred from the pit of his stomach but envy. "It's why, no matter what I have to do, no matter what names people call me…"

With a look of respect for his childhood friend, Mikado put his finger against the trigger of the gun.

"…I will deny your words with all my strength."

And a few seconds later, the dry pop of a gunshot expanded into the sky over Ikebukuro.

♂♀

Outside of Tokyu Hands

The sound of a gunshot from above reached the street in front of Tokyu Hands.

"What was that?"

Everyone present looked around for the source of the unfamiliar burst, but no one found it. The closest were a few bikers, who muttered that they heard it from up above, subsequently gazing at the expressway, the Amlux building, and the Sunshine building in turn.

That was when they finally realized that the night sky was colored an abnormally dark black.

The top of the soaring Sunshine building, in fact, seemed to be shrouded in some kind of black fog, completely hiding it from view.

"Hey, what's that…?"

The murmuring among the crowd began to spread, until it all came to an abrupt stop some fifteen seconds later.

A dark shadow suddenly raced through the group of men.

"?!"

The shadow leaped and bounced off motorcycle and car alike from roof to hood, easily speeding its way through the densely packed crowd of bikers and thugs.

"Hey!" shouted one of the bikers whose motorcycle had been used as a stepping-stone, furiously following the shadow with his eyes. "What the hell? Kill that—"

But before he could finish ordering his friends, his voice caught in his throat.

He'd heard the sound of ugly, unpleasant scraping behind him.

It was so abnormal that the bikers spun around, wondering what it was.

And when they saw what the man back there was dragging around, they lost the ability to speak.

"Hey, did you hear something?" Chikage demanded, shoulders heaving as he breathed, but no one responded.

He was like a solitary island in the sea of bikers and Blue Squares around him. Even then, he challenged his foes, not backing down from the fight.

"Hah… Ain't that a mystery. Up against every last one of you, and I don't feel scared in the least."

"Don't try to play tough with us, Rokujou! You're done for!" yelled one of the senior members of the rival Gozumezu Guns, but Chikage wasn't bothered by it.

"I'll be honest," he taunted. "I felt a lot more presence when I fought this guy who was as tough as a *kaiju*, about three months ago…"

But he trailed off. The black shadow was racing toward Chikage, rushing over the heads of the other men. It was a man dressed in black.

"…Who's that?" Chikage wondered, appraising the injured man. That man just grinned at him and surveyed the situation.

"…More people than I expected," he said. Then he noticed the crowds of red-eyed people and added, "Half of them possessed by Saika. Whatever. That suits me fine."

And with that little brag out of the way, he looked toward Otowa Street.

When Aoba saw the man, he clenched his jaws.

"Izaya…Orihara!" the boy snarled.

Just at that moment, an enormous mass leaped over the heads of the stunned bikers and flew toward Izaya.

When they recognized it as one of the motorcycles parked right in the middle of the street, even the Saika-possessed were quick to back away.

The vehicle crashed explosively against the street and slid over its surface, bits and pieces spraying off it. Izaya dodged the projectile by a tiny margin and stood in the middle of the space that had opened up in the crowd. There he awaited the monster.

Everyone present turned in the direction from which the vehicle flew and instantly cleared the path.

"Ah!" Chikage gasped.

Walking down the newly created space toward him, exuding dozens of times more intimidation than the crowd of a hundred-plus bikers, was a man in a bartender's outfit.

"It's you, Heiwajima!"

Then he turned to Aoba with a bitter smirk.

"Wait, is *that* guy the one you called in to help?"

"No. He's…not in the Dollars anymore."

"Wha…?" Chikage drawled.

Under his ski mask, Aoba's face was devoid of expression.

"In fact, I think him leaving the Dollars was one of the reasons that Mr. Mikado broke down."

After Shizuo threw the bike he had been dragging along one-handed, he continued his steady pace toward Izaya. But the other man did not attempt to leave the scene.

It was almost as though he had been hoping to lure him here from the start.

While Masaomi challenged Mikado, who wanted to be an urban legend, Izaya Orihara was challenging an established legend in the flesh.

Izaya pulled out his most trusted weapon, a large folding knife, signaling that all the little tricks were over now.

"Shall we begin?"

Despite being in the same circumstances as Masaomi, Izaya gripped his weapon for almost the exact opposite purpose.

He wanted to carve into the world the fact that Shizuo, who tried to be human, was truly a hideous monster.

♂♀

Inside the van

"Did you hear something earlier?" Anri asked with concern.

In the passenger seat, Kadota replied, "Yeah, it sounded like a gunshot."

"C'mon, man… Don't try to scare me like that…," Togusa griped, his cheek twitching.

Next to him, Anri looked at the sky through the window. Then she noticed it, too:

The sky over Ikebukuro was covered in an abnormal darkness.

When she detected the oppressive darkness surrounding the top of the Sunshine building, she couldn't help opening her mouth—to speak the name of the creature she trusted most.

"Is that...Celty?"

♂♀

In time, they gathered.
  In the place where the Dollars began.
  To bring the Dollars to their end.

And almost as if retracing the very steps of that first in-person meetup, a woman cloaked in black shadow began to wriggle and writhe. Unlike at that meetup, however, she was riding a headless horse rather than a motorcycle.
  As well, rather than racing down the side of the Tokyu Hands building, she started from the roof of the Sunshine building, the tallest in Ikebukuro.

What was once the Headless Rider was now in true, complete dulla-han form.
  And so she descended into Ikebukuro once again.
  She would display to the city the change that had come over her.

Chat room

.
.

.

The chat room is currently empty.
The chat room is currently empty.
The chat room is currently empty.

.

.

.

FINAL CHAPTER
Greener Pastures Wherever You Go

Ikebukuro—in the past

A ship rocked on the waves as it made its long voyage to Japan.
   When he wandered into the dark, afraid, the boy encountered "her."
But his fear eventually turned to trust—and trust into love.

   Then he mustered his everything to protect that love and asked a
question.

   "Hey, Celty, when you find your head, will you be going back home?"
   Shinra was only six years old. Celty responded to him by writing on
a piece of paper.
   "That's right."
   "I want to go with you."
   "…? That's nonsense."
   "Then I don't want you to go," Shinra whined.
   Put off by this, Celty scrawled, *"I am not your toy."*
   "I know. I don't care if I never see my toys again."
   "Apologize to the toy makers."
   "I'm sorry," little Shinra said dutifully, bowing to some unseen,
imaginary toy factory.

Celty noted to herself that this must simply be how children acted. She wrote, *"Why do you want to be with me?"*

"...Because we're family," Shinra said. That made sense to her.

The boy hadn't had a mother around. Perhaps he felt some kind of motherly nurture from her presence. But if she was his example of what constituted "motherly," he was likely to grow up warped somehow.

"Listen to me, Shinra. I'm not human. I can't be your family."

"Why not?"

"Why not?" she repeated, then paused her writing.

"I can talk with you like this, Celty. We live in the same place. Or do you think we can't be in the same family because you're not rejistered in the household sertifikit or the sensus?"

"Those are some very big words, you know."

Celty thought it over and answered him very carefully.

"I am too different from human beings. If you live with me long enough, you will dislike me."

"I don't know about that."

"It's true," she said, trying to distance herself from him.

Shinra fidgeted. "Then...if I don't get tired of you, will you promise to stay here?"

"If that's true, I'll consider it."

She wasn't entirely accustomed to human society yet, but over the last two years, Celty had learned much from news, television shows, manga, and other channels of contemporary Japanese culture.

She recalled a news segment where they'd said, *"Unlike pairings of childhood friends in fiction, they rarely go on to a romantic relationship in real life."* She assumed that Shinra was simply being a child and would grow out of it.

If he sees my face every day, he'll get tired of me eventually. Or...sees everything but my face, I suppose.

She added the last part as a self-effacing joke, but as a matter of fact, it was a crucial piece of information.

He couldn't see her face, hear her voice, or read her expressions. And perhaps it was this fact of life that helped Shinra hold tight to his affection for her over all those years, without growing tired of her.

To Shinra, Celty Sturluson was like a blank canvas. Bit by tiny bit, he learned what expressions she made and what elicited her happy smile, and he sketched it out onto that canvas.

After about ten years had passed, Celty had a firm image within Shinra. It was the result of seeking out her true face, not of pushing his own hopes and ideals onto her.

And perhaps that was why he was still madly in love with her now.

No matter what obstacles might exist between the two of them.

♂♀

Ikebukuro—alleyway

On a street heading toward Sunshine City from the opposite side as the shopping district, a man and woman ran into each other.

But it was not by any means a coincidence.

"…I'm surprised. You overcame Saika's curse in quite a short amount of time," said Kujiragi, who looked anything but surprised—and yet there was a faint note of it in her voice.

Standing across from her was Shinra Kishitani. Right about the time that he had identified Celty's location, he spotted a vending machine soaring through the city. Manami surmised that the vending machine was heading toward where they would find Izaya and ran after it.

Meanwhile, Shinra passed down streets with signs of destruction here and there on the way to Sunshine City.

And in the midst of that trip, Kujiragi—also chasing after Shizuo and Izaya—sensed the presence of his Saika.

"Let's see, it was…Kasane Kujiragi, right?" Shinra asked apologetically, his eyes bloodshot.

"…Yes."

"Do you have time to talk? Or would that just end up with you cutting me and kidnapping me again?" Shinra wondered.

Kujiragi shook her head. "No, I no longer have any reason to abduct you against your will," she said, staring into Shinra's red eyes. "I judge that any emotion that cannot be ruled by Saika will not be swayed by simple pain or brainwashing."

"I'm glad. I was worried you might say something like 'If I can't have you, then I'll kill you.'"

"No. I am not actually that enamored of you." Kujiragi walked toward Shinra and explained, "But…it is true that I have an interest in you. If I had to describe it, I would surmise that perhaps I am jealous."

"Jealous…?"

"As a part of my research into Celty Sturluson, I also examined you, her domestic partner. As a human who was in love with an inhuman creature."

"No mistake there," Shinra said bashfully.

"I actually did not believe it at first," she admitted. "I thought that you were acting out affection for Celty Sturluson on Shingen Kishitani's orders, in order to keep her and the valuable research she might represent close at hand."

"…"

"But the more I looked into it, the more I became convinced that your feelings were genuine," Kujiragi said. She closed her eyes and continued, her voice a monotone: "I, too, have the blood of the inhuman within me, and I have no memory of ever receiving true love from another. Even my actual mother, an entirely nonhuman being, practically abandoned me to survive on my own."

Despite her admission that she was all but nonhuman herself, Shinra said nothing. He was, of course, well aware that she was no ordinary human being.

"It was only yesterday that I finally became free from some personal business." Kujiragi looked him in the eyes. "After speaking with other Saika owners, I made a decision. If no one will love me, perhaps *I ought to love someone else*."

"And you chose me? Well, I think that's a much more positive way of thinking than deciding you don't need love, but why choose me?"

"For one thing, like I said earlier…I am jealous."

This made sense to Shinra. She was jealous of Celty, who wasn't human but was able to carry on a happy life. So she decided that she would steal a part of that happiness from Celty.

Kujiragi added, "For another…I sought some kind of return."

"Return?"

"Perhaps I was hoping that in exchange for loving, I would be loved in return. And since you are capable of loving a nonhuman... perhaps..."

She included suppositions and speculation in her statements as a sign that even she didn't understand how she felt. Still, despite her awkwardness, she was busy putting her thoughts in order.

"As I researched more about your unique nature, I began to feel a kind of envy. That you were not like other humans and you might represent a kind of hope for me. When I saw how you continued your relationship with Celty Sturluson, even after being injured by Adabashi, I felt—though I bear some responsibility for your injury, I will admit—a kind of admiration for you."

Adabashi.

He was Ruri Hijiribe's stalker, the man who'd injured Shinra terribly. But the mention of that name did not cause any particular consternation in him.

Kujiragi paused and tilted her head in slight disbelief at what she was going to say. "I became a *fan* of yours. Is that an inadequate reason?"

"..."

"So I will broach the topic again. Will you consider accepting my feelings?"

It was a simple confession of love—so very simple.

Silence enveloped the two.

In the distance, motorcycle engines roared, and there were sounds of destruction as well—but here on this street, it was so quiet that time itself might have stopped.

Then Shinra broke the long silence.

"I believe a normal human being would be angry right about now," he said, grinning lopsidedly, his eyes red. "You got me injured, abducted me for your own selfish reasons, and generally did a lot of awful stuff to me."

"..."

"But I'm just not mad at you. And that's only because I have Celty."

"?"

Kujiragi stared at him quizzically.

Shinra went on, like a rambunctious, innocent child: "Because I have Celty, I don't need anything else. It would be a waste of my time to hate other people. So it's only thanks to Celty that I can even stand here and have a pleasant conversation with you."

He looked down, then raised his head again to stare Kujiragi straight in the eyes. "The only reason the guy you like is here *at all* is because of Celty." It felt as if he was saying that as much to himself as to her. "So…I'm sorry. I cannot return your feelings."

"…"

Kujiragi closed her eyes for a few moments, then exhaled. "I understand. I am satisfied just having heard your answer clearly."

She was as expressionless as ever, but Shinra gave her a serious look as he said, "I know it's strange to say this to someone you only just met, but…you seem like a mysterious person to me. You're demi-human, and clumsy, and yet oddly straightforward, and trying to change yourself so that you're not so otherworldly."

"What are you trying to say?"

"I think that while you don't match up to Celty, you're plenty attractive yourself. It might be cruel to say this after I turned you down, but if Celty didn't exist, I might have fallen in love with you instead."

After a pause, Kujiragi said, "Are you consoling me?"

But Shinra shook his head. "I'm not that clever and considerate." He walked closer to her. "There's just one thing that I can do for you."

"…What is it?"

"I can offer you proof."

"…?"

She gave him a curious look, so Shinra leaned forward, withstanding the pain of his many injuries, and said proudly, "I am proof that an utterly ordinary human being and the world's most wondrous Headless Rider, the most mismatched couple imaginable, *can still find love together.*"

"…"

"So I'm certain that you will find the right person for you. And until then, whether it's family, or someone close, or even yourself—take good care of someone," Shinra said with a gentle smile.

Kujiragi was silent for quite a while, until at last, she said, "You're an awful person."

With the faintest hint of a smile on her lips.

*   *   *

"How could you make me like you more after you rejected me?"

♂♀

Togusa's van

"I thought I heard it coming from the building on the left…but if the sound's bouncing off the expressway, then there's no telling where it came from…"

Togusa peered through the windshield up at the buildings looming over them.

The biker gangs were gathered just a few dozen yards ahead and had practically taken over the road. No cars were moving, of course, so all the drivers, noticing the gathering ahead, were desperately trying to trickle off onto side streets.

"And you're saying the guy with the fancy hair was definitely out in front of Russia Sushi, Karisawa?"

"Yep, no question. He was with Haruna."

"…"

Anri placed her hands on her thighs, clutching the hem of her clothing.

Mikado Ryuugamine and Masaomi Kida—Izaya Orihara had likened their relationship to "balancing atop a rope on fire." With the threat of Nasujima added to the mix, Anri was fighting a powerful anxiety over a situation whose full scope she could not ascertain.

"Do you think it would be faster to get out and run?" Seiji wondered.

"Yeah, but…if there really are as many people as there were at the first Dollars meeting…," Karisawa replied.

Meanwhile, Togusa noticed a person walking down the center of the road, weaving between the cars caught in traffic. The figure's movement was awkward and halting, as though they were hurt.

What's that?

Huh? Where have I seen him before…?

As Togusa squinted ahead, the figure suddenly raised a hammer and brought it down on the van's front windshield with abnormal force.

"Wha…?!"

It smashed against the glass, sending spiderweb fractures all across the surface and turning the driver's vision through it white. There was a second impact, then a third, and big chunks of the glass fell loose.

"Y-you son of a bitch!" Togusa screamed at the man. He stomped on the gas, making to run over the attacker.

"Stop, Togusa!" Kadota shouted from the passenger seat, which was just enough to keep Togusa in his rational mind.

The attacker, meanwhile, leered at them and examined the group in the van.

"Oh-ho… Very nice… Real tasty bunch ya got in here, huh? Hey… what the hell are *you* doin' here, Namie Yagiri?"

"Izumii…," Namie said with undisguised loathing. A nervous silence ran through the vehicle.

"Huh? Izumii? Did he change up his look…?" Karisawa wondered.

Kadota grimaced. "Hah…you really slimmed down during your time on the inside. What happened to that regal pompadour you were so proud of?"

The air around Izumii seemed to chill several degrees. "Kaaadooo-taaa," he hissed with fury, staring daggers at the young man through his sunglasses. "I heard you got hit by a car, but you seem just fine to me… So I guess I oughta finish the job, huh?"

Those two statements didn't add up at all, but Kadota reached for the seat belt to undo it anyway.

"Whoa, now. Who said you could move?" Izumii pointed the hammer right at him, a vicious smile smeared across his face. "I'm puttin' on a car-dismantling show. And you've got the best seat in the house, so don't get up."

At that point, about ten more thugs appeared from other vehicles to surround Togusa's van. They all carried metal pipes, bats, shovels, and picks—implements that would indeed be useful in dismantling a vehicle.

"Hey, we've got women and children in here. At least let them out." Kadota glared without a shred of fear.

Izumii cackled and shook his head. "C'mon, dumb-ass. You know the entire reason you betrayed me is because *I don't make those kinds of concessions.* Right?"

"You son of a bitch…," Kadota growled, his brow creasing. The other man glanced at the back seat of the van.

"Okay, Yumasaki, you're in for it, too… Wait. Yumasaki ain't here…," he said curiously. Then he recognized one of the two girls back there. "Wha…?"

He opened his wide mouth into a malicious cackle. "Ha-ha… ha-ha-ha-ha-ha! You…you're Masaomi Kida's girl, huh? Okay, okay, I see. So Kadota saved your skin, and now you've been palling around with them ever since!"

"…"

Saki maintained her silence, only staring back at Izumii. As a matter of fact, they'd only just met again yesterday, but admitting so wouldn't make any difference, so she didn't bring it up.

"Hey, what if I tossed a Molotov cocktail into the van, like you folks did to me? Huh?" Izumii laughed. "I wondered what was up with the summons right after we split apart, but now it just means I get to see y'all again! I feel fate at work! Gotta thank Mikado for that!"

"…"

   "…"

      "…"

         "…?"

Aside from Mika and Namie, the entire group within the van froze.

"What…did you just say? Thank who?" Kadota grunted.

"Oops. I guess you didn't know that yet?" Izumii said, shrugging theatrically. The action caused the sternum that Chikage had injured to creak, and he scowled in pain. But it lasted only a brief moment and did not dull his enjoyment of the situation.

"I'm not the leader of the Blue Squares anymore," he said.

"What?"

"…Your buddy Mikado Ryuugamine is the one calling the shots now! Hya-ha-ha-ha-ha!"

♂♀

The rooftop of a mixed-use building

After the gunshot, only the smell of powder was left in the air.

Within its midst, the two figures did not move.

"…"

There was still a faint trail of smoke coming from the muzzle of the pistol in Mikado's hand. A little cut on Masaomi's cheek trickled blood, from either being grazed by the bullet or just the shock wave of its passage.

The sound of the shot hit him directly in the ear, leaving the reverberation of its roar rattling around in his head. Mikado felt the same thing, so for the moment, neither of them could move or speak.

Physically, they were trapped in a stalemate.

" "
...
" "
...

A moment ago, just before Mikado had fired the gun, Masaomi had bolted off the ground like a spring-loaded toy, racing for the other boy. He had tossed his crutch aside and leaped with one foot.

The knee Izumii had shattered screamed under the cast. The pain was dulled by the anesthetic, but the shock still ran through his spine and smashed into his brain.

But he pushed that unpleasant sensation down into his gut and reached over to grab Mikado's wrist. The impact of that move caused him to pull the trigger, firing the gun just to the side of Masaomi's cheek.

They froze, locked in position, for almost a full minute.

The success of Masaomi's insane one-legged jump was half thanks to good luck and half to something else coming into play. Mikado had given him an opening.

He'd moved his free hand, bringing it closer to add support to his grip on the gun. Masaomi spotted that chance and took it, rushing in to grab Mikado's right arm. He did so gingerly—if he'd done it with all his strength, the arm might as well have snapped.

Shit... You know you're not built for fighting like this, you idiot.

Masaomi gnashed his teeth, not from the pain running through his body but with anger at himself for having driven his friend to these lengths.

Once their hearing had largely recovered, his gun hand still held down, Mikado spoke. "You startled me. I wasn't expecting you to come running at me."

"...What did you do, look up how to shoot a gun online?"

"Huh?"

"Knowing how serious you are, I figured you would use both hands to steady the gun."

In a sense, it was a bet that he could make, knowing what made Mikado tick so well.

"I see… Wow, you're really something, Masaomi," he said with a grin and tried to use his free left hand to push Masaomi away.

Masaomi smacked his hand away with his own, which was fixed in place with tape and bandages. Once he had cleared it out of the way, he slammed a head-butt right into Mikado's face.

"*Hng!*"

Mikado stumbled backward, and Masaomi seized the opportunity to knock him over onto the roof with his foot. He wrenched Mikado's right wrist, causing him to drop the gun. Awkwardly, he used his shattered leg to kick the clattering pistol away; it rattled into the corner of the rooftop area.

The next moment, Masaomi straddled Mikado and promptly punched him in the face. He used his right fist, with the broken fingers taped up and secured, not caring that it was already damaged.

The physical agony of it far surpassed his painkillers, and he could feel the sensation of bone pieces sliding and shifting. But he hit Mikado again, and again, and again.

"You idiot, Mikado! You idiot! You idiot!" Tears bloomed in his eyes, and with his other hand, he lifted Mikado by the collar. "Create a place for us to come back to? Why would you go and sabotage your chances of ever coming back, then?!"

"…"

"I know I ran away for a while. But Anri was always still here!" Masaomi shouted. "I don't care if you forgot all about me, the guy who left you behind to fend for yourself! But you shouldn't be putting Anri through this kind of pain…"

Mikado's face was bruised and puffy all over from the beating. Blood dripped from his broken lips—but still he smiled.

"The Dollars…aren't going to stop now…just because I do." It was a smile not of joy but of resignation. "And that's why the Dollars have to vanish."

He reached with his free left hand and stuck it into his pocket.

"Hey, what are you—?" Masaomi yelped, thinking it would be a knife or something of that nature. The instant he looked in that direction, a sharp, heavy shock ran through his leg—and shortly after, he was hit by a wave of heat and pain unlike anything he'd felt before.

♂♀

Aozaki's office

"What the hell are you thinking, Akabayashi?"

"Something sneaky." Akabayashi, who was leaning against the wall near the door, grinned.

Aozaki glared at him as he sat down heavily in one of the chairs in the reception room. "Sneaky?"

"Yeah. About how I'm gonna carve up the Dollars."

"…Tsk." Aozaki clicked his tongue, realizing that the info was already out.

"See, I had my eyes on the Dollars, too. Did you happen to hand anything over to young Mikado?"

"…I'll explain things to the boss. I don't have to tell you a damn thing."

"Don't be cold, Aozaki. It's my jurisdiction handling the youngsters like the Dollars, right? So if I let this nonsense continue, it's going to reflect poorly on what I do."

"I never took you for the type to care about that."

It sounded like low-key banter, but Aozaki's subordinates in the room with them got a case of cold sweats from all the aural pressure that exuded from the two men. These were the Red Ogre and Blue Ogre of Awakusu, the two most ferocious of the group's lieutenants. And they were not having a friendly little chat.

"Now, now, Aozaki. I didn't come here to spar with you," Akabayashi said with a smirk, scraping the cane that he used as a weapon along the floor. "Would you mind allowing *me* to handle the Dollars?"

"…What is this nonsense?"

"Let me guess what you're thinking. You want to make Mikado Ryuugamine *disappear*, and you'll sit some other kid with ties to our family in his place. They're a weird group; it's not even clear who calls the shots to begin with. So if you get control of the Blue Squares, the most powerful faction within the Dollars, we can use them as we like."

"I don't know what you mean," Aozaki insisted smoothly.

"Look, I'm not accusing you of meddling in my business," Akabayashi continued. "My job is simply to monitor the young folks. It's not to control them. As long as they don't peddle drugs or sell to minors, I'm not going to complain. I'm just askin' you to let me handle this—the one time."

"Is this someone you want to protect?"

"…Now *that's* something I don't need to tell you."

"…"

Aozaki thought it over, then shook his head. "No. Just with the business in mind, I can overlook one kid…but *this* kid tried to shame the boss. And nobody does that without retaliation. If you wanna beg for that kid's life, go talk to the old man."

Akabayashi sighed. If he pled his case to the head of their yakuza group, he might get Mikado's life spared. But only if the boss and the other officers hadn't learned the name Mikado Ryuugamine.

The kid was too closely tied to Anri. They didn't seem to be romantically linked yet, but given that the name Saika was used in the chat room, it meant that Anri Sonohara could turn out to be a significant force in this situation.

He didn't want to consider the possibility that Anri might become hostile to the Awakusu-kai as a consequence of searching for Mikado or trying to help him. But he said nothing of that here.

"You're an old-fashioned type, you know that?" he said to Aozaki. "Shiki and Kazamoto are going to laugh at you."

"Let them. I'm too set in my ways to live any other life."

"Same goes for me."

"Says the fool who's gone soft. At any rate, the kid shot at the boss's house. That means…"

At this point, one of Aozaki's subordinates popped his head into the meeting room and approached. "May I have a moment, Mr. Aozaki?"

"What is it?"

The man approached and whispered into his ear, looking deadly serious. Aozaki's brow furrowed. He thought over what he had just heard, then snorted.

"Looks like the both of us were worried for no reason."

"?"

"Let's say that I passed a gun on to the head of the Dollars," Aozaki said coyly. "But from what my 'friend' within the police says…"

"…the gun that shot up the old man's house and the police station was a *smaller caliber* than the ones I use."

♂♀

The rooftop of a mixed-use building

"Wha…? Gaaaaah!"

At first, Masaomi thought that he'd been stabbed in the thigh with a knife or an awl. But then he sensed something wrong with his ears and realized the truth.

When the shock ran through his leg, he'd also heard a gunshot that was notably quieter than the one he'd heard earlier. He looked down and saw a small hole in the thigh of his pants, which was turning red with blood. Within that hole, heat was spreading and raging through his thigh with a mind of its own.

"Aagh…hngg…"

The smell of blood—and more powerful, of fresh gunpowder—assaulted Masaomi's nostrils. He could feel heavy sweat exuding all over his body as he tried to press down on the spot that was bleeding. Mikado chose that moment to twist loose, causing Masaomi to lose his balance and topple sideways.

"Mika…do…," he groaned, looking up at the standing boy.

Through the haze of smoke, he saw a strange object clutched in Mikado's right hand. At first glance, it looked something like brass knuckles.

"A terrorist in America used this once years ago. But…I can't remember what it was called…"

A small but eerily shaped device was fit snugly into the palm of Mikado's hand. In the sense that it fit within a hand and fired bullets, you could literally classify it as a handgun.

"It's called an HFM. A hand…something or other," Mikado said. His right eye was so swollen already that he could barely see through it.

"When I said I fired two shots, I was talking about this one," he continued, smiling. "I wanted to test it out on the way here."

And clutching that *second* gun—something Masaomi could never have predicted—he smiled down sadly at his friend, speaking as casually as if merely making small talk.

"I mean, there was no advice online for how to aim it."

♂♀

Outside of Russia Sushi

Shijima flinched when he heard the distant gunshot.

It was actually much quieter than the one just before it, but Shijima wasn't able to tell the difference. He was in too much shock to use his mind that rationally.

That crazy Ryuugamine kid... Is he actually shooting it...?

Nasujima had given him orders to hand Mikado a gun. Technically, a "gun-like" object.

"I borrowed it from Kujiragi's storage space," he had said.

"I'm good at 'borrowing' things from the office."

"It's one of the concealed-type guns that you can fit in your hand. And this one's an augmented model of one that an American terrorist once used. You can fire it normally with both hands, or you can just squeeze it in one and punch the target, which will fire the bullet."

It was a firearm out of some spy movie. That alone didn't exactly shock Shijima, who knew that there were all kinds of "hidden" guns people had invented—inside of lemons, cigarette boxes, cell phones, and so on.

But when he delivered it to Mikado and said, "I bought this for self-defense, but I'm too scared to keep it around, so I want you to hold on to it. Take it as a sign of trust," he wasn't expecting the boy to accept it with a smile.

It was clear from his mannerisms that he wasn't misunderstanding, thinking it was a toy. That was the point at which Shijima recognized that Mikado Ryuugamine was a special kind of person.

Geez, man. If he actually shoots someone, then the Dollars really are in deep shit.

Nasujima said he had a few red-eyes among the police and could have them arrest someone at random to fan the flames of the Dollars' reign of terror, but it wasn't clear that he really had everything under control.

"Mr. Nasujima, I think Ryuugamine fired the…," he started to say as he turned in Nasujima's direction, but he stopped mid-sentence. Nasujima was trembling, staring down Sixtieth Floor Street, his face pale.

"…Mr. Nasujima?"

But he ignored Shijima and stuck a thumbnail into his mouth to bite as sweat beaded on his forehead and cheeks. "N-n-no, no… N-no, th-that c-can't be… I…I th-thought h-he was in p-p-pri-pri-prison!" he stammered, the jittering extending even to his lips.

In the direction he was looking was a man with dyed blond hair. When Shijima heard the crashing earlier and saw the motorcycle skittering along the ground, he first thought some idiot of a biker had merely flipped his ride.

But now Nasujima understood.

He saw that the Grim Reaper himself had come bearing his downfall.

"Th-there's no time! Hurry! Break down the door to the sushi shop or the windows! G-go and take control of the dread-head with glasses right now!" he roared, all his calm and confidence completely shot.

And so the Saika Army surrounding the restaurant converged on Russia Sushi all at once.

♂♀

Intersection near Tokyu Hands

Izaya stood silently in the middle of the intersection after leaving Tokyu Hands, on the left-side crosswalk, where Sixtieth Floor Street and Russia Sushi's street met. From there, Shizuo approached him, step by step.

"S-so that's Shizuo Heiwajima…"

"Holy crap, he wasn't an urban legend?"

"Did he just throw that motorcycle…?"

"Look, he's dragging a vending machine behind him…"

The punks who had been so ready to pound Chikage were now hushed and awed by the threatening sight that was Shizuo.

"D-do you think that if we beat him, we'll be known as the toughest guys around?" one of them suggested. Carried away by enthusiasm, he brandished his metal bat and rushed at Shizuo.

But when he swung, there was a crumpling sound—and the bat itself broke and twisted against the side of Shizuo's skull.

"Ah, ah, aaa, aieeeee!!" the thug screamed. He stared at the bat, which was as mangled as if it were just a cardboard tube, and pissed himself.

With a rustling of air, the bikers all unconsciously drew themselves back, creating a path through the mass of humanity. But Shizuo did not pay them a single glance. His course was set. His feet moved with one purpose.

And now he stood before Izaya Orihara.

Chikage wanted to say something to Shizuo but thought better of it when he saw the man's eyes. It was clear that this was not the time to interfere except for the gravest of reasons.

While all this was happening, Izaya Orihara did not make a single attempt to escape. He twirled a knife in his fingers and soaked in the brunt of Shizuo's burning hatred.

It was only a few seconds that the two of them stood facing each other.

But it felt many times longer than that to everyone else present.

Those who knew Shizuo and Izaya and those who didn't held their breath equally.

The man in the black intended to challenge the monster in the bartender's uniform.

How would Shizuo Heiwajima's overwhelming strength be utilized? And what would happen to the man on the receiving end of it?

In the face of this coming bloodbath, neither the thugs, nor Chikage and the Blue Squares, nor even Aoba Kuronuma could keep in mind what they were doing before. They all waited, watching the scene before them unfold.

The pack of the Saika-possessed reacted largely in one of two ways.

The group with Nasujima as its mother was entranced by the appearance of the mighty Shizuo Heiwajima.

The group with Haruna as its mother quaked in fear of Shizuo, their Saika having been imprinted with the trauma of what he did on the Night of the Ripper.

So Nasujima, who was terrified of Shizuo, and Haruna, who was not, had Saika children with the exact opposite reactions—and the previously uniform actions of the Saika-possessed began to crumble spectacularly.

"..."
"..."

Izaya and Shizuo stood only six feet apart once Shizuo came to a stop.

A single step would put them within striking range.

Their eyes met.

The next moment, Shizuo swung the vending machine he was dragging vertically, like an *iai* quick-draw katana technique.

A sound of unfathomable destruction blanketed Ikebukuro.

♂♀

Togusa's van

Moments before all this—less than a minute before Shizuo and Izaya's clash, in fact—Anri felt her body seize up at the sound of the man laughing in front of the van.

"What...did he...just say?"

Why would the name Mikado Ryuugamine come up in this context?

Was this man working with Nasujima?

Questions swirled within her mind—when a new, sharp sound pierced the broken windshield, snapping her back to attention.

It's that sound again! Though it seemed a bit different this time...

This sound, combined with the new presence of Mikado's name in her mind, made Anri suddenly feel very unsettled. She pushed it all down and mustered her silent resolve.

She would control these men with Saika and have them explain as much as possible.

Suddenly, there was a bright flash in her eyes.

"I'll admit, I don't know what Ryuugamine's up to at the moment, but...hmm...?"

A few seconds before the light flashed, Izumii spotted something. A skinny man on the sidewalk, taking something out of his backpack.

"...Is that...Yumasaki?!" He couldn't understand why the man wouldn't be inside of the van, and he pointed at him for his followers' benefit. "Hey, go get... Huh?"

Then he noticed that it was a fire extinguisher Yumasaki was pulling out of the backpack.

Fire extinguisher?

Smoke screen?   *Put out.*

Yumasaki?   *No.*

Fire.

Tiny thoughts, individual flashback images burst through Izumii's mind, leading him to one answer.

"Yumasakiii! You son of a bitch..."

Yumasaki pointed the end of the extinguisher toward Togusa's van. And then...

"Here we go! It's my ultimate attack! Innocentius, king of the witch-hunters!"

With that cry, Yumasaki's fire extinguisher shot a maelstrom of flames from its tip. It was his own homemade flamethrower using the shell of an extinguisher. The flame lit everything in a red glow, covering a shocking range from sidewalk to van.

"Aaaaah!!" "Wh-what the—?!"

The thugs with their picks and metal pipes never saw it coming. They fled in panic from the van's vicinity. Yumasaki didn't specifically single any of them out for immolation, but he did spit fire bit by bit to push them back, clearing the space from one side of the van.

"Y...Yuma...saki... You bastard!" shrieked Izumii, who suffered from fire-related trauma. He hid behind a nearby car, still clutching his hammer.

"Now! Hurry! Get out of the van!" urged Yumasaki, and Kadota and the rest all poured out of the left side of the vehicle. Togusa was the slowest of them, being in the driver's seat, but they all managed to get out soon enough.

"You…! Kadota! Don't you run away from me!" Izumii hissed from behind the other car, cowering from the spray of Yumasaki's flamethrower.

The drivers of the other cars nearby all fled from their vehicles when they saw the flames, which only increased the clamor and chaos of the situation.

Kadota came gingerly to a standing position and said to the others behind him, "Leave this to us guys. You girls run for safety."

He, Karisawa, Togusa, and Yumasaki blocked the path of the thugs, creating a lane for escape.

"B-but…!"

"Just do it and leave this to the adults." Togusa grinned.

"Aw, man!" Yumasaki cheered. "I always wanted to say that! 'Go on ahead and leave this to me!'"

"Ha-ha-ha, that's a death omen," Karisawa said with a smile, despite the crowd of enemies surrounding them.

Anri still wasn't sure what to do, so Kadota continued, "This is a squabble between people who haven't grown up yet and need to get on with it. There's no reason for you girls to get infected by this idiocy, too."

He turned to Seiji, who was standing protectively in front of Mika, and said, "Take your girlfriend and get out of here. Make sure she stays safe."

Seiji considered staying here to fight alongside them, but then he glanced over his shoulder at Mika—and Namie, who was glaring at her.

I'm guessing there's no point in asking my sister to watch over her for me.

If he just told them to escape on their own, Namie was bound to attack Mika once they were alone again. Reluctantly, he came to the realization that the best choice for Mika's safety was to escape with her.

"…I will. Thank you."

"Don't thank us. I told you, we're just a bunch of idiots having a fight on our own."

Kadota turned and punched one of the oncoming thugs. It was a far more powerful punch than it had any right to be, coming from a guy who ought to be in a hospital bed. The other thugs shrank back.

He used that brief interval to yell to Saki, "Kida's surprisingly weak on the mental end…so make sure you help soothe him when you see him again."

"...I will!" Saki replied and squeezed Anri's hand. "C'mon, let's go."

"...But..."

Anri was hesitant. If she used Saika's power, she could easily defeat all these people and possess them with the blade's curse. But Kadota saw through what she was thinking.

"They're not worth the burden on your conscience."

"...!"

"Just get going! Do whatever you need to do to protect Mikado!"

"Kadota..."

Anri bit her lip and bowed fiercely. Then she turned and raced for the sidewalk with Saki.

"Hey! Wait, you bitches!" growled one of the thugs. He made to chase after them but got in only a step or two before Togusa dropped him with a roundhouse kick.

"Gahk..."

"You asshole, you didn't think you could mess up my car and get away with it, did you...?"

That kicked off a majestic round of chaos.

Fights broke out here and there in Ikebukuro.

It was like fireworks going off in a chain reaction.

They burst into motion, burning and flaming, only to go out with a whimper.

All the while unaware that a dark shadow was encroaching upon them.

The rooftop of a mixed-use building

"Mikado..."

Masaomi writhed on the ground in pain. He looked up at Mikado, who smiled down at him and said, "It's all right, Masaomi. If you tie it off and call an ambulance, I think you'll pull through."

Then, while still staring directly at his friend, he began his monologue.

"...Ah yes. I shot him."

"...?"

"I did it. I was able to shoot...Kida..."

"Mikado…?"

Masaomi kept his eye on Mikado as he fought pain all over his body—and he noticed that his friend seemed to be trembling.

"I wondered how far I would go in embracing the extraordinary. Even I didn't know what the answer would be. How far would I go, what would I have to do, to make myself stop?"

Mikado walked slowly over to the corner of the rooftop, where he picked up his first gun.

"But…even after you hit me, I didn't stop. In fact…I went ahead and shot you."

The faint smile he often wore was gone now, replaced only by deep sadness.

"If I can shoot you, then I'm sure I could shoot my mom and dad."

"Uh…Mikado?" Masaomi gasped, crawling along the floor, though it wasn't clear whether Mikado was even hearing the words.

He stared off into nothingness and continued, "I'm sure I could shoot Kadota and Yumasaki and Karisawa, too. And Kishitani, and Izaya, and Shizuo, and Harima, and Yagiri, and Aoba, and Takiguchi, and Miyoshi, and…!"

As he went down the list of close, familiar names, Mikado's voice grew more and more strained. It sounded as though he was blaming himself. But then it abruptly softened.

"Oh yeah. It's true, Masaomi… I'm certain that in the quest for my own selfish wants…"

He paused for a moment before continuing even slower and more deliberately.

"…I would even shoot Sonohara."

Through what faint light there was on the rooftop, Masaomi saw that Mikado was crying.

Then Mikado raised the original gun, the full-sized pistol, to his own temple.

"W-wait, Mikado! What are you doing?!" Masaomi cried with alarm, forgetting even his own pain. "You gotta be kidding! This is the least funny joke you've told all day!" he screamed.

But Mikado only said, "I think…I shouldn't be around anymore. I'm only going to attempt worse things…and make life worse for more people."

Tears dripped from his eyes as he put on his old smile. "So I think that I should vanish along with the Dollars."

The sight of him smiling and crying made Masaomi furious. "Don't you dare think about dying to get out of this! Look, if you die, that's not your own free will! You're being manipulated! By that asshole Izaya! I'm gonna get revenge on him! I'll kill him, even if it takes all my life!"

"…"

"So…so stop this, Mikado… Don't waste your life for such a horrible reason…," Masaomi pleaded, tearing his lungs out, slamming his bandaged hand against the ground. The agony was horrible, but he never took his eyes off Mikado.

"…"

"…"

Silence surrounded the two for a moment.

Mikado briefly closed his eyes, then said sadly, his face joyful, "Thank you, Masaomi… I'm sorry."

"Mika…do…?"

"Even at a time like this, I have to admit…I'm feeling a bit *excited* by it all… Wondering what will happen when I'm dead. Maybe I'll get to visit a world I've never seen before."

He kept the gun pressed against the side of his head, smiling to put Masaomi at ease.

"Celty exists, the Headless Rider…so maybe there is a world after death. In fact…maybe *I'll* end up being like the Headless Rider after this," he muttered to himself before looking at Masaomi again. "And the fact that I'm thinking about this stuff…makes me crazy."

"No…stop! Don't say that! You're normal! What's crazy is how we all did this to you!" Masaomi argued desperately, summoning all the strength he could in an attempt to stop Mikado.

He felt as if he might be able to get to his feet—but Mikado sensed it, too, and so he said, "Masaomi…I'm sorry."

He placed his finger on the trigger and pulled it without hesitation. The third gunshot of the night went off.

Mikado Ryuugamine's world was enveloped in total shadow.

♂♀

Intersection near Tokyu Hands

It was a battle to the death that defied the imagination.

Shizuo Heiwajima and Izaya Orihara.

There was an overwhelming imbalance between their respective physical capabilities. Izaya had been treated as an equal combatant up to this point largely because he focused on escape and evasion and attacked Shizuo in the resulting openings.

Sometimes he got Shizuo hit by a truck; sometimes he dropped him into a hole; sometimes he lured him into the midst of an Awakusu-kai battle. When Izaya used his knife to attack directly, it was usually as a preemptive measure, a kind of how-do-you-do to get Shizuo into a furious mood.

That was the only thing it would be good for, because the best he could do was get the blade about a third of an inch under his skin. Then again, a normal human being would never even bother to fight Shizuo, much less try to stab him with a knife.

At this time, Izaya had given up on his usual style of fighting.

He had chosen to use his knife as a serious weapon against this monstrous dinosaur of a man.

When the first vending machine blow came down, Izaya leaped not backward or sideways but forward. That actually put him inside, closer than the machine's attack range. But it meant that he was now close enough for Shizuo's arms to reach him, and a single misstep could easily get his neck broken.

Sure enough, when he passed inside of the vending machine's trajectory, Shizuo's other hand reached for him. Izaya dodged it by a hair and swung consecutive knife attacks.

With each piercing of Shizuo's body, Izaya felt the physical sensation of trying to stab the tires of some ultra-heavy-duty construction vehicle. He could puncture the outermost, weakest layer of skin, but no matter how much force he used, there was nothing getting past the layer of muscle. In fact, if he stabbed too deep, he might not be able to pull the blade back out.

Fly like a butterfly; sting like a bee.

It was a nice sentiment to emulate, but in reality, he was neither butterfly nor bee—more like a gnat trying to challenge a human being. A single good blow would easily destroy him, but Izaya still fought and fought.

Every single attack Shizuo made was deadly. But Izaya evaded them all by the skin of his teeth and countered with little nicks and cuts on Shizuo's body several times for each punch.

It seemed as though his plan was that even if he got Shizuo to shed only a single drop of blood each time, Izaya would eventually drain him dry.

Without planning on it, Chikage found himself in the position of observer of this duel. Upon witnessing Izaya's reckless-in-the-extreme combat style, he muttered, "Is he...*trying* to get killed?"

"If he wins, great. If he loses and dies, he probably also considers that a victory," Aoba said.

Chikage looked over his shoulder at the boy, frowning. "What? What do you mean, dying is winning?"

"Why don't you beat a man to death in the midst of an enormous crowd? You'll get arrested for murder. That's how Shizuo Heiwajima gets recognized by the world at large as a true monster. He's not a violent hero with an abnormal amount of power. He'll just be known as a bloodthirsty, unthinking beast," Aoba said with a sigh. He gazed at Izaya with mockery and pity.

"Izaya Orihara... That guy in black there hates the very notion that Shizuo Heiwajima can be treated as human. That's why he wants to trap him, to lower him to the level of a monster. So that no matter how much he might want to be human, humanity will reject him."

"How do you know that?" asked Chikage, so enraptured by the bizarre duel that he spoke to his enemy as though having an ordinary chat. Aoba gave Izaya a spiteful look.

"Because there are parts of him that resemble me. So I have a hunch."

♂♀

Outside of Russia Sushi

"There you go! You're almost through!"

Despite his hand-clapping enthusiasm, Nasujima's face was still pale with fear.

For one thing, Shizuo Heiwajima was raging within visual range. Nasujima was beside himself with terror at the thought of that power being used on him.

On the other hand, if he was fighting over there, that meant that Nasujima could do more over here without worrying about attracting attention. So despite his fear, he chose bold action.

As long as he could gain control over the man inside the sushi place named Tom Tanaka, he could use him as a hostage and possibly even as a stepping-stone to taking over Shizuo himself.

The rest was just a battle against time.

But Nasujima was unaware that the door to Russia Sushi that he had his Saika-possessed tearing down at the moment was something like the entry to Pandora's box.

After many body blows, the front door to Russia Sushi finally broke.

"Good! Get in there and take control of everyone inside!" he said, a greedy smirk on his lips, as he approached the doorway himself.

In the next moment, the shine of that smile was completely over-shadowed by literal light from the sushi restaurant's interior.

A few seconds before that, when the Saika-possessed made to pile through the open doorway, they heard something spilling onto the floor.

Before anyone could identify them as flashbang stun grenades, they were overwhelmed by light and sound, momentarily robbing them of vision, hearing, and the ability to think.

Suddenly, one of the low tables from the private booth areas of the restaurant was rushing upon them like a giant shield—and pushed the confused dolls clear out of the building like a bulldozer.

"Gaaaah!! Wh-what was that?! What happened?!" Nasujima yelped in a panic, hands over his eyes, as a number of canisters hit the ground around him.

He was blinded, his ears full of roaring echoes.

All around him, light and sound assaulted the shadowy portion of Ikebukuro.

♂♀

Outside of Tokyu Hands

There was a flash in the corner of his vision.

And the momentary loss of concentration had tragic consequences for Izaya Orihara.

When he recognized it as the effect of a stun grenade, Izaya's knowledge and experience taught him to instinctually be on guard.

The problem was, he was already dealing with something far more dangerous than a stun grenade and deadlier than potshots from a gun.

It took less than a second to refocus his every nerve on the superhuman creature before him—but even that was a fatal lapse in concentration.

Shizuo's next blow, which he should have barely dodged, nicked him on the shoulder. And though it was just the slightest of glancing blows, it sent a tremendous shock through Izaya's body.

"*Gah...*"

It was what you might feel if an express train passing through the station clipped you on the shoulder. The astonishing transfer of energy to Izaya's body sent him spinning. By the time he had recovered his balance, Shizuo's fist was careening toward him again.

"*...!*"

The timing made it impossible for him to evade it entirely. He crossed his arms to block the blow and jumped backward in hopes of deadening some of its force.

But this was not the kind of punch that commonsense actions could nullify. You don't put your hands up to block an oncoming cannonball or jump backward with the impact, expecting the result to be any different.

The instant Shizuo's fist met Izaya's arms, everyone in the vicinity clearly heard the sound of those arms breaking.

Shizuo swung through, bringing his fist downward and throwing Izaya against the ground, which he bounced off several feet in the air, as though he'd been struck by a car. If it had been an uppercut instead, Izaya might have flown to the height of one of the surrounding high-rise buildings—or so it seemed to the witnesses, such was the power of Shizuo's blow.

Izaya's resistance was not entirely in vain, however. If he hadn't given up his arms to the punch, it might have broken his sternum and obliterated his heart beneath it.

For the cost of his arms, Izaya Orihara stayed alive, leaving him capable of standing before Shizuo. But to everyone watching, it as if looked only he'd given himself a few more seconds to live.

I'm still alive.

Izaya's arms weren't just broken, they were also dislocated and dangling from his shoulder joints, but he was conscious.

He stood on the strength of his legs alone, but the shock of being struck against the ground left him hardly able to breathe.

It was a stronger blow to his system than when he'd been struck by the metal beam and knocked into the building across the street. Blood spilled from his mouth as he stared at Shizuo.

His opponent's body was trickling blood all over as well, and the overall damage seemed more than trivial. He approached, covered in red stains, step after purposeful step.

So if I'd just fought him like this from the start...I might have actually had a chance to win? The irony is rich, Izaya thought woozily as he observed his bloodied opponent.

At this point, the endorphins had kicked in, so that he barely even registered the pain in his arms and everywhere else.

Despite his frustration, Izaya smiled. He simply smiled.

More important than his own coming death was knowing that by sacrificing his own life, he would succeed at expelling Shizuo Heiwajima from human society, making him a monster.

The fact that he could prevent a future in which a monster wearing human skin strolled around society as if he were one of them was all the victory that Izaya could hope for.

This was all Izaya thought about as he stood—for standing was the only thing he could do.

Shizuo picked up the vending machine lying nearby and took another step toward Izaya.

"...Do it, monster," Izaya said with the last bit of breath from his lungs.

A shock ran through his body before he could even tell whether Shizuo heard him say it.

*   *   *

But the impact was not from Shizuo. He was still holding the machine. If anything, seeing what just happened to Izaya made him stop.

"Huh…?"

Izaya finally realized that something *else* had happened to his body. Something was sticking into his side.

At the same moment that he recognized the silver flash of a blade, he saw a shadow out of the corner of his eye.

There, standing inside the ring of bikers and punks watching the fight, was *the figure of Vorona, holding the handle of a knife without its blade.*

With cold eyes, she tossed aside the handle and brought her now free right hand up to support what she held in her left. When the crowd recognized the gun, they began to murmur uneasily.

The muzzle was pointed directly at Izaya. The people around her and behind Izaya screamed and darted to the sides to get out of its path.

"Vorona…?"

When Shizuo slowly turned to look at her, there was a troubled light in his eyes, mixed in with his battle fury. She glanced at him, then at Izaya, who was now on his knees.

"Sir Shizuo is human," she said to Shizuo. She did not know what Izaya was thinking, but through sheer coincidence, she ended up contradicting his opinions. "Necessity to become a beast is nonexistent."

Vorona pointed her gun at Izaya.

She was going to shoot him in the head and heart and eliminate him from the world forever.

When he understood the situation, Shizuo's eyes calmed, becoming clearer with reason—and he shouted at his coworker, "Stop, you idiot! Why would you let yourself be a murderer?!"

She smiled when she heard his voice, but she did not take her eyes off Izaya.

"I request your relief.

"I have always been a beast who loves killing."

♂♀

Outside of Russia Sushi

"Hey…isn't that Shizuo?!"

Tom emerged from the restaurant, making his way through the crowd of Saika-possessed who were alternately slumped to the ground holding their eyes or just plain unconscious.

The plan had been to toss stun grenades in the hope of blazing a path to escape the building, but once they were outside, it was hard to believe what they saw. As they scanned the area for the direction of least resistance, they noticed an odd clump in the crowd with a vending machine on the ground between them.

Which meant that the person in the bartender's vest beside it had to be Shizuo.

"Oh, I see Izaya, too," said Simon, whose sharp eyes were scanning the intersection. Then the crowd abruptly scattered left and right. With the sudden increase in visibility, Simon made out the figure of Vorona pointing a gun at Izaya.

"!"

His next action was lightning fast. Without a word, Simon pulled the pin from the stun grenade in his other hand. He waited a beat to time it, then hurled it with all the force he could muster toward the intersection.

"Hey!"

The grenade quickly reached the open square on the fly.

♂♀

Intersection, Tokyu Hands side

No…the end can't be this ridiculous.

The sight of Vorona's gun pointed at him filled Izaya with powerful disappointment.

But he smiled, half-resigned, and gave Vorona a direct look.

Fine, I forgive you. I love humanity.

"…You are human. Just a human like any other."

*   *   *

Vorona paused, puzzled by what Izaya had said—but unlike when she pointed the gun at Shizuo, she did not feel any hesitation about pulling the trigger. She was going to end Izaya before Shizuo could get to her and stop her.

But then something entered her vision that she didn't expect to see at all.

Before she could recognize it as the kind of stun grenade that her father's company dealt with, that she loved using—the object burst in midair barely above the ground, blinding the vicinity with light.

♂♀

Outside of Russia Sushi

After Tom and Simon rushed off in the direction of Tokyu Hands, Nasujima was left behind, his mind a toxic mix of fury, humiliation, and fear of Shizuo, whose approach he could not sense with his eyes blinded.

"Dammit…cut them! Just go and possess every last one of them, even the bikers! No more holding back! Possess every last person in this city!"

"Yes, Mother," replied Haruna, the first to respond. Because of her distance from the stun grenade, her sight was already recovering.

The crowd of Nasujima's and Haruna's Saika-possessed victims, who had previously been merely watching the events happen, now converged on the Dollars.

♂♀

Major chaos began to erupt around the area in front of Tokyu Hands.

First, a flash went off in front of the biker gangs watching Shizuo and Izaya's duel from a distance; then a group of people with red eyes rushed up on them. The bikers, plunged into the kind of terror only witnessed in zombie movies, fought back wildly with metal pipes and whatever else they had on hand.

This quickly went beyond the level of a simple skirmish. It was clearly going to end in major bloodshed, possibly death.

*   *   *

But then a miracle happened.

Though perhaps it was too visually ominous to be labeled a miracle.

A "shadow" began to descend from the sky like rain, touching and tangling up the motorcycle gangs and Saika dolls alike and freezing them in place.

Instantly, the entire crowd was nearly under the sway of this black substance—and all those people heard "her" voice in their ears.

"I understand the situation."

It was as though the shadow itself was transmitting words, a woman's voice hitting the eardrums of the entire crowd at once—and simultaneously reaching directly into their minds. Few of them had ever heard this eerie voice before.

She continued, *"Before I leave this city, I will eliminate all the trouble stemming from my body."*

It spoke clearly and briefly but with a power that resonated inside the minds of all who heard it.

"It is what little atonement I can provide for the confusion my body has wrought upon this place."

♂♀

The rooftop of a mixed-use building

All space that could be perceived was covered in shadow. It had poured down from the sky above the building, instantly coating Mikado and Masaomi.

This happened at nearly exactly the same moment as the gunshot—so it wasn't surprising that Mikado initially thought he was dead.

Ah. There isn't even any pain…

But it's so dark.

I wonder…if it'll always be this dark, forever…

Eventually, after a number of minutes, as his mind settled in, Mikado noticed tears springing from his eyes again.

Sorry. I'm so sorry, Sonohara, Masaomi…

But no sooner had the thought come to his mind than a strange voice sounded in both his ears and his mind.

"I understand the situation. Before I leave this city, I will eliminate all the trouble stemming from my body."

Then Mikado understood.

He could still feel the sensation of the gun against the palm of his hand.

Am I...still...alive...? he wondered, but without responding to this question, the voice entered his mind again.

"It is what little atonement I can provide for the confusion my body has wrought upon this place."

My...body? Mikado repeated to himself. It was an odd phrase in this case, and it put the image of someone he knew into his mind. *Is that...Celty?*

At that moment, the shadow enshrouding him softened, gave way—and the sights and sounds of Ikebukuro returned to Mikado's world.

"Mikado...? Mikado! Hey!"

He was looking at Masaomi, who was still in the place he'd left him earlier.

"Masaomi...?" he mumbled.

His friend heaved a deep sigh of relief. "I'm so glad...you're alive... You're alive, Mikado!"

"Ah..."

He looked to his right hand and saw the gun there. But the very next moment, a swarm of tiny shadows pried his fingers apart, wrenching loose both the pistol and the HFM in his other hand.

Something hard tumbled from the shadow that was right next to Mikado's head. When they saw the twisted lump of metal roll onto the ground, both boys instinctually understood what it was.

The instant he had pulled the trigger, the shadow had slipped between his temple and the muzzle of the gun, stopping the bullet before it could reach Mikado's head.

It was a feat no human being could have achieved—which was obvious, given that it was a shadow that had done it. But Mikado knew who was responsible. And before he could say that name out loud...

She descended from the sky.

Straddling a headless horse instead of a motorcycle.

Wearing pitch-black armor instead of a riding suit.

And holding a head at her side, under an arm.

QRRRRRRRRRRRRrrrrrrrrrrrrrrrrrrrrrrrrrrrrrrrrrr...

When he saw her descending to the roof down a path made of shadow, her headless horse whinnying somehow, Masaomi forgot about the pain in his leg and simply stared in wonder.

"What...is this?" Then he looked at the head she was holding and shouted, "H-hey...that head! Isn't that...Mika Harima from your class, Mikado?!"

"No...it's not, Masaomi. It looks like her, but it's not her."

Stunned, Mikado addressed the woman who descended near the edge of the rooftop: Celty Sturluson.

"Is that you...Celty?"

"..."

The eyes of the head under her arm turned to Mikado. Without emotion, her mouth opened. The words that emerged, unlike the ones earlier, were not addressed to every person touched by the tendrils of shadow. They were audible only to the young men on the rooftop with her.

"Human boy. You are...Mikado Ryuugamine."

"Huh?"

It was as though she'd never met him before. Mikado was confused.

Celty used her shadow to draw the guns closer to her. Within moments, the shadow essentially dissolved them.

"I do not know what my body said to you, but my existence is not a reason for you to desire what comes beyond death."

The separated weapon parts scattered across the rooftop.

"It would seem that the presence of my body in this city registered the strongest effect upon you."

"Effect...?"

"So, human boy, I choose to make a parting statement individually to you," Celty said, her shadow writhing around her. *"After I recovered my consciousness, I spread my shadow through the sky over this city so that I could collect information. I could not have guessed that*

I'd spent the last twenty years wandering about this distant, foreign land."

"Celty, what do you mean…?" Mikado asked, baffled.

Just then, the sound of fresh footsteps came from the emergency stairs.

"Ryuugamine…and Kida?!"

"Masaomi!"

Both of the boys turned toward the new voices.

"…Sonohara?!"

"Saki?! Why…why are you here…?"

And they weren't the only ones. Seiji Yagiri and Mika Harima were coming up behind them.

The group had been trotting down the sidewalk, as Kadota had instructed, but weren't sure where they should be heading. Should they leave Saki and the other noncombatants somewhere safe, then head to Russia Sushi, where Nasujima was located?

It was at this time that they heard a third gunshot overhead.

"?!"

And after that, the scream of a boy's familiar voice.

"Mikado!"

At the sound of Masaomi's voice, they looked up and around—until they spotted the shadow looking especially thick over one building rooftop. They rushed toward the building's exterior emergency stairs, fighting against their own unease.

And when she reached the roof, Anri was finally there. She saw Mikado, the person she wanted to see most, and felt relief flood through her. In fact, she threatened to burst into tears.

But the situation she saw there prevented her from having the moving reunion she wanted.

"Masaomi…?"

He was crawling along the surface of the roof, while behind him stood a headless horse.

Sitting on the horse was a knight, carrying a head under its arm with the same face as Mika Harima, who was just behind Anri at the moment.

"Is that…Celty?"

♂♀

Outside of Tokyu Hands

When Shizuo's vision recovered from the blinding flash, he saw a bizarre new sight around him:

A crowd of red-eyed people and bikers were tied up, their limbs tangled in black shadows. For some reason, however, *he* was unfettered and free. After a brief glance around, he saw that there was no Izaya Orihara present, just a bloodstain on the ground.

"..."

That briefly rekindled the rage that Vorona's interference had stilled, but the thought of her put her at the forefront of his mind. The place where she'd been standing a moment ago was now occupied by Tom, Simon, and Denis—caring for an unconscious Vorona.

"Vorona!" he shouted, rushing to her side, ignoring the blood dripping from all over his body.

"Shizuo... Hey, man, you all right?!" Tom asked.

Shizuo nodded. "I'm fine. But Vorona...," he prompted.

Simon and Denis offered their reassurances. "Oh, she only knocked out. When she wake up, I give her hot cup of tea."

"She's hurt here and there, but nothing life-threatening. That stun grenade hit her when she was already exhausted. Apparently, it was too much for her to handle at once."

"Why...why would she do this...?" Shizuo wondered, recalling what she'd been doing before the grenade went off.

"Well, I only saw a bit of it," said Denis, "but I'd say she didn't want you to have a murder on your conscience."

"...Oh."

This put many different thoughts into Shizuo's head. If he had killed Izaya, perhaps she would have thought that he had become a murderer to avenge her.

...I'm...still weak...

I'm sorry, Vorona.

Shizuo breathed in deep and exhaled slowly, and this time, he pushed his smoldering hatred of Izaya deep down into his gut.

But if I happen across him loitering around, I can't guarantee I won't kill him out of sheer momentum, he thought to himself, giving the scene another examination. He found his eye drawn to one sight in particular.

"...What's that?"

He was looking not at Izaya—but at an old friend in a white lab coat, walking down the middle of the street with the aid of a crutch.

♂♀

The rooftop of a mixed-use building

"I found her...my beloved."

"..."

Mika Harima met Seiji Yagiri's mumbled statement with silence. She glared at the head under the dark knight's arm. Masaomi looked at her and back, wincing with both pain and confusion.

"H-huh...? That *is* the same face, isn't it...?"

"Masaomi! Forget that—we've got to stop your bleeding!" Saki cried, rushing over to examine him. The next moment, shadows writhed around Masaomi's leg, covering up the bullet wound and stopping the bleeding.

"Aaagh!" he yelped, briefly jumping from the pain, but the next moment, the shadow wriggled in complex motions, then spat out the little bullet that had been wedged deep in his leg.

"?!"

"*I do not condone that my body should have sparked a conflict that leads to the loss of life. I cannot erase the memories of those who know me, but I will at least minimize the victims before I leave,*" said the figure, her words simple and economical.

"This isn't your fault, Celty... It's all *my* fault!"

"*Human boy. Let me ask you: If you had not met the Headless Rider, would you still be here in this place, shooting your friend with a gun?*"

"...!"

Mikado had no way to refute this. He had set up the Dollars, and when they had come together for their first in-person meeting, it had materialized the extraordinary sight of the Headless Rider and brought him into her orbit.

If that hadn't happened, then Mikado might still just be a normal high schooler right about now, and he might not have become estranged from Masaomi and Anri.

"By being in this town, my existence caused Yagiri Pharmaceuticals to go astray, Seiji Yagiri to drown in a meaningless love, and Mika Harima to give up the face she was born with."

"Meaningless love...? What does she mean?" Seiji asked. He was gazing at the living head, his face the very picture of bliss.

Celty did not reply to him. She continued her speech.

"These are only a few examples. Many people here have found their lives manipulated and twisted out of shape by the illusion of the Headless Rider."

"Celty...? What are you saying?" Anri wondered, worried.

The dullahan's head looked at her and said without any discernible emotion, *"I will be direct, girl of the cursed blade. I have no memory of living around you people. I am simply telling the truth as I have reconstructed it from the information I've collected."*

"What...?"

"It is clear that my presence has caused the gears of this city to go out of alignment. That much should be obvious, just from looking at this day's chaos alone."

"No...it's not! You're wrong! It's not your fault, Celty!" Anri shouted. "There are people whose lives were improved and saved because they met you! People like me..."

"Girl of the cursed blade, salvation is but another kind of misalignment."

"Huh...?"

"I am nothing but a system. Following a greater will, I exist within a limited area, warning chosen individuals of their death. There is no need for you humans to know the meaning behind this, and knowing it would not bring you any understanding."

She sat astride the horse, imperiously observing the shocked crowd of young people.

"I regret that you have wasted your time being manipulated by a system that was not meant to exist in this place. It is an outcome that leaves no one happy."

Then she produced a path into the sky from the shadow at her feet and pulled on shadow-made reins to point the horse toward it.

"I will return to my homeland and my purpose. By offering my words of parting to Mikado Ryuugamine, the human whose fate was most disturbed by his proximity to me, I conclude my duties within this city. Forget about me, human."

"Hey, wait…wait up!" Seiji called out, stumbling toward her, but the black shadow tangled around his foot and sent him tumbling to the ground.

"You did not fall in love with me, only an individual part of me. I have no obligation or desire to return that emotion," Celty replied robotically, in the very systematic form she had described.

"I'm not giving up! If you're going back home, then I'll go to the other side of the world for you!" he yelled, still tangled up, a true stalker.

As she watched Mika rush over to him, Anri Sonohara silently issued her own disagreements.

That's not true. Celty is lying.

The one who's had the deepest connection to her…

The one whose life was the most changed by her…

She was just about to speak out loud, to utter the name of the man who would make Celty pause, when…

"Celty…you're being a liar today."

The man spoke for himself, standing behind her.

It was not a powerful voice. If anything, it was gentle.

But it carried across the rooftop, crystal clear—and caused the headless horse to pause its forward motion.

Celty did not reply to him. She swung the reins.

"…What is it, Shooter? Move."

It was as though she couldn't hear his voice.

Instead, the man behind Anri declared, "Let's see. Did you perhaps mean, 'Move it, Shooter. If you stop now, then the point of lying will be lost'? Or am I mistaken about that?"

"…"

The head under the dark knight's arm swung around toward him. It caught sight of Shinra Kishitani dressed in his coat, looking notably *clear-eyed* and gazing right back at her.

*   *   *

"Human... Who are you?"

Anri was shocked.

It wasn't only her. Mikado, who was aware of their relationship, looked as if he couldn't believe what he was seeing.

But Shinra himself just smiled gently and said, "All right. That one's more like 'Why are you here? Seeing you only makes the parting more difficult, so I thought that pretending not to have any memory of you would make you give up! And why are you talking under the assumption that I haven't lost my memory anyway?!'"

He was speaking her mental state aloud, imagining her thoughts the way a stalker might his victim. The head did not show any emotional reaction, however.

"What? What is this human saying?"

"I don't doubt that you have recovered your memory. But I also trust you that much. I believe that you still have your memories of this city."

"What nonsense is this? I have no memory of the last twenty years."

"Either way, I don't care. It was just a hope of mine. See, simply talking with you has cleared it up for me. I *knew* you were a kind and gentle soul, Celty. You're too kind, in fact."

Shinra was not uninjured. He had dulled the pain, but his condition demanded that he stay bedridden, just like Kadota. He rapped his crutches together, however, not giving away any signs of discomfort.

"Ah, let's see. This one is more like 'Stop it! I'm not meant to be here! My presence caused you to be terribly injured, and it completely ruined Mikado's life!'"

"This is a waste of time. I do not understand what you are saying."

"'All I wanted to do was clear up the confusion in the city before I disappeared for good! I figured that if they found out I was a cold, cruel monster at heart, they would all want to forget about me! So if I act like I've lost my memory of them, they'll all give up on me! And you're the one I want to forget me the most, so why are you ruining this for me?!' ...Is that right?"

"Nonsense." Celty snorted, head facing in his direction.

But Shinra just smiled at her. "Don't be like that. Look at me, Celty."

"…"

The head was already looking at Shinra, though. It was her body that had its back to him.

"Enough, human. Your ramblings are nonsense."

"Whoa!"

She extended her shadow to spin around Shinra and tangle him up. With her back still facing him, she kicked lightly at Shooter's flank.

"Go."

Qrrrrrrrrr, Shooter trilled, stamping his hooves on the spot without stepping forward. He seemed to be pushing her, urging her, but Celty ignored it.

"Go! Yah! Yah! Move, Shooter!"

But by this point, Mikado and the others understood: Shinra was probably correct.

"Celty…"

"Wait, Celty!"

Anri and Mikado called out to her. Shooter gave another mournful whinny, then began to walk up the path of shadow stretching into the sky. Celty said nothing more; she simply rode onward up into the darkened expanse.

As though she wanted to melt into the deep of the night and vanish entirely.

Mikado and the rest, left behind on the rooftop and unable to speak their minds aloud, felt a terrible sense of powerlessness. But then a new voice joined the scene.

"Hey…was that Celty who just flew off?"

They spun around to the source and found Shizuo there, lacerations bleeding all over his body.

"Shizuo…?!" they yelped in shock.

Afterward, a single man rose to his feet and greeted him. "Hi there, Shizuo. Good timing."

It was Shinra, who had somehow freed himself from the bonds of Celty's shadow.

"Yeah, well, I saw you going up this building… Then I spotted what looked like Celty and Shooter on the roof, so I climbed up here… What's going on?" Shizuo wondered.

Shinra chuckled. "What's going on? Well, I'm about to become a villain."

"What?"

"Shizuo, do you remember the promise we made back in high school?"

"...?"

Whatever Shizuo was expecting, it was not a reference to his school days. But behind his smile, Shinra's eyes were deadly serious, so Shizuo decided to hear him out.

"...Remind me."

"That if I became a villain for the sake of the woman I loved...*you would smash me to the other end of the sky for her.*"

"...Oh yeah. I remember that."

"Now's the time," Shinra said, staring up at where Celty was vanishing into the dark of the night. "I'm about to do something terrible to Celty. But she's so kind and gentle, I'm sure that she'll forgive me for it."

"..."

"So...will you fulfill your side of the agreement and hurl me into the sky?" Shinra asked. It sounded like a joke, but Shizuo did not laugh it off.

"...Are you serious?"

"Yes."

"If you fall, you're 100 percent guaranteed to die. At that angle, I won't be able to catch your landing. Speaking of which, are you trying to make me a murderer?" he demanded, thinking of Vorona.

Shinra was quiet for a moment, then said, "Yeah, if it happens...then I'm sorry. But I trust Celty. You probably don't know exactly what's going on here, but I can put it in these terms: Do you trust me for trusting Celty?"

"..."

Shizuo thought it over, then grinned without a word. He grabbed Shinra's leg and hurled him with strength that far surpassed human limits.

"Don't regret this, you villain!" he bellowed.

And though he was injured all over and not anywhere near his peak condition, it was the most powerful throw he'd made that night, including his duel with Izaya.

♂♀

Sky

"*...Don't be so upset, Shooter,*" Celty said to her mount now that they were alone in the air. "*This was for the best. Now that all my memories are back, living here among the humans will only cause them more suffering...*"

She climbed farther into the pitch-black sky that her own shadow had fashioned as she spoke to Shooter.

"*Yes, it hurts. It hurts a lot, Shooter. I would rather never deal with human beings again if it meant not going through this feeling...,*" she said mournfully, though her head still showed not a single hint of emotion on its features. "*I just want Shinra to forget about me...but I don't want to forget...Shin...ra...?*"

She paused there.

In the sky of Ikebukuro, locked in abnormal darkness by a blanket of shadow, a blazing white light in stark contrast to the background shot right past her side.

And when she realized that it was Shinra, Celty's mind went blank instead.

"*Wha...?*"

"Hi."

"*Wh-wha...wh-wh-wha...what are you doing?!*"

As Shinra slowly arced and began to fall, Celty couldn't help but stick her hands out. Dutifully reading her mind, Shooter charged forward on his shadowy path, racing faster to catch up to the falling man.

The head spilled out of her grasp, but that wasn't a problem. Shadow tendrils extended from the severed head itself, attaching it to the sheer surface of her neck. If it wasn't going to fall, she couldn't lose it.

At this point, the soul of her head and body were completely reattached. Nothing—no saws or gunpowder—could separate her head now that it was attached by the soul that was her shadow.

All except for *one cursed sword that was said to separate the soul from the body.*

*   *   *

"…Celty," Shinra murmured as he fell.

She lunged, reaching out for him. *"Grab on!"*

At this point, there was no use keeping up her act. She was in her natural, true element now.

"Sorry," Shinra stated.

"What?"

He continued to plummet, with Celty chasing after him.

And then she saw: They were not bloodshot.

Shinra's eyes were actually glowing with red light, as Anri's had done.

And *a sharp blade extended from the palm of his right hand.*

"Oh, n…"

Silver flashed briefly in the night sky.

And Saika quickly, powerfully severed the shadow connecting Celty's body and head.

♂♀

More than ten minutes earlier

"Oh, right…Miss Kujiragi."

"?"

She stopped in the act of leaving and turned back to Shinra.

"If I wanted to rent out your Saika…how much would that cost me?"

♂♀

"_____"

Celty writhed and jerked in midair after the separation of her head and neck.

An abnormal volume of shadow spurted forth from the space where each side had been cut, and it spread through the sky over Ikebukuro with abnormal speed.

Qrrrrrrrrrrrrrrrrrrrrrrrrrrrrrrrrrr…………….

*   *   *

Her body continued spasming a little bit, but Shooter's fierce cry brought her back to her senses.

This was not the time to be asleep. As her thoughts spurred back into motion, the effects of the mental link being abruptly severed caused memories to flash back through her mind in rapid succession.

Aaah... Aaaaaaaaahhhh!

I...I...I...!

Countless memories, stretching back over decades and centuries, flooding through her, filling her mind.

She descended along with Shooter in her confusion—and as she did, flickers of a white shape began to appear in the rapid shuffle of images.

Despite the chaos, Celty reached out for the pale thing. As if to say that it was the most precious thing of all to her.

The next moment, her blindly stretching hand caught something.

It was the arm of a man wearing a white coat.

Shin...ra. Shinra...

...Shinra!

Celty's mind snapped back to consciousness again, and she sent out shadows in all directions. A cushion of darkness spread out below as they plummeted onto a corner of one of the Sunshine City buildings.

They bounced off the cushion and back into the air, and Celty still did not let go of Shinra's arm. Without Shooter's guidance, she might never have caught Shinra as he fell.

It was through a series of miracles that he avoided falling to his death. But Celty was not in the mind space to appreciate all this in the moment.

Shinra!

"Wake up, Shinra!"

Celty hopped off Shooter, pulled her PDA out of her armor—she'd been hanging on to it, just in case—and thrust it before Shinra's dizzy eyes.

"Please! Wake up! Don't die!" she typed and shook his shoulders.

He opened his eyes slowly. "No, Celty...you shouldn't shake someone with an injury like this."

"...*Shinra!*" She bopped him on the chest. "*You dummy! You big dummy! You're a big, dumb dummy!*"

"Ouch, ouch... That hurts, Celty."

"*Why? Why would you do something so dangerous?! If something went wrong...you'd be dead... You would have died, Shinra!*"

She thrust out the PDA for him to see, her body trembling.

"I refused to accept your determination," he said with a smile. "I insulted the dullahan's way of life...and the future you chose."

The doctor traced a finger softly along the nape of Celty's neck and grinned at her.

"So it doesn't even out unless I risk my neck, does it?"

Celty typed into her PDA. Words she typed at the most important moments. Words she was more used to typing than any others.

"*You really are an idiot.*"

♂♀

Outside of Tokyu Hands

"So...should I assume that the festival is over?" Chikage wondered.

Aoba smirked and replied, "I suppose it might be. Never would have counted on an ending like that."

"...By the way, how come I'm not tied up, but you are?"

Chikage had full, free motion, while Aoba, like the rest of his gang and all the other biker groups, had shadows twirled around his limbs, keeping him bound to the ground.

"Dunno. Never would have counted on finishing up our fight like this."

In fact, Celty made the decision based on Chikage's constant proximity to Masaomi, but Chikage and Aoba didn't know that, so they just assumed Chikage was lucky, and Aoba's gang wasn't.

"Finishing up, huh...? To be honest, if I'd had to fight those two big guys and all the other biker gangs, it'd probably be me on the ground right now." Chikage approached Aoba and pulled the ski mask off him.

"...!"

Aoba glared up at him, humiliated.

"But I ain't stupid enough to beat the crap out of some kid in this condition and claim I won," Chikage went on. "I've seen your face now. I'll remember it...I think. So the score between your gang and mine will have to wait until next time to be settled."

Then he looked around at the red-eyed crowd stuck to the ground and put his hand to his chin.

"So...what's up with these folks...? Their eyes are still red..."

♂♀

Sidewalk

Mikado and Masaomi walked along on the sidewalk down on the ground, Mikado offering his shoulder to his friend for support.

They were worried about Shinra after he got hurled into the sky after Celty, but they'd managed to witness him making apparent contact with her. They chose to trust that she'd help save him and went on ahead to get Masaomi to a hospital.

Shizuo returned to the area around Tokyu Hands, claiming to be worried about his newer coworker, and Seiji and Mika ran off toward Sunshine City to "check out how Celty's doing."

So Mikado and Saki each offered a shoulder to Masaomi, and they began walking in the direction of Raira General Hospital.

For quite a long time, Mikado found himself unable to speak. Celty was the very cause of his slide into the extraordinary and abnormal, but after she told him their paths crossing was without meaning and that he shouldn't die on account of her, he was left with no idea what to do next.

"Hey, Mikado," said Masaomi.

"..."

Mikado flapped his lips without words.

"How are we going to explain the gunshot wound in my leg?"

"Huh...?"

"Think about it. If they identify it as a gunshot, that gets the police involved. What if we told them...that one of those bikers over there just happened to have a gun? Then they won't know which group it was...," Masaomi joked, despite the pain that was surely racking his entire body.

"…"

Mikado looked as if he was ready to cry.

"What's this?" Masaomi continued. "Tears of joy that you got to see Anri? Better tell her you love her before I snatch her away."

"Oh, Masaomi." Saki snickered and gave him a light head-butt.

Seeing their teasing and the way Anri watched him with concern from a few steps away, Mikado looked down at the ground and muttered, "Maybe I just wanted someone to hate me. For someone to call me a villain and force me to stop…"

He felt the tears welling up and forcibly pushed his face into a smile. "It would have been nice if it were either Sonohara or Kida."

"C'mon, call me Masaomi… I don't want us going back to that awkward formal distance again. Not after everything that's happened," Masaomi said, dragging his foot while Mikado put on that forced, fake smile.

Anri felt relief flood through her at seeing them like this and managed a smile of her own, complete with tears.

"The three of us…are together again."

"Well, *four*," Saki pointed out with a grin. She closed her eyes. "Go ahead—I'll be a statue over here. You three talk among yourselves."

Anri smiled gratefully and took the lead ahead of the group. "We agreed that when we came together again, we'd talk about our secrets."

"…We did."

"What? You had a promise? Hang on—why am I the odd man out?" Masaomi protested. Mikado and Anri shared a look and laughed.

"Let's see… Who should go first?"

"It's gotta be Mikado, right?" Masaomi joked to hide the crippling pain. "I'd rather save Anri's secret for dessert."

Despite the agony of seeing his friend's state, Mikado felt the pressure around his mind steadily easing.

The ticket to the abnormal that he'd gained on the night of the Dollars' first meeting had turned into a one-way express pass after he'd stabbed Aoba Kuronuma through the palm during the Golden Week holidays.

It felt as though the things each of them had lost as the price for their actions were slowly coming back to their rightful place.

I get it now. Sonohara was right all that time ago.

Maybe a totally typical normal life that lasts forever is what's really abnormal.

Mikado thought back on the past, tears streaming down his cheeks, as he looked at her. And then…

He noticed a man approaching her from behind.

"Huh…?"

A man with bloodshot red eyes and a small knife in his hand.

The man sported a fashionable, youthful haircut, but Mikado recognized his face.

Mr. Nasujima…? Why…?

As he watched, confused, Nasujima thrust the knife down toward Anri's back, a cruel, sickening smile on his face.

———————

Unconsciously, Mikado left Masaomi's side and pushed Anri away.

Before either of them—Masaomi stumbling and Anri jolted to the side—could process what was happening, Mikado stood tall before Nasujima.

His blade dug into Mikado's stomach.

"Aah…"

A feeble gasp was all he could manage. Heat and pain shot through him from the spot where he was stabbed.

"Shit! Got in my way!" Nasujima spat with a click of his tongue and thrust the knife into Mikado's side a few more times.

There was a scream.

Was it Masaomi? Or possibly Anri?

He never found the answer.

Mikado Ryuugamine's world was enveloped in shadow without light.

Chat room

.

.

.

The chat room is currently empty.

Mai has entered the chat.

Mai: See you again later.

Mai has left the chat.

The chat room is currently empty.
The chat room is currently empty.

.

.

.

EPILOGUE

At last, Tokyo greeted the morning.

But whether the hour hand passed six o'clock or seven o'clock, the rays of the morning sun did not alight upon Ikebukuro.

Pitch-black shadow hung over the city, far darker than any cloud could make it.

It was as if the night continued onward, striking fear and unease into the citizens and making huge national news.

By noon, however, the shadow was gone, and the rest of society neatly classified it a "natural phenomenon caused by a special dust storm" so that they could continue on with their day.

But for those individuals who were most deeply connected to that shadow, it was a morning of change.

Inside a car

"…"

Through dull wits, Izaya Orihara became aware that his surroundings were shaking.

Apparently, he was sitting in the passenger seat of a car with the seat back tilted down. He looked over and saw a man with a shaved head driving in silence.

"...Is that...Mr. Kine?"

"You're lucky I happened to be nearby...if you want to call it luck."

"..."

"I'd say that with the injuries you've got, there's a fifty-fifty chance you'll make it if I rush you to a hospital," Kine estimated without a hint of emotion. "Frankly, the blunt impacts all over your body are worse than the knife wound in your gut. I'd guess you've got a couple organs failing right now. Can't believe you were able to battle with Shizuo in that state."

"..."

Izaya glanced down at his side. There was a detachable knife blade stuck in the flesh there. Only there was shadow stuck in the wound around it, holding his blood loss to a minimum.

"I wouldn't pull that out. If you start bleeding, your chances of dying go from fifty-fifty to ninety-ten."

"..."

"Before you die, thank the kid behind you. She helped carry you in here while Shizuo was blinded."

"...?"

Izaya glanced into the rearview mirror, his face pale, and saw a girl with a cold expression on her face: Manami Mamiya.

"Don't get the wrong idea. I just wanted to see your end without anyone getting in the way," she said, staring back at him through the mirror with open hatred and dismissal. "If you end up dying, I'll say, 'You got killed by a monster. Serves you right.' But if that shadow in your wound saves you, I'll say, 'Your life got spared by a monster. Serves you right.'"

"...Ha-ha... Both of those are...horrible."

"I was talking with Shinra Kishitani earlier. He told me the kinds of things you would hate."

"Damn...him..."

He grimaced, exhaled, then gazed out through empty eyes at the black sky visible through the car window. He was silent for a long while.

"What now?" Kine asked. "I could drop you off at an emergency room nearby. Or would a black market doctor I have pull with be more convenient for you?"

Despite being on the brink of death, Izaya glared at the shadow covering the sky of Ikebukuro and said, "First...take me out of this city...as far as you can manage..."

"..."

"If I'm going to die...I don't want my last moments watched over... by a monster."

He put on a brave show of smiling, but his face was getting paler by the minute. Kine said nothing and continued driving, thinking of a route that would slip them past any checkpoints set up by the police.

Eventually, their car disappeared out of the area.

Izaya vanished from Ikebukuro, taking with him any information on his death or survival.

The very info dealer who would be in possession of that info was now gone.

♂♀

In time, the darkness in the sky began to dissipate, and with it, the shadows that tied down the bikers and the Saika-possessed dispersed.

"...Huh?"

When Shuuji Niekawa became aware of his surroundings again, he was on the ground in the middle of Ikebukuro.

"What...am I doing here?"

He glanced around and saw many others looking equally befuddled.

"Let's see... I...I found Haruna...and what happened after that...?" he wondered. Then his text message alert went off.

It was from his daughter. And it was a very simple message.

"Don't worry, Dad. I'm with the one I love right now."

A very simple, worrisome message.

♂♀

Somewhere in Tokyo

Hmm...? Where am I...?
When Takashi Nasujima awoke, he was in a dimly lit room.
"...Ah...gaah...!"
He tried to get up, but his body wouldn't move. Not only that, it was racked with horrible pain.
What...? What happened...?
Despite the agony that washed over his brain like a wave, he slowly began to remember, bit by bit, the events that happened before he lost consciousness.

Fortunately for him, hiding in Russia Sushi out of fear of Shizuo meant Nasujima had escaped the binding shadows that afflicted everyone outside. From there, he wandered around in search of fresh pawns.
It was at that point that he just so happened to witness Anri Sonohara walking on the sidewalk. Plus, her attention was on someone else who was injured, so she was completely vulnerable.
Nasujima licked his lips and approached, excited to get the best pawn imaginable.
That's right. That's where that stupid kid got in the way...
He'd stabbed the boy several times in frustration, Anri Sonohara had screamed, and then she had produced a katana from her body and came slashing at him.
And then...um...I didn't get cut.
Huh? Why didn't I get sliced by her?
He felt a deep creaking in his spine and tried to go back deeper into his memories.

♂♀

The moment that Anri's Saika bore down on Nasujima, Haruna stepped in between the two and used the knife in her hand to block the sword.

"...?! Haruna!"

"No... You can't, Anri... You might be my friend, but you can't have Takashi," she said, a mixture of fury and worship in her voice.

Nasujima felt his skin crawl. "N...Niekawa...? I thought...you were under my control..."

She was silent for a moment before she answered. As her eyes sparkled like those of a girl in love, she twisted her body around and curved her mouth as far as it would go.

"Well...*isn't that what you wanted*?"

Either she was just acting, or she'd allowed him to possess her with Saika on purpose.

"I'm sorry that I couldn't always be who you wanted me to be...but I felt certain that I was about to lose you to that sneaking little cat burglar..."

In any case, it was exactly the opposite of what Nasujima actually wanted. He uttered a pathetic sound somewhere between a yelp and a shriek and turned his back on Anri and Haruna.

"Oh...! Wait, Takashi!"

Shit! Shit! Goddammit! Why?! Why did this have to happen?! I thought I had the power now! Why is this happening to me?!

Despite Nasujima's being a teacher by profession, his mental dictionary was somehow missing the phrase you *reap what you sow*. He sped along the city streets, trying to put distance between himself and his pursuer.

He spotted a van driving in his direction and stepped out into the street, waving his hands. "Hey! Stop! Let me in!"

Whether it was an ordinary civilian or a gang member, he'd stab them and take them over as soon as they got out of the driver's seat. All he had to do was stand in the road to make them stop...

"Hey, someone just jumped into the middle of the street," Togusa said, peering through the broken windshield as he drove. After the shadow descended on the city earlier, Izumii and his thugs wound up on the ground, tied up by the shadow ropes, but for some reason, Kadota's group was left untouched, so they decided to drive off and get away from the scene.

They had made it a reasonable distance away and were about to call Anri when a man suddenly stood in the road to block their path. From the back seat, Karisawa cried out, "Oh! It's him! The boss of the red-eyes! He said he was gonna do some stuff to Mikado!"

"Huh…?" Kadota grumbled. And then, "Hey…that's the guy who made the slasher *run me over*."

Something inside of Togusa snapped.

"Ah! Hey, wait, Togusa," Kadota yelled, but it was too late. Togusa jammed his foot on the gas.

There was a heavy *thump*—and Takashi Nasujima's memory of the night stopped there.

♂♀

"That's right… I got hit by that car…"

The return of that memory made Nasujima cognizant of another anomaly. His limbs were tied down to the corners of a bed with leather restraints.

"Wha…? Urgh…!"

The pain was horrendous all over. It must have been from the impact of the car.

"What's going on…? What is this place?"

From a corner of the room, a voice said, "Oh…you're awake, Takashi…"

"Huh…?"

"This is one of the little hideouts Izaya Orihara kept for himself. Don't worry. No one is coming here, and no one will hear our love-making, no matter how loud it gets…"

"Hwa—?!"

He turned his head and saw Haruna gazing at him with a blissful look in her eyes.

"I wanted to slice up the person who ran you over…but I decided to forgive them. After all, it's thanks to them that our bonds are about to become so, so much stronger…"

A knife shone in her hand.

"Aaaaah! Aaaaah!" screamed Nasujima, but Haruna just brushed his cheek with her fingers, taking it as a reaction to the agony of his injuries. Next to the bed, there was a locker which she opened up.

"Don't worry, Takashi... I'll heal you."

There were multiple shelves in the locker containing a variety of supplies, from smaller tools such as a scalpel, scissors, and utility knife to larger ones like a saw, hatchet, and chain saw. The feature they all shared in common was that they were bladed.

Haruna turned back to Takashi, carrying a bundle of the tools. "I love you, Takashi," she said.

"Ah...aaaah..."

"I'll make you forget all your pain...with the pain of my own love."

His screams echoed off the walls of the room—but this was only the beginning of a vivid and memorable period of time shared only by the two of them.

♂♀

Ikebukuro

"Yes, so the head is in transporting by the recovery team to the airport. It is to be scheduled for shipping to the headquarters of Chicago as a specimen of a special human body," said the voice over the phone in oddly structured Japanese.

Shingen replied to his wife, Emilia, with annoyance. "You called a recovery team? I don't understand how you can be so bad at cooking but so good at performing your job."

"I cannot be allowing for you to require extra workings, Shingen."

"Your sentiment is appreciated. Just stop mixing gunpowder into your cooking experiments."

Their strange form of flirting continued for a little while longer before Shingen finally ended the call and spoke to the woman in the room with him.

"You heard that. What now, Namie?"

"...I don't know what you mean."

She could have strangled him to death right at that moment, but the

Russian man with the watchful eyes behind her would have prevented any attempt. She'd been trying to recover the head before Seiji could, until Shingen caught her in the attempt and told her the spiteful news: "Nebula is in possession of the head now."

Before her irritation could dissipate, Shingen said shamelessly, "Well, regardless of what you do, your uncle was shocked into a near-vegetative state, so we drew the message 'I love severed heads' with a heart symbol on his forehead in marker, which at this point has gone past being humorous into just plain sad. We have little interest left in punishing you, as it happens."

"...And?"

"From Nebula's perspective, in fact, you had a longer and deeper fixation on that head than anyone. Wouldn't we want your expertise?"

"What? Is this supposed to be a job offer?"

"Really? With as direct as I am being with you, can't you be certain that this is a recruitment pitch? Perhaps I was wrong, and you're actually far stupider than you— Gu-gu-gu-gwaaah! Stop...stop pressing your thumb against my Adam's apple! Don't make me— Gu-gu-gu-guah..."

Namie continued to attack and harangue him until Egor finally stepped in to stop her—and by that time, the black shadow that covered the sky had vanished.

From there, the days trickled past.

♂♀

Seiji's apartment—several days later

"Are you sure about this?"

"Of course!"

"You make it sound simple, but it'll cost lots of money and time."

"I'll go anywhere that you're going, Seiji!"

Seiji and Mika were not talking about where to go on their next date this time. They were discussing the idea of going to school in America.

First, his sister had said she was going over to the United States; then Mika had told him the head had apparently been taken to Chicago.

Immediately, Seiji began to plan a way to get there using a study abroad program, and thus Mika had joined in the preparation as if she were obviously welcome.

"But...why did you tell me the head was in Chicago?"

"Huh?"

"I figure if you kept it a secret from me and went on your own, you'd have a better chance of destroying the head."

"Because even then, I'd rather be with you!" she said, giving him an utterly transparent smile.

He muttered, "The thing is...I still love that head."

"I know!"

It was a conversation they'd had a million times before, except that in this instance Seiji added, "But while I don't think of you as a lover... you are kind of like family to me."

Mika did not reply to this. Instead, she hugged him tight around the chest. Seiji didn't seem bothered by it, either. Their oddball relationship had them pointed together in the direction of the head.

Both of them knew they were in parallel with each other.

But they continued onward anyway, enjoying the warmth of their mutual proximity.

♂♀

Tokyo

When her talent agency manager told her the rumor that a suspect in the case of the serial killer Hollywood had surfaced, Ruri Hijiribe prepared herself, thinking that the time had finally come.

She'd done it to avenge her parents, but a crime was a crime. This was the time to atone for what she'd done, and she was ready for it.

The only regret she had was that she'd let the ringleader, Jinnai Yodogiri, get away—but she was no longer of a mind to kill him.

She would accept whatever happened. The only thing she wanted to do was make sure that none of it hurt Yuuhei Hanejima.

But as her manager continued to explain the situation, Ruri was left feeling baffled.

*　　*　　*

"Apparently, Jinnai Yodogiri and his secretary, Kasane Kujiragi, have been listed as suspects in the serial killings."

It wasn't announced publicly, but the police were looking for them as people of interest, so since Ruri was a former member of Yodogiri's agency, they might want to ask her some questions.

That was all her manager had to say about it, so Ruri headed out to make the trip home, uncertain of anything anymore.

I should talk to Yuuhei Hanejima, she decided and walked into the night streets around her apartment. Then she noticed a truck approaching in her direction. She moved to the side of the road to give it room to pass, but then she detected something wrong with it.

Despite the narrow width of the road, it did not slow down a bit. If anything, it seemed to be picking up speed, rushing straight at her.

...!

She was a fraction of a second too late in reacting. For an instant, she fell prey to the obsessive fixation in the madness of the man driving the vehicle.

But Ruri Hijiribe did not know that the man driving the car was a fanatical stalker of hers—the son of the man she'd killed to avenge her father: Kisuke Adabashi.

"Ha-ha...ha-haaaa...*ha-ha-ha-ha! Hya-ha-ha-ha-haaaaaaa-ha-haaa!*"

Adabashi had escaped from Izaya's hideout, dragging his broken leg behind him, and through sheer tenacity alone, he'd made his way to Ruri's location, ambushing her with a truck he stole.

Ruri had superhuman strength, but when faced out of the blue with the delusion of a man to whom love and destruction were the same thing, she was a moment too late to escape his aggression.

Just before her body was at the mercy of the mass and force of sheer violence, the owner of a strength beyond hers scooped her up, then raced up the front of the oncoming truck and leaped clear over it to safety.

*   *   *

The next moment, there was a horrendous crash behind them as the truck's front twisted and deformed against a light pole. With the sound of the pole creaking and groaning in the background, Ruri recognized who had picked her up.

"A-are you…Miss Kujiragi…?"

It was Kujiragi, the secretary of that detestable Yodogiri, who had saved her. It was hard for Ruri to process in the moment; she was utterly taken aback.

"Do you hate me?" asked the woman.

"Wha…?"

"Forgive the suddenness of what I am about to say… I am jealous of you," Kujiragi confessed out of nowhere.

Ruri summoned enough presence of mind to ask, "Um…what do you mean?" It was bafflement and curiosity that rose to the surface before hatred.

Instead of answering her question, however, Kujiragi continued her announcement. "So I have decided to steal from you. I will steal the opportunity for the serial killer Hollywood to atone for her crimes."

"?!"

"This is now my crime and my punishment to you. I will steal all of Hollywood's sins. Now you will be unable to atone for what you have done, and you never will know that peace," Kujiragi explained. She dragged the unconscious Adabashi out of the truck, hauled him over her shoulder, and turned away from Ruri. "And now, with that guilt eternally plaguing your conscience…do have a good life."

"What…do you mean? Why…why would you do this?"

"You cannot turn yourself in," Kujiragi continued, her eyes flashing red, ignoring Ruri. "I have fingers deep within both the police and the media."

Ruri flinched at the surreal look of her eyes but stood her ground. "No! Wait! What are you…?"

But without offering a single firm answer to any of Ruri's questions, Kujiragi leaped away with superhuman agility—leaving only one self-deprecating comment.

*   *   *

"I am simply an irredeemable villain...motivated by envy."

♂♀

Raira General Hospital—several days later

"I'm terribly sorry about all the trouble Mikado's put you through, Masaomi."

"But, Miss...Sonohara, was it? I'm very glad you didn't wind up getting hurt."

Two adults were speaking to Masaomi and Anri in gentle tones.

"Please, please...I hope you'll be good to our Mikado."

"We're so grateful to you for being his friends."

After Masaomi and Anri walked the man and woman back to the hospital room, they made their way slowly toward the entrance of the building.

"Was that your first time meeting Mikado's parents?" he asked her.

"Yes."

"They're almost shockingly normal, right? But they're nice. When I was a kid, I remember them getting us watermelon in the summer when I went to hang out."

The recollection sent Masaomi further into his childhood memories of Mikado's parents.

Mikado had said once that his father was the head of personnel at a printing company. He remembered the man being rather frazzled but essentially good-natured. His mother looked exactly the way that Anri imagined an "ordinary mother" would look, and she was kind enough to be concerned about Anri at a time when her own son was in critical condition.

Everything that happened was explained as an early-morning hiking expedition that had turned tragic when they'd encountered a biker-gang turf war, in which Mikado stepped in to protect them when someone turned a knife on the group.

Because the wound in Masaomi's leg did not have a bullet inside of it and the shadow had stopped the bleeding entirely, it was treated like a mystery—an injury with no clearly discernible cause.

*　　*　　*

And while Mikado Ryuugamine's life was stable for the moment, he still had not opened his eyes.

"Knowing what his parents are like, I can't help but feel like the reason Mikado turned out this way isn't because of his home life...but that it was all my fault."

"No, that's not...," Anri said, trying to comfort Masaomi, but she was interrupted by another boy who passed the two.

"Don't be so self-absorbed."

"?"

Masaomi glanced over and got a good look at who had said that.

"You're exaggerating how much influence you have over Mr. Mikado."

"Kuronuma...," Anri mumbled.

Masaomi gasped, recalling where he'd seen the boy before, and glared at him. "Aoba Kuronuma... What the hell are you doing here?"

"I'm not going to start a fight with you in a hospital. Whether you believe me or not, I'm just here to visit Mr. Mikado. Am I not allowed to do that?"

"You've got a lot of nerve...," Masaomi growled, trying to keep himself from punching him. "What's wrong...you haven't gotten him involved in enough shit already?"

Aoba sighed. "Oh no. And a very scary man already came and menaced me about that. We've largely accomplished what we set out to do, so I have no reason to force Mr. Mikado to do anything anymore."

"What you set out to...?"

"As we figured, all the uproar succeeded at getting the Dollars recognized as a dangerous, malicious group. All the ordinary folks freaked out and stopped associating with the group, and the co-webmaster named Tsukumoya deleted all the Dollars-related sites, so at this point, the name simply lives on as its own entity."

"...And in the meantime, you Blue Squares get to walk free. After all, that was the *Dollars'* work," Masaomi spat.

Aoba smirked and shook his head. "The truth is, I wanted to swim with Mr. Mikado. The fish tank got a lot bigger, and the visibility improved with it."

"Hey..."

"But I don't know if things are going to work out that well anyway. I've certainly attracted Chikage Rokujou's attention, for one thing... And from what I hear, Libei Ying, the boss of Dragon Zombie, is back in Japan. And your least favorite person, Ran Izumii, is still up to something, so there's no resting easy for us. Not to mention the Yellow Scarves." Aoba shrugged.

Masaomi glared at him and declared, "If you try to drag Mikado into any more shit or use what he did as leverage to screw him over, I'm going to destroy you guys for good."

"I'll be careful." Aoba sighed. Lastly, he gave Anri and Masaomi one true little smile. "And just so you don't get the wrong idea... I really do have great respect for him."

Once Aoba had moved on to Mikado's hospital room, Masaomi spat, "Be careful, Anri. You go to school with him, right?"

"Yes, but...I was mostly surprised that he seemed different from usual..."

She'd heard about the younger boy's true nature, but actually seeing it in person for the first time had left Anri a bit shaken.

Masaomi decided to get back to the topic at hand. "Hey...what'll you say to Mikado when he wakes up?"

"Well..."

There was no sign of that actually happening yet, but they had faith. They knew he would regain consciousness. And that was why it would be important for them to know what to say when he did.

After a bit of thinking, both Masaomi and Anri arrived at the same answer.

♂♀

When they walked out of the hospital entrance, Saki was waiting.

"Oh, you're here?"

"Yep. I didn't want to intrude on the three of you and your private time," she said with a gentle smile.

Masaomi rolled his eyes. "Don't get all weird on me. You're going to make it hard for me to introduce him to you once he does wake up."

Anri listened to Saki and Masaomi talk with a grin on her face but paused when she realized that someone she recognized was approaching from the front gate of the hospital. In fact, though she had no idea, it was the same "very scary man" whom Aoba had just been talking about.

"Yo, Anri."

"Mr. Akabayashi? Why are you here?"

Masaomi was wary of Akabayashi, perhaps sensing that he was no ordinary civilian—but after a brief introduction from Anri, he and Saki left, looking rather relieved to be going. Once they were gone, Akabayashi said, "I just wanted to give my thanks to the kid who risked his life to save yours. Is he still under?"

"Yes…"

"Ah. That's too bad," he said, shrugging. In his head, he replayed the negotiations he'd had with Aozaki a few nights earlier.

Aozaki didn't want to give up on his plans for Mikado and the Dollars, so Akabayashi had made a suggestion:

"*I know what kind of business we're in. I'm not asking for mercy or obligation in lettin' the kids go.*"

In fact, it was less of a suggestion that he had for Aozaki than a simple deal.

"*I'll give you a part of what I'm dealing in now… Nothin' fancy, merely a chunk. Would you consider withdrawing from this matter in exchange for that?*"

Aozaki glared at him with surprise and suspicion, but once he understood that Akabayashi was serious, he thought it over and eventually accepted.

"*You really have gone soft. A part of me was actually hopin' we might finally settle this score, once and for all.*"

But Akabayashi snorted and grinned in his self-deprecating way.

"*Just the opposite. I ain't senile enough that I'd put the burden of us killin' each other on some kid's back. It's a grown-up's duty to see that a child gets back to safety when he's in danger of losing his way, that's all.*"

Then he shrugged and added one last wry sentiment.

"Except I don't pull him back with me—I just push him to where he ought to be."

"By the way, I was hopin' to ask you something again, Anri."

"What is it?" she replied.

Akabayashi paused a moment. "Do you love this Mikado Ryuuga-mine kid?"

"...!"

Her eyes went round, but after a moment, she nodded firmly. "I'm not entirely certain myself...but I think maybe I do."

"And that's...*your* opinion? Not influenced by anything else?"

"Huh...?"

She wasn't sure what he meant at first, but then she gasped.

Akabayashi knew her mother. Maybe he knew about Saika, too.

But rather than follow up on that suspicion, Anri firmly told him, "Yes, mine... That's my feeling."

"All right, then. I've got nothing more to worry about." Akabayashi said not another word hinting at the presence of Saika. He rapped his walking stick with a satisfied smile. "Enjoy your youth while you've got it."

And reflecting on his past, he spoke his own unvarnished truth.

"I never had the chance myself."

♂♀

Several weeks later

"Goodness, look how deep into autumn we are," murmured Karisawa as sunlight streamed into the van.

"...It's the middle of goddamn summer," Kadota snapped, now healed up and out of the hospital for good.

Karisawa and Yumasaki protested against this. "What do you mean, Dotachin? Hot and cold weather mean nothing to the indoor types!"

"That's right! Obviously, the only real indicator of autumn is when that season of anime begins!"

Togusa was finally in a better mood these days, now that the windshield and everything else in the van had been repaired. "You guys are indoor types? The ones who hitch rides in my car to get to Animate all the time?"

"Oh, by the way," Karisawa said, completely ignoring that comment, "I heard that Ruri Hijiribe's stalker finally got arrested."

"Yep. The bastard's name is Kisuke Adabashi. I can hardly even believe that he was trying to run her over with a truck! Apparently, a passing fan dragged him out of the vehicle, beat the shit out of him, and left him half-dead in front of the station."

"Left him?"

"I mean, what they did is still assault. No point in getting yourself arrested for it," Togusa said. His smooth manner suddenly turned feral as his eyes gleamed with murder. "But if it was me, I wouldn't have turned the guy in at all. I'd grind him into meat."

Kadota sighed. "And here we are, back to the usual."

He watched the scenery of the city trickle by through the windshield and found a smile naturally coming to his lips.

"But I guess I kinda like this vibe."

♂♀

Outside of Rakuei Gym

As the van carrying Kadota and his friends passed by the gym, a few girls and one adult woman popped out of the door.

"You did great today, Akane! You beat a boy two years older than you! It's the arrival of a promising future star! There's a new heroine in the world of wooden-staff combat!" chattered Mairu Orihara.

"N-no, I just got lucky," stammered Akane Awakusu, her face flushed.

Kururi softly rubbed the girl's head. "...Fortune... Momentum..." [Luck is also a part of skill.]

"Y-you're embarrassing me," Akane insisted, shaking her head.

Then the assistant instructor who attended to the three of them approached. "I wouldn't say lucky; that was the kid's fault," said Mikage Sharaku. "He got lazy against a female opponent and earned what was coming to him. But...you get passing marks for taking advantage of the opportunity he presented."

Then she addressed her newest apprentice directly. "Now, Akane, you've joined the gym at a young age, and you take your practice very seriously...but what is it you intend to do with this skill?"

"...There's a man I have to beat..."

"Ooh. A bully in your class, I'm guessing?"

Akane shook her head and said, in a tiny voice, "Sh...Shizuo Heiwajima."

Mikage's face went slack for a moment, and then she burst into laughter.

"Ha-ha-ha! That's perfect! You couldn't ask for a bigger goal!"

When Akane's face went even redder and she stared at the ground, Mairu and Kururi stood up for her.

"Hey, you shouldn't laugh at her, Mikage!"

"...Awful..." [The poor thing.]

"Oh! Sorry, sorry. I didn't mean to insult you."

The grown woman thought about the man who had challenged that monster single-handedly and then vanished from the city. She murmured wistfully, "I can make you stronger. Strong enough to defeat that monster? I don't know...but I'd sure love to see that for myself."

♂♀

Inside Russia Sushi

"Kchoo!"

A muffled sneeze echoed off the walls of Russia Sushi.

"Oh, Shizuo, you catch cold? That happen when you don't get nutrition. When eat our sushi, sick children become healthy children. Fish children are roe; chicken children are eggs. You eat all the children, feel better!"

"Way to make me lose my appetite," Tom grumbled to Simon. He turned to Shizuo. "You all right? It's about that time of year that everyone gets sick."

"Oh…I'm sure it's just someone spreading a rumor about me. You know how that superstition goes."

"Ah… Maybe it's Vorona, telling her dad and his buddies all about your heroic exploits."

"Don't tease me about that… I didn't do anything that anyone would call heroic," Shizuo muttered, head downcast.

Just the other day, Vorona had gone with an acquaintance she called Slon back to Russia. She claimed it was something about facing her father and her past self, but Shizuo didn't pry into it at all. When he looked into her eyes, he saw a special kind of resolve there and knew that it wasn't his place to intrude upon her struggle.

Still, he did have some parting words.

"I'm not gonna ask for details…but you are an important coworker of mine. I'm your senior here, so if you ever need help, I've got an ear to listen."

Vorona grinned at that, then admitted, *"If the possibility for me to visit this city again is approved…I will desire a battle upon our reunion."*

Shizuo was a bit nonplussed by the use of the word *battle*. But she continued, *"I wish to speak with you in direct terms, at risk of my very life… To experience the joy of existing in this world is my desire."*

Denis sensed the feelings that were running through Shizuo as he recalled that conversation.

"Don't worry about her," he said. "Her old man acts cruel and stubborn, but he's much more compassionate than you'd think. Once she finds the right timing, she'll be back here to visit."

Shizuo admitted, as much to himself as to Denis, "The truth is, it's thanks to her that I can act like a person at all… And I feel bad that I never got to thank her for that…"

Simon piped up. "Shizuo is genuine human being. We guarantee it. Genuine, sunshine, coastline, gold mine. We offer all the best fish, no fakes. Moonfish, negitoro, halibut, mahi-mahi nigiri, conger, sea snake, everything good, make you happy, make you full."

He was clearly just reading the names of the sushi off the list on the wall, but before Shizuo or Tom could reply, a peculiar sound reached their ears.

*   *   *

Qrrrrrrrrrrrrrrrrrrrrrrrrrrrrrrrrrrr...

It appeared to be coming from the expressway between Russia Sushi and Sunshine City—an eerie engine sound that resembled a horse's whinny. Shizuo, Tom, Denis, Simon, and even the other employees and customers grinned a little.

As if they felt an irreplaceable measure of reliable familiarity in the urban legend, that absolutely abnormal being, still around and wandering the city in broad daylight.

♂♀

Tokyo

A motorcycle without a headlight stopped on the side of the road.

"You should be all right after coming this far," Celty typed into her PDA. Seeing the message from the back seat of the motorcycle, Shinra gave her a big smile.

"Thanks for the huge help, Celty. My broken leg isn't fully healed yet, so I wouldn't have been able to get away on my own."

"I can't begin to imagine what you did to get both the Chinese mafia and the Asuki-gumi chasing after you," she typed, exasperated.

Shinra gleefully answered, "The vicissitudes of life are woven of fortune, good or ill. Sadness and gladness succeed each other. To have the pleasure, you must endure the pain. There doesn't need to be an answer to explain days like this."

"I feel like the only thing you'd ever weave is disaster..."

"Whatever do you mean?! Just going on a drive with you like this is the greatest bliss I could possibly hope to grab, Celty. And I say that because what I'm grabbing is your body, eh-heh-heh-heh-heh-heh-helb-grbl-guh!"

She used her shadow to clamp down on his face and typed out, *"Then you'll need to suffer to balance things out."*

It was just like always—silly, idle flirting.

When they were done, and Shinra was free of his shadow shackles, he said to her seriously, "Hey, Celty."

"What?"

"Tell me the truth. Do you still have the memories of your head now?"

"Why would you ask this?"

Shinra hadn't touched upon the matter ever since the night in question. Part of that was because his injuries had festered and his broken bones had come loose again, but even after he had recovered somewhat, Shinra still hadn't asked about Celty's memories.

He must have decided that this was the right moment and summoned up the determination to go ahead with it.

"It's not like when it got severed while you were asleep. If it happened when you were wide awake, though…"

"That doesn't actually matter," she typed out before he had even finished asking the question. She wasn't trying to shut him up to hide the truth. She was putting her honest feelings into each word and relating them directly to him.

"I'll always be with you."

"…"

"If you can sense a person's feelings that accurately, don't embarrass me by forcing me to type this out, you jerk."

"…Celty!"

Out of an abundance of emotion, he clutched her around the midriff from behind. She hastily sent out shadows to pry him loose.

"Control yourself, you idiot! We're in public," she typed, her fingers pausing partway—she'd spotted a familiar face in the process of looking around.

"Yo."

It was a traffic officer on a motorcycle, grinning at her.

"Puttin' on quite a show, huh, monster?"

"Um, this isn't—"

"I hate to ruin your blissful display…but are you aware that this road, upon which you are engaging in a public display of affection, does not allow parking?"

The officer, Kuzuhara, was no longer smiling now. More engines roared all around them, and many more white police motorcycles appeared.

Shinra timidly asked her, "Um…what's going on here, Celty?"

"Shinra."

"What?"

"Don't die."

Before he could so much as emit a questioning peep, Celty's shadows were spreading around them, seeking a rapid escape. Shinra nearly passed out from the phenomenal roller-coaster Gs he pulled, strapped to her back, as she raced away.

Celty Sturluson was not human.

She was a type of fairy commonly known as a dullahan—found from Scotland to Ireland—a being that visits the homes of those close to death to inform them of their impending mortality.

The dullahan carried its own severed head under its arm, rode on a two-wheeled carriage called a Cóiste Bodhar that was pulled by a headless horse, and approached the homes of the soon to die. Anyone foolish enough to open the door was drenched with a basinful of blood. Thus, the dullahan, like the banshee, made its name as a herald of ill fortune throughout European folklore.

But that was all in the past.

Now she was a living urban legend and a woman leading a happy life in love with a man named Shinra Kishitani.

And so wishing and hoping that this happiness would continue indefinitely…

…the living legend spent another day racing through the city.

♂♀

Another day, another month

How much time had passed?

The boy woke from long dreams of darkness and opened eyes fuzzy with sleep.

The light was blinding, his vision still unclear.

When he craned his neck, he heard a nurse speaking with alarm.

"Mr. Ryuugamine opened his eyes…
"Call the parents at once…"

Then he thought he heard voices calling his name.

"Mikado!" "Mikado!"

A boy and a girl. Familiar, fond voices.

"...A...auh..."

He couldn't speak words; his tongue felt stiff and clumsy.

Over agonizing moments, he finally gained enough control to make himself understood.

"...Masaomi...? Sono...hara...?"

They were practically grunts—just exhaled air. But the boy and girl understood what he said, and they squeezed his hands tight.

"Welcome back, Mikado."

"It's good to see you again."

Through vision hazy with blinding light, he sensed their voices—and before he could even process what this meant, he was aware that tears were running down his face.

They never stopped.

Whether ordinary times or extraordinary, he sensed that behind their words was what he always wanted.

The boy's tears kept falling.

♂♀

This is a twisted story.

A story of twisted love.

With the whinnying of an urban legend,

or with a boy's tears,

or with a return to normalcy,

or with the disappearance of a mastermind,

or with the premonition of a new story—

this story of twisted love now comes to a close.

For their love is no longer twisted in the least.

C A S T

Mikado Ryuugamine
Masaomi Kida
Anri Sonohara

Izaya Orihara
Shizuo Heiwajima

Celty Sturluson
Shinra Kishitani

Kyouhei Kadota
Walker Yumasaki
Erika Karisawa
Saburo Togusa

Mika Harima
Seiji Yagiri
Namie Yagiri

Aoba Kuronuma
Chikage Rokujou
Saki Mikajima

Vorona
Mikage Sharaku
Kasane Kujiragi

Durarara!!–The End

AFTERWORD

And that is the end of *Durarara!!* as the story of the Dollars and Yellow Scarves.

It's been a very long journey.

My original plan, starting with the fourth volume, was to do a story set two years after the third volume, without Mikado's group, and based around a completely different plot kernel—but instead, it turned out to be a massive thirteen-volume epic centered around the trio of teenagers.

The story of Mikado Ryuugamine, Masaomi Kida, and Anri Sonohara will reach an end here, but I hope that you will imagine them on the other side of this story, making new connections and weaving a new tale.

Incidentally, while I did not touch upon the past of Kine and Mikage Sharaku very much, I was going to write about that in a book that was scheduled to be published last year, except that certain publishing conditions did not line up for it to come to fruition. Please wait for that.

Now, in the process of getting my mind out of *Durarara!!* mode, I had a meeting with my editor, discussing whether to move next to *Vamp!*, or *Baccano! 1935*, or maybe *5656! Two*, or *Vamp!* or *Hariyama-san*, or a new series, or *Vamp!*, or...

This is how that conversation went.

Me: "As for my next plans..."

Editor: "About that. April 2014 is the tenth anniversary of *Durarara!!*"

Me: "Right."

Editor: "So let's do *Durarara!!* next, as a ten-year memorial project."

Me: "Right...? ...What?! Wait, but I just finished wrapping it up, at least for now...and it's *Vamp*'s tenth anniversary, too..."

Editor: "Well, if this is the end of Part One, we should do another one now for the anniversary, to let the fans know that Part Two is going to keep the gravy train rolling!"

Me: "I...I see... I didn't think of it that way..."

*   *   *

So in the coming spring, I'll be starting up *Durarara!! SH*, the continuation of the series.

This is the story I initially wanted to write starting in Volume 4, a depiction of the ordinary life of Ikebukuro two years after the Yellow Scarves incident in Volume 3. I would love it if you'd follow along with me!

And as for what the *SH* stands for, I intend to make that clear within the story and my afterword, so you'll have to check it out to find the answer.

And in coordination with this, there will be all kinds of things to announce and promote on the tenth anniversary ahead. I hope that you all enjoy *Durarara!!* Year!

First of all, there are new *Durarara!!* comic adaptations coming out in the pages of the *Sylph* and *Dengeki Maoh* magazines!

These will be an adaptation of the PSP game *Durarara!! 3way Standoff—Alley—* by Izuko Fujiya and a chibi-style spin-off called *Minidura* by Yoko Umezu!

There's also Akiyo Satorigi's *Durarara!! Yellow Scarves Arc*, covering the events of the main story, running in *G Fantasy*!

Also, for the Blu-ray release of Suzuhito Yasuda's own *Yozakura Quartet* series, we have a special limited-edition bonus: a collaboration manga of *Yozakura Quartet* and *Durarara!!* I love doing collabs like this and can't wait to see the finished product!

And in even more news, in Sega and Dengeki's crossover fighting game *Dengeki Bunko: Fighting Climax*, Shizuo Heiwajima will be appearing as a playable character, with Celty as a support character! He's got some extreme stats as a fighter, so if you have the chance to play, try him out and rage to your heart's content!

And from what I hear, there are other tenth-anniversary plans I still don't even know about yet. We'll be saving some of those for the release of *Durarara!! SH* and some future Dengeki events, so keep your eyes peeled!

And lastly, I must deliver my acknowledgments.

To my editor, Papio, and everyone at ASCII Media Works and the printers, I am so sorry for all the trouble I've caused throughout the entirety of this first part of the series!

I am full of gratitude to all the readers who have stuck with me for nearly ten years to read this story about a rather unique take on the district of Ikebukuro in Tokyo.

And I am overflowing with thanks for my illustrator, Suzuhito Yasuda, and all the other people involved in making the anime, manga, and games, for sharing the world of *Durarara!!* with me and helping to expand it further than I could ever do on my own.

In the process of writing about a sprawling cast of characters interacting on the streets of Ikebukuro, I myself became associated with so many wonderful people in return, and it is this that is my greatest reward from the series.

I am grateful to my friends, acquaintances, and family, for all their emotional support.

And though I said this already, a true thank-you to all the people who enjoyed and supported the story of the Dollars, Saika, the Yellow Scarves, and the Headless Rider, as well as the three high schoolers and the many, many characters surrounding them!

I hope that we will meet again soon.

December 2013—Ryohgo Narita